PRAISE

"A beautiful story following several characters on a poignant journey at a week-long wellness retreat. A story of second chances, healing, redemption, and awakening! Loved it!" — *Amy Impellizzeri*

"*The Retreat* is a compassionate story of women's friendships set against the backdrop of bourgeoning self awareness inspired by a spiritual retreat in Costa Rica. While the women confront such universal themes as death of a parent, illness, abandonment, romantic relationships and choosing a life path, there is an interweaving of basic spiritual teachings that are simply stated and easily understood. An engaging novel for the spiritually curious." — *Krista Anderson-Ross*

"Michelle Davis continues to bring clarity to the characters in this second book of *The Awakening Series*. The struggles are authentic, and the 'spiritual awakenings' each character experiences are true to life. Admittedly, I was not anticipating how much of an impact reading this story had on me to be accepting/unprejudiced/unbiased to beliefs and practices that are not mine. Yet, I felt a bonding with each of the characters and gleaned a much deeper understanding of where I am in my own spiritual journey." — *Gail Porazzo*

"I loved Michelle's uplifting book following the lives of five women attending a retreat in Costa Rica. Every person had a unique reason for attending the retreat although I saw that they were all seeking something similar; clarity with their reason for being." — *Kelly Swisher*

"I really enjoyed following the spiritual journey of the women in *The Retreat*, all the while learning about various Ayurvedic practices. Each of the women have their own obstacles in life and their own beautiful way of overcoming them. The details in this book really take you into Nueva Vida and the Costa Rican jungle to give you a look into what a holistic wellness retreat experience might be like."
— *Katie Dwyer*

"A truly uplifting and thoughtful novel that has inspired me, through the characters and story, to look deeper into my journey in life! — *Sue Davis*

"So much about *The Retreat* resonated with me. I was whisked away into the lives of the characters, all seeking answers and life transformation. I doubly enjoyed the bits about Central Oregon, as I have just finished my fifth year in the wonderful town of Bend. I loved it!" — *Elizabeth Vanderliet*

"A wonderful read opening the conversation to an awareness of spirituality beyond ourselves. In a world that teaches us to think with our heads, this teaches us to lead with our hearts and listen to our intuition." —*Alexis Kelly*

"*The Retreat* is a wonderful story about women and friendship, love and loss, and how to figure out what we want in life. In this book the characters go to a retreat in Costa Rica to meet with various healers and get answers to questions that have been blocking them in their lives. The journey to go into your internal landscape is scary for these women and they step up beautifully to find the answers. If you're looking for clarity in your own life this book is a must!"
— *Molly Cornell*

The Retreat

MICHELLE DAVIS

The Retreat by Michelle Davis

First Edition 2023

Copyright © 2023 Michelle M. Davis
Cover Design by Lieve Maas
Edited by Julie Swearingen and Alison Cantrell
Front Cover Photo by Content Pixie on Unsplash

Printed in the United States

ISBN: 978-1-7344619-6-1

Library of Congress Control Number: 2023901448

For more writings by Michelle Davis, please visit:
www.michellemdavis.net

*"Your visions will become clear only when
you can look into your own heart.
Who looks outside, dreams;
who looks inside, awakes."*

—C.G. JUNG

*"Awakening is not changing who you are
but discarding who you are not."*

—DEEPAK CHOPRA

*"That is the real spiritual awakening,
when something emerges from within you
that is deeper than who you thought you were."*

—ECKHART TOLLE

MAGGIE
Monday, February 22

I tiptoe up the stairs. The frayed burgundy runner silences my footsteps, yet it does nothing to dull the echo of my accelerated heartbeat. Something's off. Trying to pinpoint the source of this unsettling feeling, I attribute it to that supersize gas station coffee I bought earlier this morning.

The plan was to return last night … after skiing. However, we were having so much fun—and checkout wasn't until today at ten—so there was no real reason I couldn't stay and drive back early this morning. I pause when I reach the landing, noting my throat feels tight. How strange.

Mom's usually up, sipping her second cup of coffee while completing the *Pittsburgh Post-Gazette*'s sudoku puzzle. She's always been an early riser. In fact, she rarely sleeps past 4:45, which seems silly because she doesn't need to be at work until eight o'clock.

I glance at my phone, noting it's already 6:28. While I'm thankful my mom was able to sleep in for a change, somehow my body doesn't *feel* like this is a good thing.

But the extra rest will be good for her. She's constantly moving, doing, helping others. Still, I wish Mom took better care of herself. Not only does she worry nonstop about Granddad and me, but she's also the one who keeps that law firm running. As administrative assistant to the lead partner, Mom's constantly fixing, planning, and solving other people's problems. I let out a small laugh, knowing they'd be lost without her. But the tightness in my throat returns, causing me to involuntarily gulp.

Sadly, my mom, who will soon turn forty-six, already has creases on her forehead and lines beneath her eyes. Almost five inches shorter than me, Mom barely weighs 110 pounds. Last week I noticed how her skin's beginning to sag around her joints. I keep telling her to eat healthier meals and exercise—or at least walk daily. But she says that's not in her DNA. I guess she'd rather spend time taking care of people. Still, despite her doctor's warning, she continues to smoke half a pack each day.

But can I blame her? Mom's life has not been easy. However, that's mostly because of me. I clench my jaw, acknowledging that had I not been born, her world would be completely different. Instead of working fifty-hour weeks, she'd probably be living in a beautiful house in the suburbs, with a doting husband, several children, and lots of cats. For a moment, I allow myself to smile. But reality returns. My mother is stuck in a monotonous life that revolves around responsibility and duty. While I've considered moving out on my own, I'm afraid Mom would be lonely. And after all she's given up for me, the last thing I want to do is leave her.

Of course, my father—whoever he is—remains a mystery. No one in my family will discuss "the situation." All I know is what my grandmother shared before she passed. Mom was seventeen when she became pregnant, she had me, and that was that. And there's *never* been any mention of my father—who he was, why he didn't stay with Mom, or where he is now. Whenever I asked, all I got was a tight-lipped nonresponse. Finally, I gave up and focused on being grateful for the family I had. Still, I spend many nights lying awake wondering who my dad is and why he left.

Reaching the second-floor landing, I make a right and head down the hall toward the stairs to my third-floor bedroom. Oddly, my heartbeat seems to be pulsating even faster.

It's when I come to my mom's room, where the door's slightly ajar, that something tells me to pause. I look in, expecting to see our cat, Felix, snuggled against my mom's feet. But the lights are off ... and the bed is made.

Suddenly, my racing heartbeat comes to a screeching halt. I throw open the door and turn on the lamp atop her nightstand. As soon as the light shines, Felix pokes his head out from under the bed. He cautiously walks toward me and begins to circle my legs. It's then our adopted tabby emits the strangest sound.

What's happening? This cat never leaves my mom's side. Adrenaline spikes through my veins, jolting my heart back into a rapid rhythm. Mom *must* be home ... I just parked my car behind hers ... on the street in front of our house. I run toward Mom's office at the end of the hallway, then to the bathroom. She's neither place. Quickly, I check the third floor, but everything's exactly as it was when I left Friday afternoon.

Sprinting down the stairs, I flip on the switch as soon as I reach the landing. My eyes scan every inch of our small living room. But it looks as it always does.

There is only one remaining room where she could be. Yet, the kitchen is dark. Hesitantly, I force my legs in that direction, but what is normally a five-second walk now feels like eternity. Slowly, I turn on the light.

As soon as the hanging lamp's golden glow illuminates the space, my heart swiftly plummets into my stomach ... Mom is lying on the pale blue linoleum floor, her head tilted to the right. I move toward my mother, kneeling next to her before touching her ashen face. It's cold. I gasp. Felix, who's been following my every move, rubs against my arm, then lets out a chilling moan. He knows.

I cannot remember what happens next. All I recall is how, in a matter of seconds, my entire world falls apart. Everything shatters, as my pillar of strength lies lifeless. Collapsing next to my mom, my body heaves up and down as unimaginable sounds exit my mouth. Felix nudges my shoulder with his head, as if asking for comfort. Sobbing as I gather him in my arms, tears fall onto his soft, striped fur.

At some point, I let go of the cat, stand up, and reach for the phone to dial 911. Swallowing several times before I'm able to respond to the question of, "What's the emergency?" I finally say, "I've just found my mother … on the kitchen floor … she's not breathing." I am unable to use the word *dead*.

The EMTs arrive within minutes. Maybe that's one advantage of living in a city. I watch in silence as they do their job. Once they cover my mother with a faded yellow sheet, the oldest in the group approaches me.

This man, who seems to be in his early forties, gently places his hand on my shoulder, tilts his shaved head, and softly asks, "Can you tell me what happened?"

I nod, but before I can speak, my body begins to shake, and more tears pour from my eyes. The EMT leads me out of the kitchen, away from my mother, and toward the dining table. This man pulls out a chair, helping me to settle into it. Then he sits next to me.

"I know how difficult this must be," he begins, his eyes softening. "My name is Tim." He pauses, offering a sad yet compassionate smile. Instead of pushing me, Tim patiently waits, allowing me to gather myself.

Using the backs of my hands, I wipe my eyes before lifting my chin to look at Tim. Knowing he's only doing his job and I must answer his question, I begin to speak.

"I'm Maggie … I was away this weekend … went to Seven Springs with some old college friends. I had texted my mom … that I was going to stay one more night … then drive home early today before work. But she never responded … I just figured she hadn't looked at her phone … or maybe she went to bed early." I pause. "Mom's not a big texter." Shaking my head, I chastise myself for not calling instead. But I was busy … having fun … thinking only of myself.

My throat becomes even more constricted than before, as I suddenly realize I could have prevented this. If only I had driven back last night. Even if she had already fallen, I could have called an ambulance, taken her to the emergency room … saved her.

"It's all my fault." My voice quivers as I cradle my head with cupped hands. "I should have returned last night … like I'd planned … then she'd be all right."

"Maggie," Tim says, once again placing his hand on my shoulder. "It would not have made a difference if you had returned earlier. It looks like your mother died suddenly … most likely from an aneurysm or a heart attack. Even if you would have been in the room with her, there would have been nothing you could have done to save her."

"But she's only forty-five," I stammer, using the present tense because I cannot refer to my mother in the past.

Instead of responding, Tim remains quiet as that caring look returns to his face. I suppose he's used to comforting people in times of crisis.

After several minutes, Tim proceeds to ask more procedural questions. I do my best to provide him with accurate answers, though I honestly cannot be certain of anything that is coming out of my mouth.

Having shared the "what's next" steps, Tim offers to call someone—a friend or family member—to come and stay with me. I thank him for his kindness but quickly let him know I'm OK. I tell Tim my boyfriend lives close by, and I'll reach out to him as soon as everyone leaves.

I guess Pete, my boyfriend, is the only person I could call. My grandmother is gone, and my grandfather is in a care facility—he has Alzheimer's. Now it's only me. I have no brothers or sisters. And Mom's only sibling died years ago.

I watch Tim and the others wheel my mom's body toward the door. Before they go, I slowly walk toward the gurney, lean down, and place my cheek over her covered torso. No doubt a part of me hopes to hear a heartbeat, making this all a huge mistake. But her body is still, cold. She is truly gone.

The EMTs carry Mom toward the ambulance. I remain on the front porch, watching. As they shut the van's back doors, Tim pauses to look toward me. I swear I see tears in his eyes. He must be one of the real people, the ones who truly care.

I nod my head, then turn as my own tears begin again. After locking the door behind me, I head toward the couch, sit down, and tuck my knees into my chest. Wrapping my arms tightly around them, I begin to rock back and forth. Felix jumps up onto the sofa and nuzzles his tiny gray body next to me.

Instead of calling Pete, I remain on the sofa. I need to be alone. Besides, I don't want Pete here right now. Things haven't been too great between us lately. That's one of the reasons I was so happy to be away with my girlfriends—having fun—without him.

Besides, Pete would only complicate things. Sure, he's one of the sweetest guys I've ever known, but he'd work too hard at telling me everything would be OK … that he'd take care of me. I let out an exhausted sigh.

The truth is, I never wanted Pete to take care of me. This relationship has only continued because I've lacked the fortitude to end it. The guilt of breaking up was too much. Staying together was easier. However, last night I swore to my friends I was finally going to leave him. It seems the only right thing to do—for him and for me.

But dealing with Pete will have to wait. I turn my head toward the kitchen, which is now starkly empty. Moving my hands to my forehead, I dig my fingers into my scalp. Why did this happen to Mom? Last Wednesday she shared the firm had hired a recent graduate to work as her assistant. I thought she'd finally have more time to relax, maybe go to the gym, try yoga … take better care of her health.

But that will never happen. I shift closer toward the arm of the sofa, pull a throw blanket over me, and shut my eyes. Though I know this is not a nightmare, the little girl inside wants to pretend it is. Then all I'd need to do is wake up … and my mom … the only parent I've ever known … would still be alive.

MARLEE
Saturday, April 17

*S*tay home.

It's been weeks since Margaret, the degrading voice inside my head, spoke. I thought she was gone, but apparently she's not.

My jaw tightens as I blankly stare at the opened suitcase in front of me. Glancing at my watch, I inhale deeply, shut my eyes, and try to envision the upcoming week. Unfortunately, this trip will not be a blissful seven days away with friends sipping cocktails poolside. No, Sophia, Annie, and I promised Juliette we'd go with her to Elevar, a holistic retreat held in Costa Rica. According to the hotel's website, this experience will help "unveil your inner-knowing and guide you toward your destiny." I gulp.

While a vacation sounds lovely, I wonder whether Elevar is meant for me, or I for it. Most likely, it's designed for the "awakened," enlightened individuals like Juliette, who know their dharma—a new word I learned, which means "your soul's purpose."

Tucking a strand of loose hair behind my ear, I admit to having no clue about my dharma, except maybe to be Tom's wife and Patrick's mom. I walk to the closet, pull a rain jacket from a hanger, and stuff it into my bag—just in case it actually rains in the rain forest.

Why are you really going, Marlee? Remember … you can't find your soul's purpose without facing your fears. Are you ready to explore those dark shadows, the ones you've buried deep inside for so long?

Damn that Margaret. Reluctantly accepting my demeaning inner voice is back and speaking without invitation, I release a huge sigh, then walk into our bathroom. A sudden heaviness bears down on my shoulders when I zip closed the toiletry case that's next to the sink. Will Margaret tag along to Costa Rica? Or can I mandate she stays here, in Pennsylvania? However, as I return to the bedroom and shove the flowered case into the corner of my carry-on bag, I remind myself *I* have absolutely no control over *her*.

Why does this nagging voice still inhabit my mind? I've made so much progress and certainly don't need Margaret telling me what is and is not in my best interest. Besides, I'm no longer the same person. I squeeze my eyes shut, remembering who I was *before* that weekend at Eagle's Landing, my family's home in the Pocono Mountains.

It all began when Brad, my editor at the *Inquirer*, asked me to write an article highlighting holistic healing options in the Philadelphia area. But for me to properly compose a convincing piece, I needed to do some research.

Still, regardless of how much I read about the topic, I felt stuck, unable to understand the nuances of these practices. This confusion only forced me to dig deeper, prompting me to meet with local healers and learn—firsthand—exactly what they do.

These unusual and somewhat uncomfortable experiences unknowingly led me to see myself from a totally different perspective—as I truly am, not the version of Marlee I'd spent years unconsciously crafting for others. Slowly, I began to uncover shadows and discover self-limiting beliefs and sabotaging patterns. By learning *what can be*, I realized how I'd been living in the dark … paralyzed by fear for most of my life. Gradually, a light within began to flicker. My days now seem to flow with more grace and ease.

Never in a million years did I expect so much could change. However, once I started down this path, *everything* began to shift. Besides finding close friends—something I've always struggled with—I started to face my fears and deal with uncertainty. I've adopted yoga, meditation, and Ayurvedic practices. Plus, I receive monthly Reiki and gemstone healings. Perhaps this explains why I feel happier and my relationship with Tom has never been better.

It's difficult to capture the impact from these past months. And this glimpse into what *can be* has only caused me to want to know more—like why the intuition that suddenly appeared that weekend in the Poconos now seems to have vanished. Unlike with Margaret, that voice felt real, pure, true. I release a sigh and utter a quick prayer that my intuition isn't gone forever. Biting down on my lip, I force my travel pillow into my suitcase before securing it shut.

My mind returns to brunch at Parc, the weekend after we returned from Eagle's Landing. That's when Juliette asked Sophia, Annie, and me to go with her to Elevar. Juliette's description of Nueva Vida, the resort where we'd stay, sounded so peaceful and restorative. But there was more. She raved about the different presenters—I believe she called them healers—claiming this experience would be magical and help take us to the next level of our spiritual path. That's why I agreed to go.

However, as our departure date grew closer, I'd started to sec-ond-guess my decision. I'm not so sure I want to dig deeper. What if I discover things about myself I don't like? Besides, am I willing to let go of what feels comfortable? My life's good—no, it's *great,* better than it's been in ages. Do I really want more?

Do you?

Suddenly my head begins to throb. I wish *she* would go away.

Digging the pads of my thumbs into my temples, I accept it's too late to back out. Like it or not, in several hours, my three friends and I will be headed to Costa Rica.

I scan our bedroom before turning off the lights, conceding the next time I'm in this space, I may be a very different human, altered in unforeseen ways. Shaking off this thought, I pick up my carry-on bag and drag my suitcase out of the room toward the wooden stairway of our restored farmhouse. Hopefully the noise from the wheels will not awaken Patrick.

When I reach the first floor, I see Tom standing at the kitchen island reading the paper, a mug of coffee in his right hand. He insisted on driving me to the Philadelphia airport, claiming it was on his way to work. But that's not true. It's a significant detour.

My heart warms as Tom looks up from the newspaper, walks toward me to give me a kiss, and says, "This trip is going to be a good thing." My husband wraps his arms around me, pulling me into his chest. The unusual upbeat tone of his voice must mean he's concerned. Then again, last night after dinner, I admitted my hesitations about attending the retreat.

"You'll have time with friends, away from Patrick and me." Tom pauses as he traces his finger across my lips. "You don't have any old boyfriends in Costa Rica, do you?" He raises his eyebrows. He's referring to my last trip with Juliette, Sophia, and Annie to the Poconos—when I bumped into Travis. But it was so much more than *bumped into*. Travis became part of our team that proved his sister-in-law didn't murder Wyatt, the man she was secretly seeing. That weekend is when I discovered my intuition—leading me to the information that connected the murderer to the crime. While it was only two months ago, our three days at Eagle's Landing seem like another lifetime.

The tension in my shoulders dissipates. "Nope. That was it. No old boyfriends in Costa Rica." I nestle my face into Tom's shoulder, inhaling his musky scent. "I'm going to miss you. You know that, don't you?"

"And I'll miss you." Tom pulls back and looks into my eyes. "So, when you return, will I recognize you?" he jokes. Yet a part of me wonders if he, too, is unsure about the impact this retreat might have.

"Maybe I'll come back as the new and improved model, Marlee 2.0," I say, attempting to smile. However, a lump suddenly appears in the front of my throat, as I know this is absolutely feasible. And if I return changed, will Tom like the new me?

***

After a bumpy landing, the Boeing 737 taxis down the runway. I gaze at the majestic palm trees gently swaying in the distance. Juliette, who is next to me, sits upright, eyes shut. Her lips turn slightly upward, and the muscles in her face appear relaxed. It's as though she's returning to someplace familiar. Or perhaps she's meditating. Looking farther to my right across the aisle, I see Sophia and Annie, seated next to one another. They're engaged in conversation, most likely about Annie's pregnancy.

Resting my head back into the somewhat faded, royal-blue leather headrest, I allow my mind to wander to the upcoming week. Maybe I'm imagining it to be more than it really will. Besides, Annie's here. And if my nervous friend can handle this retreat, there's absolutely no reason why I should have *any* reservations.

However, as the plane pulls into the gate, waves of anxiety travel to my belly. What's really going to happen these next seven days? Will I be ready for whatever lies ahead?

It's at this exact moment the other voice appears—the sweet, guiding tone I have not heard for weeks.

What if this week is exactly what you need?

Although thrilled that what I believe to be my intuition has finally made itself known, I'm caught off guard by the wording— *what you need.* Why does this exact phrase keep reappearing? Sophia and Juliette have asked me that. And so did Sabrina, during our first gemstone healing session.

Releasing a sigh, I pause ...

What exactly *do I need*? Could I be missing something big, like a significant realization or a "connect the dots" aha moment? Then again, what if I'm ignoring a shadow, a side of myself I'd rather not see? I let out another sigh, hoping whatever it is *I need* will be nice, gentle, and easy to accept.

While a part of me is curious, perhaps even wants more out of life, I have no idea what "more" equates to. Maybe there's a way to achieve a higher level of thinking—or being. I bite my lower lip, knowing I'm overanalyzing the situation. Stop it. Life is good. Everything's *working*. What could I possibly *need*?

The voice whispers ...

For us to grow and become our higher selves, our time on Earth requires more than merely going through the motions and completing the daily "to-dos." There's something else to discover. This is your purpose.

My throat tightens. Could this be true? *Is* something bigger available? And if so, might I find it this week? Is it possible to release my fears, let go, and learn to trust the unknown? Or is that too much to ask?

***

The Customs' line resembles a switchback of humanity moving at a snail's pace. Stop. Breathe. This is supposed to be a vacation. Or maybe it's time away to dig deep within—and discover *what I need*. Regardless, I may as well relax and accept our exit from the San José International Airport will require both time and patience.

While I hate to generalize, it's as though three types of people wait in line: Costa Rican citizens—individuals, couples, and families with children; loud tourists wearing khaki shorts, flowered shirts, and big hats; and the posh people—possibly from Europe,

LA, or New York—dressed in androgynous black clothing, their eyes shielded by dark designer sunglasses.

We don't fit into any of these categories. I guess we're just four women from Philadelphia visiting this beautiful land, hoping to expand our consciousness and discover a new way of being. I roll my eyes and laugh aloud. But my heart skips a beat when I realize I've repeated verbiage from the retreat's website.

"Follow me … this way," Juliette loudly commands as she leads us to the end of the queue.

Looking over my right shoulder, I spot Annie struggling to manage her large canary-yellow hard-shelled roller suitcase along with the sizable matching carry-on. I turn around and take several steps toward my pregnant friend to grab the smaller of the two bags, the one that required two of us to shove it into the plane's overhead compartment. If this is how Annie travels on her own, I can only imagine what she'll pack once she has the baby.

Finally situated in the Customs' line, we have a moment to catch our breath. While I'm dripping in sweat, astounded this international airport does not appear to be air-conditioned, Sophia looks fresh as can be. Gracefully poised, in high heels nonetheless, she appears as though she's stepped out of a fashion magazine. With her jet-black hair casually styled in a tight chignon, my somewhat older friend's wearing high-waisted navy pants and a crisp white linen shirt. I cannot detect any sign of perspiration or impatience. Instead, Sophia calmly waits with a blissful look on her face, as if there is nowhere else in the world she'd rather be.

"Is the line always this long?" Annie, who appears more affected by the heat than I, asks. Almost four months into her pregnancy, Annie must be exhausted. Sophia picked her up at 4:45 this morning. Our first flight departed at 7:15 for Houston. Then, after a two-hour layover, we finally boarded the plane to Costa Rica.

"This is my fourth time here, but it will only be my second at Nueva Vida," Juliette announces as she wipes beads of sweat from her forehead before twisting her flaxen hair into a knot at the nape of her neck. "Now that I think about it, Customs is usually backed up. Seems like most flights arrive around this time." Juliette glances at her watch. The biggest smile comes across her face, and her turquoise eyes illuminate almost as brightly as the still-new diamond ring she proudly wears. "But once we're at the resort, this line will be the last thing on your mind. Trust me." Placing her right hand on her hip, she offers her trademark smirk.

One hour and seven minutes later, a tall man exuding minimal expression stamps my passport. Eager to finally exit the airport, we follow the crowd toward "Ground Transportation."

A warm breeze greets us as soon as we walk out of the sweltering building. The air feels refreshing, in a tropical sort of way. Ahead, a sea of men dressed in white shirts and black pants hold signs bearing the names of various resorts. I scan the crowd, hoping to see "our guy." After a few minutes, we spot a short, smiling man with a "Nueva Vida" laminated placard.

Our driver, who introduces himself as Carlos, grabs Annie's yellow case, then waves for us to follow him. Annie takes her carry-on from me before falling in line behind Juliette, who confidently strides down a cement sidewalk that leads to the parking lot. Several minutes later, I spy a van with our resort's name scripted on its side. After Carlos hoists our bags into the back, he opens a side door, then offers us cold bottles of water from an Igloo cooler. In almost perfect English, he explains that our hotel has a filtration system, but whenever we are outside the resort, we must only drink bottled water.

Carlos turns on the engine before returning to the side of the van with a small step stool. He motions for us to get inside.

"I will return shortly." Sign in hand, Carlos retraces the path back to the terminal. Apparently, we aren't the only guests he's transporting to Nueva Vida.

The cold blast of air-conditioning feels amazing as I climb aboard the van. I suggest Annie and Sophia take the first row, then I settle into the second. Juliette plops down next to me.

Ten minutes later, the side door opens, and a tall, willowy blonde, dressed in slim-cut jeans and a white short sleeve tee, carefully climbs into the van.

"Hi, I'm Maggie." Her voice is soft yet sweet.

While I'm no expert when it comes to women's ages, I'd guess Maggie is in her mid to late twenties. Yet, I can't help but notice a sadness about her. While naturally beautiful, her face appears drawn and her eyes tired, as though she's in need of sleep. Or perhaps she's going through a troubling time and is coming on this retreat in search of answers. Still, it could be she—like me—is merely apprehensive of what lies ahead.

After the four of us introduce ourselves, Maggie makes her way to the back of the van, setting her embroidered backpack down on the unoccupied third row. Her gentle sigh suggests she's also had a long day of travel.

As we begin the drive to Nosara, Juliette exclaims, "This is going to be awesome! You guys are going to love the morning workshops. But it's the private sessions with the healers that will blow your mind. When they tap into you … well, that's when the magic happens." Juliette speaks one hundred miles an hour, and she's quite loud. "I think I'm most excited to meet with the channeler, Daniel Goodman," she adds before flipping her hair in a nonchalant manner.

Suppressing a giggle, I gently nudge Juliette, as if to remind her we're not the only ones in the van. But when I turn in her direction, she seems oblivious—or unfazed—loudly continuing where she left off.

"Daniel's from Chicago. When he channels, he says things twice … first quickly, and then he repeats the words, enunciating each carefully so those present can better hear the message. I've read several of his books and seen him on YouTube." Juliette's tone is crisp and animated. Unsure how Maggie, quietly seated in the row behind us, may embrace the concept of channeling, I place my hand on Juliette's leg, again as a reminder it's not only the four of us in the van.

"I can't wait to hear him," a tender voice from the back of the van says. I feel my shoulders relax. As much as I love Juliette's spirit, sometimes I'm concerned she may overwhelm others with her endless energy and woo-woo ways.

***

The ride to Nosara is anything but comfortable. My body rocks back and forth as the van's wheels traverse endless potholes, noisily bouncing from the undulations of the run-down gravel road system. I worry a bit about Annie and the impact this ride may have on her. But when I crane my neck forward, I see she's asleep, her head resting on Sophia's shoulder.

Finally, after more than two hours, Carlos turns left onto an obscure driveway that leads us into the dense jungle. Noting the sun appears to be lower in the sky, I reflexively check my watch. It's close to five. I remember reading Costa Rica does not practice daylight savings time.

As I glance out the van's window, it's abundantly clear we are far from civilization. I turn to look at Juliette. Earlier she was overflowing with energy, but now every muscle in her body seems to have softened. However, when the van makes a right and proceeds down a cobblestone path, Juliette's face lights up.

"Welcome to paradise," Juliette says, grinning ear to ear.

Ahead of us lies a large white building peppered with bright orange terra-cotta roofs and open-air patios. On the upper levels, private balconies overlook the rain forest. My eyes scan in both directions, entranced by the flowering bushes, palm trees, and pots laden with exotic plants. To my left is a large pool. Lounge chairs, covered with crisp white towels, await their next guests. Across from the pool are endless paths leading to unknown destinations. Then I notice the people. Whether sitting alone on wicker chairs, gathered with others on the balconies, or walking along the stone pathways, all appear at peace. Perhaps Juliette's right. This place may be close to paradise.

One by one, we exit the van. Carlos begins to unload our luggage, placing our bags on a large metal luggage rack before wheeling it away. An elegant woman with shoulder-length graying blonde hair and deep blue eyes walks toward us. She's wearing a stylish white pant suit, but it's her stunning amethyst necklace that catches my attention.

"Welcome, my friends. We are thrilled you have joined us. My name is Dominque." The woman pauses as she opens her arms in a hospitable manner. "My husband, Francisco, and I are the owners of Nueva Vida. Please, follow me." With a glimmer in her eyes, she motions for us to walk up the cobblestone driveway toward an archway covered in magenta bougainvillea. One after another, we enter the registration area. Gray marbled flooring beautifully accentuates the deep mahogany furnishings. White orchids are everywhere, adding a fresh, organic feeling to this space.

"Please have your passport and visa ready for when you check in," Dominique says, then gracefully sits behind a polished wooden counter and begins to type on a keyboard. "What is your name?" she asks with a tilt of her head. Sophia, who is first in line, steps toward the counter and hands Dominique her travel documents.

As Sophia checks in, Juliette, who's next, walks toward the man seated beside Dominque. I listen as she speaks to the handsome older gentleman with thick salt-and-pepper hair. "Hello, I'm Juliette Greene. I've been here before, two years ago. But this time I've brought three of my friends." Juliette stands tall and proud, as if a self-appointed ambassador for Nueva Vida.

"Welcome home," the refined gentleman says. His eyes softly twinkle before they narrow. "Yes, I remember you." He smiles. "I believe when you were last here you had recently opened a yoga studio, am I not correct?"

Juliette nods as she stands a bit straighter, no doubt happy this man recognizes her.

"I trust your business is a huge success." He pauses, then adds, "Please know how happy I am to see you again."

Several moments later, Juliette turns toward me with a devilish look on her face. I watch as she returns her passport and visa to her purse before placing a key tied to a leather cord around her neck. She softly whispers in my ear, "He's the shaman. Wait till you have your one-on-one session with him. He's gonna tell you things that will rock your world." Juliette's eyes widen—as if having my world rocked will be a good thing. She winks at me, then moves out of the way so I can approach the man—rather, the shaman, which I believe translates to a medicine man of sorts. But what is she talking about? We have a one-on-one session?

"Hi, I'm Marlee … Marlee Ryan." I hand *the shaman* my passport and visa.

"Welcome, Marlee Ryan. My name is Francisco." He reaches his hand over the counter to greet me. As his hand embraces mine, an impish grin forms on his face, revealing perfect white teeth. I'm puzzled by his sophisticated appearance—this man doesn't match any image of shamans I've seen. Besides, aren't they supposed to have some mystical name? "Francisco" sounds normal to me. In fact, this man reminds me of Ricardo Montalbán, the actor from *Fantasy Island*, a show we'd watch as kids.

"I see you are staying with Ms. Greene … in one of our tree houses," Francisco casually mentions as he begins typing on the keyboard in front of him.

"A tree house? Oh my gosh, there must be a mistake. I remember all four of us booked rooms in the main building." I wave my hand in a flowing manner, suggesting I belong upstairs, not in the jungle, where monkeys and other wild animals roam.

The man's eyes brighten as he slowly shakes his head. "There is no mistake. Ms. Greene called several weeks ago to alter the reservation. In fact, I remember her insisting on this particular guest suite. It overlooks the ocean and is only a seven-minute walk from here. Trust me—the view makes up for the slight inconvenience." The shaman named Francisco stares deeply into my eyes, and a wave of calmness comes over me. "Do not worry, Ms. Ryan," he says, momentarily pausing after speaking my name. His eyes continue to penetrate mine, as if he's sensing—and possibly easing—my fear of sleeping in a jungle. "It is totally safe. In fact, it is *perfect* for you. Exactly what you require." Offering me a brief grin, he hands me a welcome packet along with a key on a cord, identical in appearance to Juliette's. I glance toward Sophia and Annie, whose room keys are attached to small wooden squares with a number etched into each block. But then my chest tightens as I realize *what you require* is basically the same as *what you need*.

"Please do not fret. You and Ms. Greene will not be alone. In fact, there is a woman staying in the tree house next to yours. I believe you shared the airport transport this afternoon."

He must be referring to Maggie. I exhale, somewhat comforted Juliette and I are not completely by ourselves in the jungle. While we didn't talk much during the van ride, I sensed something quite lovely about Maggie. She appeared more mature than a typical woman her age. But then again, I'd have to say the same for Juliette. Yet Maggie's almost Juliette's opposite. Confident beyond her years,

Juliette seems to know who she is and what she wants. However, I suspect Maggie's slowly evolving, quietly finding her own voice as well as her direction. I shake my head, wondering if perhaps Maggie and I have a few things in common.

Forcing myself to smile, I politely thank the shaman, then quickly walk toward Juliette.

"A tree house, seriously?" Annoyed, I dangle my "room" key in front of her face.

"Well, if I told you, you would have switched the reservation back. Anyway, I've always wanted to sleep in the rain forest. And since Sophia insisted on rooming with Annie, you're stuck with me … in the tree house." Juliette smirks, then raises her eyebrows in a snarky fashion.

"Fine. Whatever. I can handle it," I say as I tuck a loose strand of hair behind my ear. At least that's what I tell myself.

After explaining our "room situation" to Sophia and Annie, we agree to first unpack then meet at six thirty for a drink. According to the welcome packet, dinner service begins at seven; however, there appears to be a lounge area adjacent to the restaurant, so we plan to meet up there.

As my two friends who are staying in a *real* room head toward the elevator, I reluctantly follow Juliette out of the reception area, past the pool, and toward the sign stating "BEACH."

Juliette, who clearly knows her way around the resort, carefully points out various buildings—where we'll go for meditation and yoga, the huts for massages and other spa treatments, and even the way to the sweat lodge, whatever *that* is. As we follow the stone path, my eyes drift upward. Sheltered within the jungle's thick branches are tree houses. But instead of looking rickety or unsafe, they seem warm, cozy … almost enchanting. Wooden stairs zigzag up from the ground in the most casual yet elegant fashion, connecting to a deck equipped with two rocking chairs and a small table.

These elevated rooms do not seem to have glass windows; instead, there are framed openings adorned with wooden shutters.

Suddenly, the sound of crashing waves fills my ears. Though not visible, the ocean *must* be nearby. I inhale deeply … salt air.

"We're here. What do you think?" Juliette asks in a somewhat dreamy voice while tilting her head toward the sky.

Lifting my gaze, I take in our "room." But instead of feeling the jaw pain I often experience whenever I'm in an uncomfortable situation, I notice my shoulders gently slide down my back and realize I'm beginning to smile. Maybe staying in a tree house won't be too bad after all. Appeasing Juliette with a grin, I eagerly follow her up the wooden staircase to the threshold of our "home away from home" for the next seven nights.

"This is so cool," I unexpectedly blurt out, causing Juliette to beam in an "I told you so" fashion.

Before taking in the features inside of the tree house, I find myself drawn to the far side of the room. Mesmerized, I approach the glassless "window." About six hundred feet away lies the ocean. As I watch the day's last sunbeams bounce off the water's glassy surface, any remaining tension from today's travels dissipates. Shifting my eyes to the right, I spy the most immaculate beach. The surf turns over in a rhythmic manner, splashing on the white sand. It appears to recycle its crests every eight seconds.

But it's the people—young and old—who capture my attention. Families swim in the waves, gather around bonfires, and play soccer in a nearby open field. Suddenly, the chaos of Customs and the bouncy van ride vanishes, only to be replaced by an unfamiliar state of serenity. No doubt I have not experienced this sensation for quite some time. Perhaps I'm due.

After several moments of blissful silence, I turn around to examine our room. There are two queen beds, each covered by a cream quilt and several seagrass-green throw pillows. A wooden fan silently swirls above. To the right are two wicker chairs, separated by a small glass table. This could be the perfect spot for a cup of coffee … or maybe journaling. I see our suitcases atop wooden luggage stands at the ends of our beds. Was it difficult for Carlos or another resort employee to lug our baggage up those narrow stairs? But this is their job, what they do each day. It's me who finds the concept of residing in a tree foreign.

Twenty minutes later, after unpacking our belongings and checking out the rest of the room's amenities—a hammock on the back porch, a beverage refrigerator stocked with water bottles and dark chocolate, and a bowl of fresh tropical fruit on the counter—we leave to meet the others. Perhaps staying here won't be too bad after all.

***

Juliette and I spot Annie and Sophia seated at a U-shaped teak bar. As we take the two empty stools next to them, the bartender—a young blonde dressed in black pants and a white cotton shirt—pours rosé for two middle-aged women seated to our right. I watch as they clink glasses in a toast.

"Isn't this place delightful?" the slightly rounded woman dressed in a T-shirt and khaki shorts asks in an Australian accent.

"Yes, it is quite charming. I'd read the glowing reviews. Yet this resort most definitely exceeds my expectations." Wearing an embroidered shift dress, the smaller woman removes her sunglasses, and I notice she is blind in one eye.

Both women wear matching wedding rings. I wonder if they're celebrating the beginning of a well-deserved vacation away. Or perhaps, like me, they're not quite sure why they're here.

The bartender then turns toward us. "What can I get for you?" she asks in a sweet yet confident manner. Her unfamiliar accent and tall stature suggest she is not Costa Rican. Glancing at the name tag pinned to her blouse, I see her name is Alana Martin and she's from Portugal.

"Club soda, please ... with a lime," Annie responds.

"I would like a glass of sauvignon blanc," Sophia says, looking elegant as ever in a white halter sundress. Her long dark hair falls gracefully over her perfectly squared shoulders.

"What signature drinks do you have?" Juliette, dressed in gauzy teal pants and a black tank top, asks as her eyes light up. "I remember last time I was here they served these amazing guaro sours," she adds. She begins to play with the beads of the labradorite mala hanging around her neck.

"We still do," Alana says, grinning, then tilts her head toward the left. Two couples are drinking delicious-looking light green cocktails garnished with lime.

"Two please." Juliette then turns to face me, "This drink is beyond amazing, Marlee. Guaro comes from Costa Rica. It kinda tastes like vodka, but it's sweeter."

Although my first instinct is to tell Juliette I'll order for myself, I take a breath as well as a step back to consider the situation.

When Annie presented the idea of going to Costa Rica to her husband, Jonathon, he expressed concerns. He worried about her—being three and a half months pregnant and almost forty-five years old—traveling in a developing country. However, Sophia, who is an internist, promised Jonathon she would watch over Annie this week.

Since Sophia feels it's her responsibility to ensure Annie's well cared for, I guess that leaves me to be Juliette's bestie. Fully aware of Juliette's assertive side, I remind myself of her many positive traits. Incredibly intelligent, Juliette has her doctorate in philosophy from Yale. And this amazingly energetic twenty-eight-year-old studied at an ashram in India and now owns her own yoga studio. Juliette's also trained in energy healing, and she's always the first one to offer help to others.

While I'm happy to room with Juliette … even if it is in a tree house in the rain forest, she must let me make my own decisions, at least allow me to order my own drink. Nevertheless, I can't deny the soft side I have for Juliette. Knowing she's only being who she is, I choose to surrender and let her call the shots … at least for now.

"That sounds wonderful," I say, swallowing a bit of my pride yet resigned to go with the flow. Meanwhile, Alana's busy muddling sugar and lime juice in two rocks glasses. Next, she adds a healthy pour from a bottle of guaro liquor before topping it off with a squirt of club soda. She hands the picture-perfect cocktails to Juliette.

Several minutes later, we leave the bar area and move to the patio. Adorned with exquisite potted plants and soothing water fountains, this beautiful outdoor space appears as a gateway to the lush rain forest. I gaze ahead, entranced by the grandeur of this exotic jungle. The intensity of each color appears to be magnified tenfold. Green leaves transform into sparkling emeralds, and the orange and purple blossoms appear iridescent. My nose twitches as I detect an unfamiliar sweet scent. Most likely, it's from the flowering foliage. While I'm wondering what exactly lives in this tropical forest, a loud rustling startles me. Reflexively, I turn my head to the left toward several swaying trees. Then suddenly, out of nowhere, there's a loud screech. Three more follow. My head swivels back and forth, searching for the source.

"Those are howler monkeys," Juliette casually says as she walks toward the wooden railing. "If you look carefully, you can see them … Watch … up in those trees." She points at moving branches as she speaks.

While Sophia and I move to the balcony's edge to scan the jungle's tree line in hope of spotting the monkeys, Annie stays put on the sofa.

"They aren't harmful," Juliette says to Annie, noting her hesitance. "In fact, the monkeys are more afraid of you than you are of them." And with that statement, she flips her flaxen hair before motioning for Annie to join us. Still, Annie remains seated, clutching her glass of club soda.

When I finally see the monkeys—eight in all, some slightly hidden by tree branches—I gasp, eyes wide in awe. The largest, who is obviously a male, begins swaying through the trees. Grabbing branches with his nimble hands and tail, he effortlessly glides across the jungle's ceiling as thunderous screams emanate from his mouth. Immediately, I'm reminded of old Tarzan movies. Yet this is a true primate, not a man swinging on a rope across a Hollywood set.

Earlier this month, while researching Costa Rica, I discovered an informative article about howler monkeys. Apparently, their cries are not meant to intimidate. Rather, they're a communication model for calling to one another, mating, or establishing territory. But what seemed most fascinating is you can hear these primates from up to three miles away. That must explain their name.

Out of the corner of my eye, I watch as Annie slowly inches closer to the railing. Maybe she merely needed time to warm up to the concept of monkeys in our backyard. However, when I turn toward her, it's evident she's focused on the tiniest howler hanging onto its mother's neck. Gradually, the muscles in Annie's face relax, and her lips form a curious smile. Of course. Annie's connecting to the baby howler. I suspect this little one's activated her maternal instincts, sensations Annie once doubted she could feel.

After several minutes of being entertained by the monkeys, we—and several other guests who had migrated to the railing—return to our seats.

"Shall we move to the dining room?" Sophia asks before taking a final sip of wine.

"Please, I'm starving," Annie announces as she rises.

It's then I note a small rumble in my stomach. Dinner sounds wonderful, especially since I haven't really had much since the protein bar I ate right before we landed. Plus, while it's only 7:15, my body thinks its two hours later.

We place our glasses on the bar counter and thank Alana before heading toward the dining area.

Unsure of what to expect regarding the food at this resort—the website only stated there would be organic meals prepared with a Blue Zone influence—I wonder if the kitchen is strictly vegan. But maybe not. When I googled "Blue Zone diet," the articles stated fish and meat are included on occasion.

While the others find an empty table, I head to the buffet, too curious not to check what's for dinner. Only then do I realize Nueva Vida's website totally understated its culinary offerings. Of course, I have yet to taste the food, but everything looks amazing. White cards placed in front of each dish share the names as well as the ingredients. There's shrimp, marinated in a verde sauce and sprinkled with fresh herbs; an assortment of roasted vegetables, some of which I've never seen before; rice mixed with beans, peppers, and onions; ceviche; and containers of warm tortillas next to bowls of gallo pinto.

Already, I'm mentally calibrating how to replicate these dishes once I return home. My mind crafts tentative recipes, though I suspect I'll need to make substitutions as certain ingredients will be challenging to find in Pennsylvania. Still, I bet I can come close.

"Wow," a wide-eyed Annie says as she takes a plate, then adds generous helpings of shrimp, vegetables, and the rice medley. I can tell she's famished. But then again, she is eating for two. I momentarily recall how much I consumed when I was pregnant with Patrick. But that was so long ago, almost another lifetime.

"Now do you trust me?" Juliette grins as she begins to help herself to the roasted vegetables. "I told you this place was fabulous.

And wait till you see the desserts. Just because we're on a retreat doesn't mean we have to starve ourselves." She winks, then heaps gallo pinto on top of a corn tortilla.

I motion for Sophia to go before taking a plate. Helping myself to a bit of each dish, I make a mental note of how I suspect it was prepared.

Moments later, the four of us are seated, devouring our dinner. Everything I put in my mouth exceeds all expectations. There's little conversation, only questions such as, "Have you tried the shrimp?" or "What spices do you think the chef used on the roasted vegetables?"

However, when a gorgeous man who appears to be in his mid-thirties approaches our table, we all pause, place our forks onto our plates, and stare. Sexy as hell, jet-black hair clearly accentuates his dreamy crystal-blue eyes. And his fitted chef's jacket makes it obvious this man is not only incredibly handsome but also quite fit.

In the most delicious French accent, he says, "I hope you are enjoying your meal. May I introduce myself? I am René Moreau, the head chef at Nueva Vida." With that, he gives a slight bow, the entire time maintaining eye contact with Juliette. Right before me, the overly confident, newly engaged Juliette turns a deep shade of crimson.

"Chef Moreau, have you published any of your recipes?" I ask, hoping to distract his attention away from my young friend who is soon marrying Michael, an orthopedic surgeon in my husband's practice. "I would love to try them when I return home."

"Regretfully, I have yet to create a ... what would you say ... a cookbook? But it is my hope to do so some day." His voice inflects at the end of the sentence. And although he answers me, I may as well be invisible. His gaze is fixed on Juliette.

As soon as he's gone, Juliette says, in an indignant fashion, "I think I was just eye-fucked."

Unable to contain ourselves, we burst into laughter, only causing Juliette's face to redden more. "Seriously, who does he think he is? Didn't he see the ring on my finger?" she protests, but the entire time she seems to be flattered by his attention.

"Don't be offended," Annie says, giggling again. "Feel lucky the yummy-looking chef has a thing for you. I mean, he certainly wasn't looking at me, a chubby pregnant lady." She laughs again.

"Nor was he paying attention to me. I assume I am a bit too old for him," Sophia says as she arches her perfectly formed eyebrows, then purses her brick-red lips in a demure fashion. "He is *very* good looking." With this statement, she bats her eyelashes, causing me to laugh.

Even though we seem to be behaving like a bunch of teenage girls, I have an urge to add my two cents. "And despite that I'm the one who asked about his recipes"—I inhale loudly—"he barely acknowledged me. I guess I'm not his type." I fully exhale, then shrug my shoulders, all while looking mischievously at Juliette.

By now, Juliette no longer looks insulted. Instead, her eyes are sparkling though her face is still red, causing me to wonder *if maybe* she's flattered by his attention and finds him *a bit* attractive.

"Consider it a compliment. Anyway, don't you think Michael still gets stares at the hospital?" As soon as the words come out of my mouth, I realize my error. Suggesting to my beautiful yet jealous friend that other women flirt with her fiancé was a huge mistake. No doubt my comment will only add fuel to this fire. Juliette furrows her brow, looking as though she may erupt.

Fortunately, I'm saved from Juliette's wrath when Francisco enters the dining area and announces this evening's "Welcome Talk" will begin in ten minutes. I take this as a cue to go to the dessert table. After grabbing a plate of tres leches cake, I proceed to the beverage station where I fix myself a cup of herbal tea. Sophia and Annie follow me, leaving Juliette alone to brood. On my way back to the table, I swing by the dessert station again to grab another plate of cake, then place it in front of Juliette. Maybe she'll take this as a peace offering of sorts.

"Hey, I'm sorry. There is absolutely nothing for you to worry about. Michael adores you," I quickly say before the others return with their desserts and beverages.

Juliette scrunches her nose, then takes a bite of the cake. Speaking as she eats, she says, "I want to trust him. It's just that, well, with his history, I still wonder if ..." But she refrains from finishing the sentence.

"Come on. You know he's not that type. Sure, when he was single ... but now he's committed to you. Asking you to marry him was a big deal for Michael."

Juliette tilts her head as she swallows. "What do you mean?"

"Let's just say that he and Tom talk from time to time. Now it's you who must trust me ... Stop worrying. Besides, 'your shaman' is going to begin soon." I motion with my eyes to the front of the room. Francisco, holding a glass of what appears to be ice water in one hand, stands at a podium. After taking a sip, he places the glass on the dais, clears his throat, then speaks.

"Welcome. I am so very happy each of you chose to join us ... not only here at Nueva Vida but also for our newest retreat ... Elevar." A vibrant glow comes over his face.

"As you may know, *Elevar* is Spanish for 'to elevate.' And that is our greatest hope for the next six days ... that each person here elevates to a higher version of themselves." This shaman who looks like a normal man takes a moment before continuing. "Now, of course, elevation means something different for each of you, as every person's reason for attending is unique. It would be ignorant of me to plan a retreat assuming each one of you required the same healing. Of course, that is never the case." His head tilts, and for a moment, his eyes blink shut a bit longer than normal. I wonder where this is going.

"You"—Francisco pauses as he takes his time to look at each table—"are here for a specific purpose … though I suspect many of you are still unaware of this particular reason." He smiles, in a knowing way. "For now, it is not important to know the *why*. All that matters is you have made a pledge toward your personal growth." Again, he stops to smile. It's as though he is purposely connecting with each of us.

"I promise this week will be filled with unexpected experiences. Some will be joyful, and others …. well, they may test your resolve. Over the next six days, presenters will share their truths and talents through both workshops and private healing sessions. During your stay, our caring staff will do its best to make you as comfortable as possible. But in return"—he again takes a moment, scanning the room for emphasis—"I ask one thing … that you trust us." Pause. Nervously I look at Sophia as I wait for the shaman to continue.

"This is not a small request, as one's trust is sacred and should never be taken for granted. But as we guide you into the unknown to help you unveil your shadows, heal your wounds, and lift … or elevate … to new possibilities, you will come to understand that personal transformation is worth any discomfort it may initially cause. The work can be difficult. And some pain may be necessary for growth to occur."

Annie kicks me under the table, causing me to flinch. I look in her direction. She is visibly shaken. I place my hand on her arm, hoping to calm her nerves.

"Part of this week's *assignment* is to accept the mystery, the uncertainty that lies ahead." Francisco chuckles before saying, "I will not tell you what to expect. It is better for you to discover your path on *your* terms." He stops and takes another sip from his glass, then glances at his watch.

"It is now time to introduce this week's speakers. Each will offer a morning workshop. While there is no prescribed format for presenters to follow, sessions will last approximately two hours. There may be a talk with time afterward for reflection and questions. Or perhaps you will be asked to participate in various activities." He pauses. I look at Juliette sitting on the edge of her chair, seemingly over her anger and now entranced by Francisco.

"These morning workshops serve as an introduction to each healer's specialty. However beneficial the group experience may be, the *real work* occurs at the individual level."

I glance around the table. Sophia looks as calm as ever, but Annie's eyes widen with each statement the shaman makes.

"We *encourage* our guests to sign up for private sessions with our presenters. These one-on-one meetings are what allow you to go deeper. With the guidance of a trained professional, you will be supported to look within … and discover *what you need*." I again flinch upon hearing this all-too-familiar phrase.

"And, of course, as promised, I will meet with every guest for a personal healing session. This is my gift to you." Those in the room begin to applaud. Juliette's particularly enthralled, clapping louder than most. But Annie sinks even deeper into her chair.

"And now, permit me to introduce you to this week's presenters." As if on cue, a group of men and women join Francisco at the podium.

"Elevar's first speaker will be Sonya Roberts. The lovely Sonya will unveil the mystery behind astrology and how the movement of the planets impacts our daily lives." A woman, looking to be in her early thirties, confidently waves to the group. Tall and stunning with long tousled blonde hair, the astrologer in a crinkled indigo sundress appears totally comfortable and at ease. I find myself drawn to the moonstone pendant that graces her neck.

"Sonya will explain natal charts, help you understand the influences of the moon, and show how planets interact with one another." This astrologer appears to have a glow, or aura, around her. I suspect she truly does have a special gift.

"On Monday, we'll hear from Conor Kelly." A young strawberry-blond man takes a step forward and smiles. "While in his final year of dental school, Conor discovered he had an unusual ability … He can see what has not yet occurred. Conor uses these premonitions to assist his clients with life decisions."

Annie's eyes bulge when she hears this. But, of course, she's recently discovered her own psychic abilities. I'm guessing she will want to attend this session.

"Next, the lovely Lindsay Keeler will share with you the world of Sound Healing. Through drums, gongs, and other instrumental effects, you will experience the numerous benefits sound and music can have on the body. Lindsay's husband, Jack, is a close friend of Dominique's and mine. Jack now practices functional medicine and relies on the combination of traditional medical training, holistic knowledge, and his gifted intuition to heal others. Together, Lindsay and Jack are a most powerful couple." Francisco turns and winks at a man in the audience who is surely Lindsay's husband. It's then that a pretty young woman dressed in a long flowing flowered skirt and a white tank top steps forward. She appears a bit tentative, as she swirls loose strands of her blonde hair around her fingers. However, the man, whom I assume is Jack, beams. No doubt he's quite proud of Lindsay.

"On Wednesday, we are thrilled to present Daniel Goodman, a first-time guest at Nueva Vida. Be ready to encounter the world of channeling. You do not want to miss this session," Francisco says with a wink as a somewhat balding Black man, dressed in a dark gray long sleeve shirt and khaki pants, hesitantly takes a step forward. He smiles, but only momentarily. Clearly, he's uncomfortable in the spotlight.

"Anahata will lead Thursday's session. Unlike the other workshops, this will be a powerful cleansing ritual designed to help you release toxic emotions so you can better integrate everything you will be encountering this week." This thin older woman wearing a lavender sari does not move. Instead, she stares straight ahead as if she is not only here but also somewhere else.

"On Friday, I will conduct the final workshop. While retreats calm the mind and revive the soul, we must inevitably return to our homes, families, and workspaces. To prevent us from resuming old habits and patterns, it is important to make conscious decisions if we hope to maintain our transformation. We will discuss how to continue your life but at a higher level." Francisco takes a sip of water.

"Many of our presenters have books and other materials you may wish to purchase. All items will be available for you to peruse both during their workshops as well as at our gift shop." He smiles momentarily at a woman standing next to Dominique. "And finally, before we end tonight, I'd like you to meet our resort's staff."

"First, Chef Moreau." The man who apparently "eye-fucked" my friend smiles broadly, then unabashedly grins in Juliette's direction. Despite our best effort to contain our smirks, three of us giggle like little girls. However, our fourth blushes, biting her lower lip as she stares down at her left hand.

"Helping him in the kitchen is Victor Jimenez, better known as Vic. Born and raised in Nosara, Vic and his wife have two precious little boys—who happen to be our godchildren." Francisco beams when he shares this. "You may see these two children running around our property from time to time, most likely getting into mischief." The shaman affectionately smiles as Vic bashfully nods his head. Francisco then says something quietly to Vic, causing him to laugh aloud. I watch as Vic's thick black curls bounce up and down on his forehead. Imagine having a shaman as your children's godfather.

"I am pleased to introduce Isabella Pérez to you. Isabella is a dear family friend, and we are thrilled she recently became the manager of our new gift shop, which is located on this floor next to the elevator." A very attractive middle-aged brunette wearing a tailored black skirt and a sage blouse offers a broad smile, then waves to the group. She has the most beautiful cheekbones I've ever seen. Yet I couldn't help but notice how Dominique gently touched Isabella's arm during Francisco's introduction. But, of course, earlier Francisco mentioned Isabella was a family friend.

"Alana Martin, from Portugal, is our talented barista and bartender. Whether it is a latté you desire or our signature cocktail, the guaro sour, Alana is the woman to see."

Juliette nudges my arm and mouths, "I told you they are known for that drink."

"Our café bar is open from nine in the morning until nine at night. For those early risers, our kitchen will have coffee and a continental breakfast available from 5:30 a.m. until breakfast service begins at eight o'clock. Additionally, should you like to purchase food or beverages for your room, that can most certainly be arranged through the front desk."

"And finally, what would our resort be without the talented members of our spa as well as our health and fitness team? Led by Dr. Jack Keeler"—Francisco momentarily pauses as he motions to Jack who is seated next to Lindsay—"our professionals are highly trained to help you relax, rejuvenate, and meet your wellness goals. Additionally, Jack is available for private consultations. At Nueva Vida, we are committed to assisting you with healing your body, mind, and spirit. While Jack's staff is not with us tonight, you will be able to meet them tomorrow. Each morning, Eduardo leads a group meditation at seven, followed by yoga with Kali from seven thirty till eight thirty. I encourage you to try both, even if these practices are new to you." Francisco pauses, smiles, then pauses once again. This seems to be an ingrained habit. Or perhaps he does this with intent.

"Sabina and Angelica are our holistic therapists who offer a variety of spa treatments. Consider booking an appointment with each of these wonderful ladies, as their unique healing gifts will surely enhance your week's stay."

Again, Francisco takes a moment to gaze around the room. I'm beginning to think this behavior is deliberate. Maybe he senses apprehension and wants to personally connect with each guest, to provide a bit of comfort. I'm certainly unsettled about what may transpire this week.

A calmness comes over the room. Could this be Francisco's doing? Still, I can't help but think this man doesn't appear or behave how I envisioned a shaman would.

"You may be wondering about me. After all, I know I don't fit into the mold of a traditional shaman." His enchanting smile brightens the room, as the guest laugh softly. But I'm not laughing. Instead, I'm stunned, wondering if he just read my mind. But that would be ridiculous. I'm sure it's only a coincidence.

"Like each of you, I have my own story," he says, then looks toward his wife who is now glowing. Perhaps this is rehearsed, something they repeat to every group.

"Many years ago, I knew a little girl who lived in my neighborhood of Las Condes ... in Santiago, Chile. I remember she always wore her hair, which would become almost a white blonde during the summer, in two pigtails. In fact, I think I got into trouble for pulling those pigtails once or twice." Everyone laughs.

"Well, as the years passed, we each went our separate ways. I attended medical school, then married a beautiful woman during my final year of residency. My wife and I remained in the area, as I accepted a position in the oncology department at Clínica Las Condes. We had a perfect life. That is until my wife developed cancer." He stops, looking down at his hands folded on top of the podium. Before continuing, Francisco takes a sip of water, then clears his throat. "Despite my profession, there was nothing I could do to help her. Within six months, she was gone." A heavy silence fills the room. Suddenly, I feel lucky about how my bout with breast cancer turned out.

"I felt lied to, cheated, angry. What I had learned at medical school could not save my wife. But deep inside, I knew there must be other ways to heal the sick."

"I spent the next six months researching practices not recognized by modern medicine. Only then did I realize I had focused on relieving my patients' symptoms. But to truly eradicate the source of illness, one must treat the cause—be it physical, emotional, or energetic—not only the effects." As he speaks, I turn my head toward Sophia, who is now sitting up straight, captivated by Francisco's every word. Knowing she's recently decided to add holistic methods to her medical practice, I assume his story deeply resonates with her.

"Concurrently, I noticed something shift within me. Nuances I'd never seen. I was better able to understand people … the 'whys' behind their words and actions. But then this sensation grew … to the point where I could not only comprehend another's motives, but I could also predict what lessons lie ahead for them … their karma." Francisco stops for a moment, as if to gauge the group's reaction. He then continues.

"Perhaps this new awareness combined with my need to understand how to treat the causes, not merely the effects, of 'dis-ease' … when trauma from our energetic body impacts our physical body … are what led me to the jungles of Peru." A smile returns to his face.

"Of course, this was not easy. I had to show the local shamans I was committed. More importantly, *I* needed to believe I could learn their ways. Eventually, one took me on as his apprentice, and I spent months listening, studying, and assisting in ceremonies. I followed him throughout the jungle, procuring precious plants to make the medicine. I learned the *icaros*, a term for their chants, and devotedly practiced their rituals." Francisco exhales loudly.

"Saying this came naturally would be a lie. I had to unlearn so I could finally *see*. Eventually, I began to *know*. Three years later, I was allowed to lead one of the retreats. There were twelve people coming for five days of healing. Ten men and two women. I believe you can guess the identity of one of the women." With his left hand, he gestures to Dominque, who slowly nods her head as if to corroborate his story.

"Immediately we recognized each other from our childhood. As you might imagine, she was quite surprised to find me … in the jungle … conducting her healing session. Dominique thought she was getting a Peruvian shaman, not the grown-up version of a little boy who used to tease her on the playground." By the grins and nods of those in the room, it's apparent everyone is enjoying this story.

"It is then I learned the lovely Dominique had just left a marriage and, like many of you, was searching for answers. Before the end of the first day, I felt something in my heart I never expected to experience again. I'd like to think she had a similar reaction, though she claims it took her a bit longer." I hear laughs and watch as several of the couples shake their heads, suggesting they had a similar experience.

"After the final day of the retreat, I told Dominique of my feelings. I never expected to fall in love, especially with a woman who came to the jungle for shamanic healing. But I did … and it was at this time she admitted she was in love with me." Francisco walks over to Dominique, takes her hand, then leads her to the podium.

"Good evening," Dominique addresses the group in a refined and elegant manner. "What Francisco says is true. After twenty years of being married to a very powerful man, I realized I was living a lie. I could no longer ignore the affairs, pretend to be the doting spouse, and stand by his side as he spoke lies. I wasn't a weak woman by nature, but I had allowed myself to become one. Luckily, I woke up, before it was too late," she says.

"Our daughter was attending college in the States, leaving only my husband and me at home. Despite my family's objections … they were quite concerned about me damaging my, or perhaps *their*, reputation … I left my husband." She raises her eyebrows in a disapproving fashion. It's at this moment that I connect the similarities between Dominique's and Sophia's mannerisms. Although Dominique is lighter in complexion and somewhat shorter than Sophia, they could be sisters.

"It was several months later that I traveled to the rain forests of Peru. Francisco has already shared what transpired during the retreat." She pauses, and a faint blush comes across her face. "When it was time to return to Santiago … of course, no one knew where I was … I'd told friends and family I traveled to a spa in Belize …" Juliette let's out a snort, causing everyone to glance back at our table. "I found I did not want to leave … this man nor the jungle." Dominique continues without missing a beat. "I extended my stay, and Francisco spoke to his shaman, requesting his blessing for time away so we could sort through our situation. We found a lodge within several hours and spent the next ten days together figuring out what had happened between us. After intensive inquiry, both alone and together, we knew our answer. Neither of us wanted to return to Santiago. I desired a fresh start, a second chance of sorts, and Francisco realized his calling was to heal, but as a shaman, not a medical doctor," she says.

"And that is when we decided to create our own retreat center, a resort where we could give others their own second chance. We considered the name Segunda Oportunidad, but felt it limiting. Francisco and I wanted our guests to return multiple times, so we christened our new venture Nueva Vida … or 'New Life' … in honor of *our* new life together as well as the new life we hope to offer to those who visit." Dominique reaches for Francisco's hand, then gives it a squeeze. "And then the unimaginable happened. My daughter, Camille, and her boyfriend moved to Nosara. Together, they designed and built an elementary school, one based on the foundations of both the Montessori and Waldorf methods. They gave our community the most beautiful gift, benefiting our children in so many ways. And last year, they married … and are now expecting their first child." Dominque pauses, and a huge smile comes across her face. Francisco wraps his arm around his wife, kissing the top of her head. "Should you be interested in learning more about this beautiful project, please see me and I will connect you with Camille," Dominque adds, sounding like a proud mother.

I turn and see Annie's on the edge of her chair. She must have sensed my glance, as she then turns toward me and mouths, "I want to see that school."

I smile. It's nice to see Annie interested in something besides work.

"It is our greatest hope this upcoming week assists you in uncovering pieces of yourself you've hidden, ignored, or perhaps forgotten. It is through our journey inward that we realize what *can be*." Dominique pauses, perhaps permitting us time to grasp the impact of her last words.

"As Francisco shared earlier, please participate in the meditation and yoga sessions as they will prime your mind and body to receive the many gifts from this week's presenters. And remember to pamper yourself. You may sign up for spa treatments by visiting our front desk, or you can reserve your appointments online. Some of you have booked in advance, but there are many openings available. The same is true for private sessions with our presenters. Remember, we are always here to help you manage your schedule."

Then Dominique takes a deep breath before continuing. "Francisco also mentioned the healing sessions he offers to each guest. For those new to Nueva Vida, you may be wondering what this involves. My answer is that it depends *on what you need*," she says with a twinkle in her eyes.

Goose bumps form on my arms. Why does this phrase keep appearing?

"But do not worry. Francisco will know, and he will design your time together so he can help heal those areas that hold you back from achieving your dreams." Dominique's face softens. She then adds with a smile, "Please, enjoy yourselves tonight. I've asked Alana to remain until ten o'clock, in case anyone would like to mingle."

"They are both incredibly fascinating," Sophia whispers as people begin to leave their tables, some for the elevators, and a few for the bar area.

"Of course, I'd never say I told you so," Juliette begins, no doubt squelching a desire to add *but I did*.

"I'm still not sure I want to meet with Francisco." Annie's voice sounds timid.

"Annie, you do you. Don't if it makes you uncomfortable," Juliette says with a shrug of her shoulders.

"But do not disregard it either." Sophia's tone is motherly, a role she seems to be fulfilling a lot when it comes to Annie.

"But it could be *uncomfortable*."

"Uncomfortable is not a bad thing," Juliette adds as she walks toward four empty seats by the bar. "Maybe experiment a bit, do things you normally wouldn't try. After all, once the baby arrives, you won't have this opportunity for a while."

I refrain from giving Annie advice as I, too, am leery of my upcoming shamanic session. While quickly reviewing the welcome packet before leaving our room, I saw a note stating I'm scheduled to meet with Francisco on Monday afternoon—less than two days away. This reminds me, we must book our other sessions.

"When we get back to the room, do you think we should go online and sign up for spa treatments? I'm not sure what else I want to do. The presenters sounded so interesting," I say, trying to be up-beat but anticipating some may be too "out there" for me.

"Oh, you don't have to worry about that," Juliette proudly announces as she runs her fingers through her hair. "I took care of setting up your schedules ... Not only spa treatments, but I also booked our sessions with the presenters, or healers, whatever you choose to call them." Juliette pauses for a moment, smiling at the three of us, as if expecting a heartfelt "thank you." When no one speaks, she says, "It's my gift to you ... for agreeing to come along on the retreat. I wanted to make sure you have the best experience."

"What did you sign me up for?" I ask, instinctively clenching my jaw.

"It's a surprise. I'll share your itineraries tomorrow at break-fast," Juliette nonchalantly says as she catches Alana's attention. But then her nose begins to scrunch a bit. "You all trust me, don't you? I mean, you know I'd take care of you, match you with the healers best for you."

I watch Annie's brows furrow. Even Sophia shows an unusual display of annoyance as she purses her lips.

"How do *you* know what's best for *us*?" Annie tentatively asks, her hands grasping the rounded edge of the mahogany bar.

Immediately, Juliette's body slackens. Perhaps she now realiz-es she's overstepped a boundary, one of the cardinal sins in friendship. "I'm sorry," she says, her eyes welling with tears. "I didn't mean to be controlling. I only wanted to make things easier for everyone."

Alana, who is approaching us, pauses, then quickly busies herself by tidying up the cocktail napkins. No doubt she picked up on the tension.

"Maybe if you tell us now, then perhaps we can all relax." It's Sophia who speaks as she turns to face Juliette.

"OK, but first let's order a glass of wine … and, of course, a club soda for Annie. Then I can show you the emails I saved on my phone." With that, Juliette turns toward Alana and begins to speak.

"Did I hear her correctly?" I whisper to the others. "She decided all of this… like she did with switching my room … without asking?"

"I believe she did," Sophia says, but her voice does not waver. It's then her emerald eyes begin to sparkle. "Perhaps this is meant to be." She lifts her shoulders in a slight hunch. "After all, would you have opted to meet privately with healers… or stay in a tree house … had Juliette not taken the liberty to choose for you?"

Sophia's right, but that's beside the point. Juliette was presumptive in scheduling everything, even if it does make it easier for us… or, more likely, pushes us out of our comfort zone. Resigned I have absolutely no control over what happens this week, I let out a brief sigh. Perhaps this is the Universe nudging me to let go and surrender to what is, something I struggle to do.

Ha! You can tell yourself anything you want, but you know the truth … You're too scared to let go … because you're afraid that God does not exist.

Damn that Margaret. Why can't she stay silent? But then my throat tightens. What if she's right?

MAGGIE

Sunday, April 18

Beautifully nestled among palm trees and beds of tropical plants, this bamboo structure appears more like a shed than a building for meditation and yoga. But once I'm inside, it's clear the space was expertly designed and constructed for mindful movement.

Black yoga mats, placed in the shape of a perfect circle, take up most of this room. To my right are shelves filled with bolsters, blocks, blankets, and additional mats. On the opposite wall hangs mystical artwork. Immediately, my attention goes to a watercolor of lotus flowers depicting the seven chakras. Then my eyes travel toward a gold-framed oil painting of Ganesh before spotting an intricate pen-and-ink sketch of Buddha in a garden. I smell sandalwood. Looking for the source, I see incense burning on top of a bronze plate in the center of the circle.

After removing my flip-flops, I step upon the cool cork floor. It's as though someone's meticulously considered every detail of this space, anticipating what's necessary for those who enter to let go and relax. Just then, I hear the most delightful sound coming from behind me. Turning around, I discover several brass chimes hanging by the open-air windows. In an unconscious response, my shoulder blades slide down my back as I let out a faint sigh.

"Please, find a place that speaks to you." A tall, swarthy man with wavy shoulder-length brown hair emerges from a closet tucked behind the shelves. He's wearing flowered board shorts and a white tank top. But it's his turquoise necklace that calls my attention. Perhaps it's the contrast of the vibrant blue stone against his tanned skin. Then again, it could be the energy of the gemstone—serenity and peace—a state I truly desire.

I sit directly across from what I suspect is our instructor's space. At the top of each mat lies a perfectly folded striped yoga blanket. Tufted meditation cushions, ranging in colors from pale blue to deep purple, sit in front of the blankets. I watch as the man goes to his phone and taps it several times. Soft music fills the room. The melody sounds familiar, yet I cannot place it. Maybe it's a song I've heard at my yoga studio in Pittsburgh. Then, as if on cue, a gentle breeze sounds the chimes, creating a graceful flow of vibrations from the outside into the studio.

As I settle on the bolster and shut my eyes, I try to unwind. But despite the calming environment, my body's returned to its "new normal"—anxious and stressed. With my shoulders hunched close to my ears, thoughts ping-pong throughout my head. But of course. Every time I sit to meditate, that monkey mind reappears. Jumping from one idea to the next, this untamed animal makes my search for peace an impossible quest. Nevertheless, I do my best to dismiss the internal chatter and focus on my breath.

Several minutes later, I slowly open my eyes and glance about the room. All but two of the mats are taken. To my left are the four women from the van ride. I smile in their direction, offering a small wave of acknowledgment. As one of them—I think her name is Marlee—returns the gesture, an unexpected warmth fills my body. Strangely, I find it calming. Is this coming from Marlee, or am I finally beginning to relax? All I know is she seems kind, in a maternal sort of way. With that thought, my throat constricts.

"Good morning," says the instructor, sitting cross-legged on his mat. His accent is slow and thick. "My name is Eduardo Feria, and it is my pleasure to welcome you to morning meditation. Each day, we will practice for approximately thirty minutes. If this is new to you, no worries. Please, make yourself comfortable. And should sitting on a mat be difficult, you may lie down ... Whatever is easiest for you."

All at once, the participants begin to move, adjusting their bodies in various ways. While several choose to recline on their backs, most sit, either on their mat or atop a bolster. I use my bolster, doing my best to lengthen my spine while allowing my knees to fall toward the ground. After closing my eyes, I slow down my breath, conscious to take long inhales and exhales.

Several minutes later, Eduardo speaks: "I've chosen a guided meditation for this morning, as it is a wonderful introduction for those new to the practice. All you must do is listen to my voice." He pauses, causing me to wonder whether his smooth accent might help calm my mind, releasing those endless unsettling thoughts.

"After our time together, my dear friend, Kali, will be offering an hour-long Vinyasa yoga class. I encourage you to participate in both morning offerings while you are with us at Nueva Vida. Starting your day off with meditation and yoga helps you open and become more receptive to the morning's presentation. And, should you have any other healing sessions during your day, I suspect this will enhance those experiences as well. Perhaps a week of meditating together will encourage you to adopt this practice into your morning routine." His voice inflects up, as if he's hoping we'll become regular meditators.

While I've been doing my best to sit in silence each morning, meditation continues to feel awkward. But maybe practicing with Eduardo will help. Hopefully he'll share some strategies that resonate. As I exhale, wishing I was better able to meditate with ease, Eduardo rings a bell, signaling our practice has begun.

Moments later, another sound—a soothing vibration—replaces the stark silence. This muted melody appears to swirl, almost as though it's dancing in circles. I crack open my eyes to find Eduardo playing a singing bowl. As he circles the rubber mallet around the beautiful crystal bowl, my chest pulsates. Could my heartbeat be resonating with the bowl's vibration?

"Let's begin," he says, his voice smooth and inviting.

I feel myself slowly melting as my bottom sinks deeper into the bolster. When Eduardo speaks, my mind drifts to former times and different locations. Some memories are pleasant, others not. Yet Eduardo keeps bringing me back, centering me on the present moment with his words and the whirling music. My mind repeats this process for the course of the entire thirty minutes. Finally, after a long pause, I hear the same ring that signaled the beginning of the meditation.

Remaining seated, I reach for the journal I'd placed next to my mat and begin writing.

> I just finished our first meditation class. Surprisingly, it was not as difficult as I anticipated. Eduardo's voice and the beautiful singing bowl gently guided my straying mind back to the present, keeping me from those dark places I no longer want to visit.

I momentarily put my pen down, hesitant to write more about this topic. Too many pages of my journals are filled with these same sentiments—catalogs of the pain and regret I've felt the past two months. I physically shake my head—as if doing so will help me shift gears—then I pick up my pen and continue.

> I don't know why it's so difficult for me to just be. I'm so used to doing. Sitting on my meditation cushion has always been hard. But afterward, I usual-

ly feel calmer, even if my mind was all over the place. So I guess it's worth the effort. I just wish I understood the process better ... knew how to release the fears buried inside. I try to delve into these elusive emotions that swim so close to the surface of my consciousness. But just as I'm about to see what is there, they evade me, diving deep below, disappearing into the dark recesses of my mind.

How do I see them for what they are? I want these destructive feelings out of my body. But if they don't stay still long enough for me to grasp their meaning, how can I ever release them?

I look up and see Marlee walking toward me.

"Hey," I say, closing my journal.

"I wanted to say hi." Marlee smiles before adding, "I think you are staying in the tree house next to us." Her voice is warm yet reserved.

"Really?" I apologize for not knowing we were neighbors. "I've kind of been … preoccupied."

"I know," she says, then sighs. "Being here, away from normal life, well, I guess it takes a bit of time to unwind. And staying in a tree house was not part of the original game plan. We were *supposed* to be in the main lodge, with Annie and Sophia." Marlee rolls her eyes a bit but then her face relaxes, as if she's at peace with her accommodations. "However, Juliette's been to this resort before and wanted to experience sleeping in a tree house. I believe she booked it on the sly." She raises her eyebrows. "At first I was upset with her, but the space is actually pretty cool." Grinning, Marlee lets out a small chuckle.

"I agree ... plus the view of the ocean ... I've never seen anything like it. And to fall asleep to the howler monkeys, well ... this is so very different from life in Pittsburgh." While I say this, the truth is, I didn't sleep very well last night. I never do.

Our conversation subsides when a petite blonde dressed in tie-dyed yoga pants and a midriff top walks into the room.

"That must be Kali," I say.

"Then I guess it's time for yoga. Maybe we can talk later," Marlee says before returning to her mat.

"Do you like the room set up this way, or should we move the mats into rows?" Kali asks the group with a slight wink before turning toward Eduardo and shaking her head, suggesting they have an ongoing battle regarding mat placement.

"Yoga is better in a circle," he teases, making me wonder if there might be a bit more to their relationship.

Following Kali's lead, everyone picks up their mat and finds a new spot, lining their sticky mats in rows toward the front of the room.

"Ah ... that's much better. Now we can move without bumping into each other," she says as she begins to pass out cork yoga blocks. I catch her glancing in Eduardo's direction, her eyes filled with mischief. Maybe they're just buddies and have some private joke between them.

"I hope everyone feels rejuvenated after yesterday's travels. And, of course, I'm sure meditation with Eduardo helped you to center and ground." I watch as Eduardo holds his hand at his chest, then slightly bows in Kali's direction. Instead of leaving, he takes a yoga mat from the shelf and unrolls it, filling an empty spot in the last row.

"Let's lie on our backs, with the soles of our feet together in Supta Baddha Konasana. Gently place one hand over your heart and the other on top of your stomach. Now slow your breath." The room becomes silent. A calming binaural beat begins to play from the speakers in the ceiling. "Even out your breaths. Inhale through your nose, then gently exhale through your mouth." She waits for us to follow her cues. "Begin with three counts in and three counts out. When that becomes comfortable, consider stretching to four counts, then five."

Kali guides us in Pranayama breathing, explaining how to constrict our throat muscles and breathe through our nose to make a sound like the waves of the ocean. After several minutes, she tells us to extend our arms and legs, then pull our knees to our chest before rocking up and down our mat, eventually landing into a forward fold.

Kali's instructions are clear and concise. Her playlist perfectly complements the sequence of poses. We hold various postures, but not for too long. She offers adaptations, allowing options for both the advanced and the beginners.

Listening to Kali, I become lost in the movement, focused on my breath and oblivious to those around me. After several balancing poses, we lie down on our mats, completing twists and backbends. Finally, we arrive in Shavasana, or Corpse Pose.

Several minutes later, we turn on our sides in a fetal position, symbolic of a rebirth of sorts. Finally, Kali asks us to sit cross-legged at the top of our mat.

As she places her hands in a prayer position at her heart center, she bows. "The light in me honors the light in you." There's both conviction and ease in Kali's voice, making me believe she's speaking her truth.

Sounds of "namaste" fill the room before people begin to stand and roll up their mats.

"I knew this would be amazing," Juliette, the youngest of the four women from the van, declares. "But now I'm starving, aren't you?" she asks her friends as she picks up her perfectly rolled yoga mat and places it on the shelf.

While food sounds nice, what I really want is coffee. Because I was up half of the night, trying to figure out what I should do once I return to Pittsburgh, I slept through my first two alarms. There's a coffee maker in my room, but I had no time to make a cup before meditation.

***

Upon entering the dining room, I spot Marlee and her friends busily chatting in the buffet line. Wondering what's in store for breakfast, I'm happy to see large bowls filled with papaya, mango, melon, and berries. But it only gets better. Farther down the table are platters of scrambled eggs, roasted vegetables, and diced potatoes. Plates laden with yummy-looking baked goods complete the buffet. Suddenly, I'm famished.

After filling my plate, I head toward the beverage station and fill a large mug with dark roasted coffee. A sign notes it was locally harvested.

"We have an extra seat at our table … if you'd like to join us."

I turn around. It's Marlee.

"Thanks," I say, truly appreciating her offer. While I deliberately came to this retreat alone—so I'd have some time and space to figure things out—I'm not sure I want to be by myself during meals. Grateful for the invitation, I join them, sitting next to the woman with midlength strawberry-blonde hair. Luckily, she introduces herself, as I've forgotten her name.

"I'm Annie," she says, with the kindest eyes. "I know we all met yesterday, but I was exhausted. Plus, I'm horrible with names," she adds with a slight giggle. We take a moment to reintroduce ourselves.

"Do you know much about astrology?" Marlee asks as she pulls a printed copy of the week's schedule from her canvas tote.

"Only a little bit, but it really intrigues me. I read my horoscope every morning," I say before adding, "Actually, I signed up for a private session with the astrologer." I do my best to smile. However, I'm somewhat hesitant to hear what's "in the stars" for me. But then again, I never saw the last two months coming. And with all the decisions ahead, a private astrology reading might provide some guidance.

"Don't worry, Maggie. It's going to be awesome. In fact, I think we should all get our charts read while we're here," Juliette says matter-of-factly. She reminds me of my college roommate, Tara—beautiful and bold—a girl who knew how to have fun but maintained strong and uncompromising boundaries. If Juliette's anything like Tara, I suspect there's more to her than what appears on the surface.

A bell rings, causing everyone to stop talking. I look up to see Francisco standing by the buffet.

"Good morning. I trust everyone slept well."

Most likely everyone but me, I think, hoping I didn't actually say these words aloud.

"Our first workshop will begin in fifteen minutes. It will be held on the third floor in the main conference room. Please feel free to replenish your beverage before joining us upstairs." With that, he smiles, tilts his head, then leaves.

I place my hand into my backpack, ensuring I've brought my journal and zippered case filled with pens and markers. Sometimes I like to doodle while others are speaking. It helps me focus.

After returning our empty dishes to the small window that opens into the kitchen, we thank Vic—who is busy rinsing plates—

refill our mugs with coffee, then follow the others upstairs. The five of us find a table in the back right corner of the conference room. Positioning ourselves so we each have a clear view for the presentation, we observe Sonya Roberts, the astrologer, sitting at the long wooden table in the front of the room.

Even though I've never heard of this woman before, I sense an unusually strong connection, as though we've already met. Of course, that's ridiculous. Still, this is not the first time I've felt a premonition like this. There have been many other instances—it's like I know someone although we're complete strangers. I let out a sigh, remembering the one mailman who filled in for our regular carrier while he was on vacation. While I'd never laid eyes on this person before, it was as though I could read his mind, feel his emotions … but I had to have been imagining it all.

"Good morning." Sonya's words halt this frustrating exercise of trying to explain these odd connections I feel with strangers. Her tone is crisp and uplifting. "I'm Sonya. Ready to delve into the world of astrology?" Suddenly, a picture of an elegant ballroom—seemingly from a distant time, perhaps the 1800s by the dress of the people in the room—runs through my mind. It feels as though Sonya and I are there … together … in this scene. Shaking my head, I wipe the silly thought from my brain, forcing myself back into the present moment. I really must get more sleep tonight. It's beginning to affect my thinking.

"While there are multiple ways to introduce astrology, I'd like to start with the natal chart, as it symbolizes how we begin our life on Earth." She smiles warmly, wipes a stray blonde hair from her forehead, then sits on the edge of the rectangular table.

"Each human has their own unique birth chart. While this may sound complicated, it's really quite simple. Your birth chart is a picture of how the sky looked the moment you came into this world." She springs to her feet, picks up a rolled-up poster, then tapes it onto a whiteboard at the front of the room. Looking closely, I see a large circle divided into sections with multiple concentric circles, lines, and symbols.

"This is my birth chart … or natal chart. It's easy to create. All that's needed to calculate a birth chart is the exact time a person was born, as well as the day, year, and location. Of course, years ago, it took a great deal of time to compute this configuration. But now, we merely input the information into a program, and instantly we have a document containing vast amounts of knowledge, revealing your strengths, challenges, points of resistance … and so much more. Think of it as a blueprint to your life." She offers the crowd a quirky smile, causing me to nervously wonder about things my chart might reveal.

"What if you don't know the exact time you were born?" a woman with a thick Australian accent asks. This seems to be a valid question.

"If you are unsure, we approximate the time. While the skies are always changing, we can get a good reading by making a 'best guesstimate.' However, the more precise the information is, the more accurate the reading," Sonya says in an unfazed tone, as if someone asks this question at every presentation.

"I'll use myself as an example. I was born on June 8, 1988, at 5:27 a.m. in San Diego, California. And this is what the skies looked like when I came into the world." Sonya waves her hand toward the poster taped to the board.

I strain my eyes, hoping to decipher the symbols. But we're in the back of the room, making it difficult to see the small details. Luckily, Sonya's one step ahead. In a casual manner, she begins to distribute a handout to each person. When she walks by our table to pass out what I assume is a copy of her birth chart, she pauses.

"You look incredibly familiar," she says to me with the warmest of smiles. "Have you been to one of my workshops before?"

Taken aback that she's verbalizing what I've been feeling, I refrain from admitting the same sensation. Instead, I only shake my head. "No, this is my first real exposure to astrology." Still, there is a familiarity to this woman, though for the life of me, I cannot place from when or where it stems.

Once everyone has a copy, Sonya waits, most likely so we can take in the information. Finally, she speaks: "As you can see, there are twelve sections of the outer circle, each representing a sign of the Zodiac. The next circle shows which planets were positioned in those signs at your birth. Then, the third circle shows which house corresponds to each sign." She pauses, again allowing us time to digest this information.

"Many people are familiar with the signs of the Zodiac. Most know their Sun sign, the sign of the month they were born. However, there is so much more to astrology and our natal chart than just Sun signs. We also have a Rising sign and a Moon sign. Additionally, there are the houses that come into play. My guess is many of you are unfamiliar with the Twelve Houses." As she says this, I scan the crowd, noting many heads nodding in confirmation.

"OK, then let's start with the basics … There are twelve signs of the Zodiac, twelve houses, and ten planets on this chart." She pauses to take a sip from the mug sitting on the table. "If you look on the back of the sheet, it lists the different houses and explains which areas of our lives each rules."

I flip the paper over and scan the back. While some of the houses sound benign, others appear dark, dealing with death, taxes, debt, and other things I view as negative aspects of life.

"Everyone's chart has all twelve houses; it's where they fall that makes each of us unique," Sonya continues. "Think of the natal chart like a clock. The house located between the eight and nine o'clock portion of your chart is your First House, and it addresses your personality, appearance, mannerisms … how you approach life. It's positioned in the sign that was rising in the east when you were born, your Rising sign. This signifies the beginning of your Zodiac wheel. Your Second House then follows the first. For example, if your Rising sign is Aquarius, then your First House is in Aquarius, making your Second House in Pisces, the sign that follows Aquarius on the wheel. Does this make sense?"

Instead of glancing at the room, I look at the people at our table. Everyone nods except for Annie, whose eyebrows furrow as she keeps flipping her paper over, as if trying to make sense of it all.

"But there's more," Sonya says with a quick wink. "We have the ten planets that affect our life. Their influence, like everything else, is based on their location in the sky at the time of our birth." She walks toward the poster she taped to the board. "The Sun, which represents the self, or the ego, sits in the Zodiac sign of the month you were born." Sonya then begins pointing to different markings on her birth chart. "Of course, there are other important planets, such as Venus ... known for symbolizing love ... and Pluto, representative of death."

Upon this statement, heads turn, and I hear slight mumblings around me.

"Don't worry ... not *your* death, but endings, destruction, stuff like that." While Sonya speaks in a lighthearted manner, just the word *death* invokes pangs of anxiety. But Sonya remains upbeat as she says, "Remember, it is the interplay of the sign, the house, and the planets that matters most." She then picks up her mug and stares into the cup as if whatever is inside will tell her what's next.

Annie, now wide-eyed, loudly whispers, "This is so confusing." Sophia smiles in response, resting her hand on Annie's arm, perhaps to reassure her.

But Sonya's far from done discussing the birth chart. "Rarely do we have planets balanced throughout our chart. Usually, the areas of our chart with the most activity are the areas of our life that have the most meaning." I wonder what part of my chart is most active.

"If you look at your sheet, you can see that I'm a Gemini because my Sun is below the Gemini sign ... the symbol that resembles a roman numeral two." Sonya pauses to point to the taped poster on the whiteboard. "In addition to the Sun, I have my Ascendant, or Rising sign, in Gemini, making this my First House. Mercury and Venus are also in Gemini. Chiron's there as well. While not one of the ten planets, Chiron is important. It's our Achilles' heel of sorts, our weak spot. The position suggests that I have some tenderness regarding First House elements ... personality, appearance, temperament ... so there's a lot going on," Sonya says with a capricious laugh. "According to my chart, I'm a bit curious about how things work. In general, I tend to be adaptable and versatile, but these qualities suggest I may have difficulties focusing on one thing. It's as though I'm a 'jack of all trades, master of none.'" As she tosses her head back, her long flowing hair responds by falling into her face. Sonya pushes it aside before saying, "The truth is, I sometimes get lost in my head and am interested in too many things. It might also explain my fascination with astrology." She shrugs her shoulders in a nonchalant manner, as if that's just the way it is.

I look closely at Sonya. This woman, who is a bit older than me, seems airy yet grounded. And despite her claiming she's "a jack of all trades and master of none," I suspect she's pretty accomplished at whatever she attempts.

Sonya continues to delve into the various houses and planets in her natal chart, sharing that if we book a private session with her, she will create a report about our birth charts and explain how the various elements impact us.

Suddenly, my stomach flutters, causing me to wonder what my upcoming session with Sonya will entail. Will she be able *to tell* what I've been through simply by reading my chart? I don't know much about my birth chart, except that I'm an Aquarius. I exhale, reminding myself the reason I signed up for this session ... I'm hoping this astrologer can give me guidance ... so I can make the best decisions when I return.

Next, Sonya transitions into the moon's cycles, explaining how the moon looks full when the Earth is between the sun and the moon because that's when we see the sun's light shine on the moon's surface. When this happens, the full moon is always in the opposing sign to the current Sun sign. For example, if it is Leo season, a full moon will occur in Aquarius, as that is 180 degrees away on the Zodiac wheel. We learn that during full moons, we can melt down obstacles, releasing what we no longer want. And if we can focus on elements associated with the house opposite of the current sign—where the full moon is occurring—we have a better chance of letting go in an area that needs our attention.

Then she explains the significance of a new moon—when the moon is between the sun and the Earth and we cannot see it. During this time, there is no light shining on the side of the moon facing Earth, causing the moon to appear as if it is not there. New moons are the perfect time to set intentions, begin new ventures, or reignite stagnant projects. Basically, it's an opportunity to call in what we want, especially in the house that it coincides with.

But what do I want? So much has changed, do I really know what I desire?

I force my thoughts back to the presentation, accepting that if I am to fully grasp these concepts, I must give Sonya my full attention. To keep my brain focused, I pull my journal and colored markers from my backpack and begin to take notes.

Sonya has a way of explaining astrology in an understandable manner. As she describes the meanings of the planets in her chart, I realize this really isn't scary—it's fascinating. Slowly, I relax, becoming more comfortable about our upcoming session and what my natal chart may reveal. Hopefully, it will help me better understand myself, my strengths, and my challenges—or opportunities, as Sonya calls them. Apprehension dissolves, allowing curiosity to take its place.

After forty-five minutes spent explaining the various aspects—the relationships between planets, such as oppositions, squares, conjunctions, textiles, and trines—Sonya wraps up the presentation. But before we end, she passes out packages of Starbursts attached to her business card. How clever, I think, as I open a cherry-flavored candy. Popping the red square into my mouth, I momentarily return to my childhood, and remember eating Starbursts at the pool with my mom. We'd go to our community's pool every Saturday during the summer months. But then, in an instant, this memory disappears as I'm reminded she's gone forever.

After Francisco graciously thanks Sonya and provides details about this afternoon's activities, he heads toward our table.

"Ladies, I hope you enjoyed this morning's workshop."

"Sonya's incredible," Juliette says, fully animated and looking perkier than normal. She seems to light up in Francisco's presence. It's as though she's searching for his approval.

"Wonderful. I am so pleased her presentation resonated with you." Francisco's tone is even, measured. While he acknowledges Juliette, he does not seem fazed by her attention.

"She is quite gifted in her knowledge," Sophia says, sitting erectly in her chair. This refined woman has a way about her. She's wise, worldly, and elegant—a modern-day Grace Kelly.

"Marlee," Francisco says as he offers a broad smile, "I look forward to our session tomorrow afternoon. Ms. Greene asked that I set aside an additional thirty minutes for our time together. She claimed we would have a great deal to discuss." I watch as Francisco turns toward Juliette and gives her a brief nod.

Wide-eyed, Marlee looks at Juliette, then raises her eyebrows. However, Juliette merely shrugs her shoulders and smiles sweetly at Marlee.

While Juliette's response seems to profess her innocence, I have my doubts. And I can only guess how Marlee must feel after learning she has an extra-long session with this man.

Francisco, who seems quite aware of this silent interaction between Marlee and Juliette, only says, "I will meet you tomorrow at two by the reception desk." His smile is tender, almost fatherly.

Yet Marlee appears anything but reassured. While she nods her head in response, her congenial expression seems forced, as if rooted in fear rather than a genuine anticipation. Regardless, Francisco gives Marlee an impish wink, then briefly bows before leaving to speak with other participants.

"I guess I'm first to meet with the shaman," Marlee gulps, looking down at the floor. "And for ninety minutes."

"I know it seems unsettling, but trust that your time with Francisco will be wonderful," Sophia says, most likely hoping her words will calm Marlee's trepidations. "I suspect you may learn something to help you connect your dots." Sophia tilts her head in a most curious fashion.

Annie places her hand directly on top of Marlee's hand. "Don't worry. It'll be great." But then her voice becomes shaky. "I see him on Thursday." She offers a crooked smile. In the softest whisper, I hear her say, "I'd cancel if I could, but Juliette would be pissed at me."

"Can't believe you get to go first," Juliette says, sounding like a little kid. I'm amazed she didn't apologize or explain why she asked Francisco to add extra time to his session with Marlee. But then I sense desire in her voice. Juliette *really* wants to meet with him. Perhaps she thought she was doing Marlee a favor by arranging for an extra-long session.

"I already started writing a list of questions for my session on Friday," Juliette announces as she pulls a piece of paper from a binder that's on the table in front of her.

"I need to come up with questions?" I ask as I take a swig of my lukewarm coffee before gathering my items and placing them in my backpack. Annie's now standing behind Juliette, looking over her shoulder to see what questions she'd written.

"No ... but I want to be totally prepared for when I meet with him," Juliette casually says as she closes her binder, then pushes her chair back from the table to stand. "I mean, Francisco's utterly amazing. He'll tell you so much—that is, if you want to know. This is my second time here, so I've already done one session with him. I learned some serious shit about myself. Literally, it's changed my life." She tosses her head back and lets out a wicked laugh. As much as I think I like Juliette, she also kind of scares me.

It's then the ethereal astrologist walks over and says, "Maggie, I wanted to say hello before we meet tomorrow."

"Hi," I respond, before adding, "How did you know who I was?" Could she be psychic too?

Sonya merely chuckles. "After looking at my schedule for Monday, I asked Francisco who you were." She then squints her eyes and gives me the sweetest smile. "Have you been to Nueva Vida before?" Only now do I notice her tone is deeper, more mystical one-on-one than it was when she was presenting.

"No, this is my first time," I say, noting my voice cracks a bit. Why am I nervous around her? She seems so nice.

"This is my second time in Costa Rica, but it's my husband's fifth. He's a huge surfer and insisted on tagging along so he could ride the waves in Nosara," Sonya says, her words instantly relaxing me. I watch as her blue eyes, framed by her beautifully bronzed face, glisten as she talks about her husband. By her comments, I suspect they have a solid marriage.

"Does he also follow astrology?" I ask, curious if this is a mutual interest.

"He's always asking what to expect," she says with a laugh, "but he doesn't care to learn the whys behind it ... if that makes sense." She gives me a quick wink. "Are you married?" she asks, prompting me to glance down at my naked left hand.

"No ..." I pause, thinking of Pete. Conscious this relationship is going nowhere, I let out a slight sigh, knowing ending things won't be easy.

Suddenly conscious of my actions, I ask, "Is there anything I must do before our appointment?"

"All I need is your birth date, as well as the time and place of birth." Sonya takes a small notepad and pen from her purse, then looks up at me.

"February 16, 1992. Oh, and I was born in Pittsburgh, Pennsylvania ... at 7:28 a.m."

Sonya smiles. "Perfect. I'll prepare your report this afternoon. We'll be meeting in the small building to the right of the yoga room. Do you know where that is?"

"I think so," I say, remembering I saw a hut-like structure next to the studio.

"Wonderful. And please, don't worry about anything. Having your astrological forecast read is not scary ... In fact, most people find the information enlightening, even empowering ... that is, if you allow it to be." With that, Sonya turns and seemingly floats out of the room.

"She's awesome," Juliette says. "Maybe I'll see if she has any openings this week. I've had my birth chart read several times before, but I'd love to get her input ... 'cause each astrologer seems to have a unique interpretation of the meaning behind me being an Aries and my planetary placements."

Of course, Juliette's an Aries. That explains her independent, bold, and somewhat brazen characteristics.

Juliette then totally shifts subjects and says, "Let's have lunch by the pool ... meet at twelve thirty? I'm famished."

I watch as Marlee, Sophia, and Annie glance at each other and shrug their shoulders. It's as though Juliette—the youngest of the four—is their self-declared leader. I suppose she's always that way.

***

The last time I wore a bathing suit was this past summer. Pete and I had gone to the Jersey Shore to visit one of my college friends. Her parents were renting a house for a month in Sea Isle. I exhale loudly. While this was less than nine months ago, it's as though it happened during another lifetime. I remember returning late that Sunday evening, and Mom was still awake, waiting up for me. She always worried whenever I was away. That familiar heaviness in my chest returns.

It's Juliette who brings me back to the present when she asks, "Maggie, are you coming?"

As the three of us walk to our tree houses, I have a sudden urge to know the story of how Juliette and Marlee met. "So how long have you two been friends?" I'm curious about their relationship, especially considering the age difference.

"Not that long," Marlee answers. "We met four months ago ... at a holiday party." She turns toward Juliette and smiles.

"True, but we became super close really quickly," Juliette chimes in with a gleam in her eyes. "You see, my fiancé, Michael, works with Marlee's husband, Tom. They're both orthopedic surgeons at Jefferson Hospital in Philadelphia. But when Marlee, Annie, and I met that night, Michael and I had just started to date exclusively." She twists her flaxen hair into a ponytail, securing it with a scrunchy from her wrist before adding, "But it wasn't until we all had dinner at Marlee and Tom's home the following month that I got to know Sophia. And before that night was over, Marlee invited us to her family's home in the Pocono Mountains." She pauses, looks at Marlee, then says, "Do you want to tell her the rest, or should I?"

Marlee stops walking. It's then her expression turns uncharacteristically serious. "Maggie, this may sound super strange to you, but while we were on our 'girls' getaway weekend,' we kind of, um, well, we ..."

"Solved a murder," Juliette jumps in and finishes Marlee's sentence.

"What?" I ask, feeling my jaw drop, astonished these four women could have been involved in a criminal investigation.

Marlee gives Juliette a glance before explaining: "It's a really long story, and we can share it when we get to the pool, but the main gist is that weekend, Annie discovered she had a gift of sorts ... She's clairvoyant ... and, well, she was able to see what had actually happened ... uncover the missing pieces of a crime ... that involved people none of us knew." Marlee's expression shifts, as if she's embarrassed or concerned I won't believe her.

I pause, allowing myself a moment to take in this information. Annie's clairvoyant? Growing up, my best friend's mother could see things, so the concept is not new to me. Yet I would have guessed Sophia or Juliette would be the clairvoyant one, not Annie. She seems so timid, scared of her own shadow. How could Annie have handled visualizing a murder?

Juliette and Marlee continue looking at me, as if gauging my reaction. "I think it's amazing. But didn't the police question her clairvoyance?" I ask.

"To our surprise, the chief of police trusted us. Of course, he didn't understand it, nor did he really want to, but everything Annie said panned out." Marlee's voice is calm, though somewhat distant, as if she's returned to that weekend in the Poconos.

"But it wasn't only Annie," Juliette says, a somewhat mischievous grin emerging on her face. "Marlee was quite the detective herself. She also discovered a gift that weekend. Marlee learned how to hone her intuition."

"Really?" I ask, wondering exactly what occurred.

"It's hard to explain," Marlee begins. "*Something* inside told me where to go in the victim's house to find important documentation that ultimately implicated the murderer and provided motive."

"Wow, what was it?" I ask, curious to know more.

"Letters … the murderer, Caroline Rhimes, threatened to expose Wyatt Bixby for having an affair with a married woman. But apparently, Wyatt retaliated after he received the blackmail letters, hiring a private detective who discovered embarrassing information about Caroline. Her blackmail letters and Wyatt's written response to them provided enough motive for the police to arrest Caroline. And when they did, they found the murder weapon in her trunk. Still, something seems to be missing. There must be more to this story," Marlee says as she stares at the ground, looking a bit defeated. "I suppose it will always remain a mystery."

"Regardless, I'm in awe that you and Annie were so integral in solving a real murder."

"Juliette helped too," Marlee says. "She does energy work, and she was able to pick up on some clues that were critical to the case."

I turn to look at Juliette, who is now beaming with pride.

Shaking my head, I say, "Wow … what a way to begin a friendship. I guess the four of you will forever be bonded."

Juliette and Marlee look at each other and laugh. "I believe so," Marlee adds as she begins walking again. Perhaps that explains the unconditional trust between the four of them. Despite Juliette's somewhat assuming behavior, the others seem to accept her as she is.

Before I know it, we're at our respective tree houses.

"I need to make a phone call," I say, "but I'll meet you at the pool shortly." I smile, then purposefully climb up my stairs.

***

Lying on my bed—curled into a fetal position—I'm embarrassed I lied when there was no reason to. The truth is, I don't have anyone to call, except maybe Pete. But soon Pete will no longer be part of my life.

I certainly don't mean to dismiss Pete, but it's not fair to expect him to be someone he isn't. As much as I'd like him to be *that guy*, he is not. Pete's kind, sweet, thoughtful. Yet there's no true spark between us, at least there isn't on my end. And Pete always defers to me, wanting to make *me* happy. Maybe I should be grateful about that. Many women would. But I'm not. I need more.

We met at a bar in Shadyside three years ago. He was a left wing for the Pittsburgh Penguins. I'd be lying if I didn't admit this impressed me, mostly because he didn't seem like the asshole professional athlete type—the ones who act as if they're God's gift to women. Pete was never that way. Immediately I saw his soft and caring side. That's what drew me to him.

Several months after we began dating, he had a serious concussion while attempting a goal. He got hit from the side and fell hard on the ice. That play ended Pete's career. Now he sells cars for the largest Ford dealer in the area. At first, they capitalized on his professional ice hockey status. But now, two years later, the attention seems to have faded. So has Pete's drive. I've tried to help. A tear falls down my cheek. Then another. I'm not sure if I'm sad for Pete or for the fact that our relationship is going nowhere. I know what I must do. But he's been so supportive of me. It seems cruel to end it now. Plus, then I'd truly be alone. I sigh, knowing I cannot ignore what already is.

And then my mind shifts to my bosses' offer.

Sandy and Mark, the couple who owns the architectural firm where I work, recently decided to relocate to Bend, a small town located in the center of Oregon. After skiing at Mt. Bachelor this past winter, both fell in love with the place. Three weeks ago, they flew back to scout out possible locations for their business—and themselves. Besides being avid skiers, both are mountain bikers, and they love to camp. Plus, since I've known her, Sandy's expressed concerns about her boys growing up outside of a major city. She wants them in nature, not glued to their PlayStation. According to Sandy, besides being a playground for nature enthusiasts, Bend has wonderful public schools. I sigh, knowing I'd probably love it there. I think back to how our conversation began.

Three days before I left for Costa Rica, Sandy asked me to stop by her office before leaving that day. When I walked in, she and Mark were seated at the table in the corner. Immediately, I sensed a seriousness in the air. She motioned for me to join them.

Sandy shared that as much as she and Mark loved Pittsburgh, after weighing the pros and cons of relocating, they'd decided to move to Bend. I remember the glow on her face when she shared this. Then she explained that many people were moving to Central Oregon, creating a huge demand for new construction as well as renovations, both requiring architectural plans. While there are several firms in the area, by no means are there enough to handle the volume of work.

Sandy told me more about the town. Once she finished describing how amazing Bend is, Mark quickly added how much they both wanted me to come with them. He said I possess a strong expertise in LEED, an area in which neither of them has much knowledge. But more importantly, he claimed they enjoy having me be part of their team and have a great deal of respect for me both personally and professionally.

Mark's eyes narrowed, and the muscles in his jaw softened as he said, "Please, consider coming with us, Maggie."

Sandy added that there would be a generous relocation stipend as well as a salary increase if I chose to join them. I could tell both really wanted me to accept their offer.

At first, I was speechless. Leave Pittsburgh? I'd lived my entire life in this city. Born in Brookline, I then went to college at Pitt, a short drive from my home. I'd never been west of Minneapolis. Oregon was on the other side of the country. How could I move there?

Sandy must have noticed I'd mentally checked out because she gently touched my arm, bringing me back to the present. Without missing a beat, she shared that they'd found a perfect office space in a beautiful modern building located at the edge of town. Sandy then pulled out her phone to show me pictures. The view from what would be my office was spectacular—it overlooked a gorgeous river. And even though it was late March, I could see paddleboarders on the water and tons of people walking, biking, or running on the path that paralleled the river's bank. But there was more. In every photo, the sky was robin-egg blue, and the sun was shining, something that rarely happens during March or April in Pittsburgh.

I noticed Sandy look toward Mark, then she cleared her throat. Leaning closer to me, she said, "I know how much you've been through ... and all you're currently dealing with." She paused, then inhaled before continuing. "But maybe it's the perfect time to try someplace new. Plus, we'd be there to help in any way." With that, she turned toward Mark, who nodded in agreement.

"Thank you," I said while biting my lower lip. "I'm flattered. There's a lot to consider ... and I promise I'll think hard about it." Though at the time I had already made up my mind. I couldn't go.

"That's all we can ask." While I suspect Mark sensed I'd say no, his eyes still twinkled, as if imploring, *Please give it a try. I promise. It will be a good decision.* "Take your time, Maggie. You don't have to give us an answer right now. Let's revisit this after your vacation." Mark gave me an encouraging look before placing both hands on the table, as if to suggest the meeting had ended.

Back in the present, I look at my watch. Fifteen minutes have passed, enough time to have made my imaginary phone call, that is, *if* I had one to make. Pushing myself up from the bed, I walk toward the wooden bureau and pull a black bikini from the second drawer. After changing, I take a white cover-up from the closet, slip into flip-flops, and grab a hat and sunscreen from the top of the bureau. But before leaving, I pause and stare into the mirror. As if on cue, my eyes fall toward the floor, away from my reflection. The woman in the mirror seems serious, sad, unsure of herself. But then again, I guess I've always been that way.

MARLEE

Sunday, April 18
Monday, April 19

All thoughts of Margaret's unnerving comments fade as the sun's intense rays warm my body. After the long, cold winter, I crave light and heat. Totally relaxed, my body sinks into the lounge chair, and my mind swims in a sea of nothingness.

While the ocean is nearly a quarter mile away, salt air fills my nostrils, reminding me of past weekends spent at the Jersey Shore. But the beach here is different. I pause, recalling Juliette's and my walk this morning before meditation. Unlike the smooth New Jersey beaches, this sand is grainy and does not stick to my feet. Plus, the water here is crystal clear. We even spotted schools of fish swimming in the shallow surf.

I exhale, acknowledging how special this place truly is. Actually, it's amazing ... exactly as Juliette promised. I suppose that wasn't the only correct statement she's made. For a moment, I allow myself to imagine, *What if this week could change me inside and out?* Then I remember tomorrow's session with Francisco.

My past one-on-one experiences with healers have been impactful. But having a session with a shaman is an entirely different level of work. What will he tell me? What should I tell him? Do I explain Margaret and how she harshly criticizes me? If so, do I also let him know about the other voice—my intuition—the one that's challenging to hear? Luckily, I don't have to make any decisions now, so I do what I always do whenever I'm uncomfortable—I push these unsettling ideas out of my head. But aren't I "stuffing," avoiding the inevitable?

"Is anyone planning to go on the garden tour?" Annie asks, pulling me back from my internal dialogue.

"What time is it?" Juliette, who has on the tiniest white bikini I've ever seen, casually asks.

"The tour doesn't begin for an hour and a half … It's at four o'clock," Annie, covered in SPF 70 and seated under an umbrella, says. She insisted on bringing a maternity bathing suit, even though she only has a tiny baby bump. However, she looks adorable in the pink polka-dotted, skirted one-piece.

Sophia, wearing a slimming navy bandeau, adjusts her Prada sunglasses higher on the bridge of her nose before saying, "I plan on going, Annie. I am fascinated by the wide range of plants on this property. No doubt Dominique will offer incredible insights as to why she chose each variety." Sophia then returns to her book, a thick hardcover titled *Integrative Medicine*.

"I'm in," Juliette responds before reaching inside of the tote sitting next to her lounge chair for a yoga magazine.

"So am I," Maggie sweetly adds. "I had planned to run this afternoon … because I was a bit hesitant to run alone before this morning's meditation class … but I really want to learn more about this property."

I, too, agree to go. A tour of the gardens sounds lovely. However, I'd rather get a glimpse of René's kitchen. I bet he'd let me see some of his recipes, especially if he knew about my passion for cooking. For a moment, my thoughts go to Tom and Patrick, hoping they remember to defrost the meals I prepared for them. Still, a part of me suspects they will opt for takeout.

Everyone becomes quiet, and the five of us settle into tranquility, lulled by the water gently cascading over the infinity pool's edge. Within moments, my mind becomes silent, and I drift off to sleep.

***

Juliette, Maggie, and I are the first to arrive. While waiting for Sophia and Annie to join us, I find myself staring at Maggie and Juliette chatting. Somewhat shy, Maggie's slowly coming out of her shell. I suppose the four of us can be a bit overwhelming, especially Juliette. Still, it's as though Maggie wants to be with us. Coming here alone must be difficult. I wonder if there's a particular reason she's chosen to do so.

Just as the tour is about to begin, Sophia and Annie appear. Annie looks flustered, which is becoming her new norm.

"Good afternoon. I trust everyone had time to relax after lunch," Dominique says to the small group assembled outside of the reception area. "I thought I'd begin by showing you our garden and explain how René incorporates our organic produce into his recipes." Dominique's words draw my attention. And I can't help but notice how Juliette perks up when Dominique mentions René. Maybe my friend wasn't annoyed with the attention he gave her last night after all. I let out a chuckle as I follow Sophia down the cobblestone path.

When we arrive at the top of a short but steep hill, we discover the most magical fenced-in vegetable garden. Meticulously built raised plots house rows of plants. I spot green beans, carrot tops, scallions, tomatoes, and zucchini. To the right, I see sprawling leaves with small melons visible under wilted yellow flowers. The aroma of the emerging vegetation cannot be denied. Suddenly, I have a strong desire to create a meal using these amazing ingredients.

After Dominique concludes this portion of the tour, we proceed down the path to the beach. Only then do I see the gorgeous purple orchids that have been grafted onto palm trees. I can't believe I didn't notice them before. Perhaps it's because I've been looking down, at my feet. Had I taken the time to *look up*, I might not have missed them. Realizing how unaware I am of my surroundings causes me to wonder what else I've been missing.

However, one thing I do notice is a strange connection between Sophia and Dominique. Sophia seems to naturally anticipate the direction the tour's about to head before Dominique says or does anything. And they make a lot of eye contact, as if to confirm some sort of bond between them. Earlier, I'd picked up on their physical resemblance, but there appears to be more beneath the surface. Maybe it's their mannerisms, the way they hold themselves, move, and interact with others. I shake my head, convinced I'm missing something deeper.

***

While impossible to imagine, this evening's dinner exceeds the delicious dishes René prepared last night. I suspect his herbs and spices are key to his sublime cooking. And I'm not the only one who appreciates his skills—all five of us return for seconds. I'm happy our foursome adopted Maggie. She's a breath of fresh air that adds a softness to our group. Plus, Juliette appears to be on her best behavior when Maggie's around.

As soon as dinner's over, Francisco announces that Kirtan will be offered upstairs, encouraging everyone to attend.

"What's Kirtan?" Annie asks, a quizzical look on her face.

"I believe it has something to do with music," Sophia says.

"You're absolutely right." No doubt Juliette's an expert on this too. "Kirtan is like a back-and-forth sing-along. The leader, who is called a wallah, chants a phrase. Then we respond by reciting the same words back to him. Oh, and there're different kinds of musical instruments for everyone to play."

When we enter the upstairs room, it's apparent Juliette is once again correct. There is a large woven basket containing all sorts of percussion instruments. Some are traditional, similar to cymbals and tambourines. Others appear new to me. A woman motions for each of us to take an instrument from the basket. I choose a caramel-colored gourd, then run my fingers across its smooth, lacquered finish.

She directs us to sit in a circle. Folding chairs are available, but we opt for the multicolored cushions. The woman then distributes sheet music to each participant. Looking closely at the paper, I'm able to read the notes but do not recognize any of the words.

A short dark-skinned man, cloaked in a soft gray tunic and black pants, bows to the group, then begins to chant. At first his voice is soft, but slowly it grows in intensity. The words are not in English or Spanish—which I kind of speak. I suspect he's singing what's written on the sheet.

"It's Sanskrit," Juliette shares, perhaps aware of my confusion.

When the leader pauses, those in the room repeat the words. Trying my best to chime in, I struggle with the pronunciation. In search of assistance, I glance toward Juliette, who is shaking a tambourine as she effortlessly recites the phrases.

This back-and-forth exchange repeats itself for the next forty minutes. Some of the songs are slow; others keep a rapid pace. I lose myself to the pulsating rhythm. As I'm mindlessly shaking the lacquered gourd, the tightness in my shoulders seems to subside, and my body sways back and forth. Enveloped in this perfection of peace, I become one with the moment.

When the chanting finally stops, the room becomes still. The wallah nods his head, and the audience begins to clap. Yet we're more than an audience; we've been participants, cocreators of this back-and-forth performance. And this was more than merely chanting and making music. There seems to have been a transfer of energy between the wallah and those present.

My thoughts are interrupted when people rise from their seats and begin to chat in a festive manner.

"That was incredible!" Annie has a huge smile on her face. "And do you know what?" she asks, wide-eyed. But before I can ask what, she says, "I think I felt the baby kick."

Sophia, who is always within earshot of Annie, comes closer, then places her hand on Annie's belly.

"I do not feel anything," Sophia says after several moments.

"The baby isn't doing anything now. It was only during the Kirtan." There's no question in Annie's voice whether the baby kicked, nor the cause.

Sophia merely smiles, as if proud of the progress Annie's making in her pregnancy. At first, Annie was terrified when she discovered she was pregnant. Never in a million years did she or Jonathon believe they could conceive a child. In fact, the idea of motherhood overwhelmed Annie. But now, she seems to be easing into her upcoming role.

"I don't know about you, but I'm exhausted," Juliette says. "Ready to call it a night?" she asks, looking in my direction.

Suddenly feeling tired myself, I agree. But before we head back to the room, I approach Maggie, remembering she mentioned wanting to run but feeling hesitant to go alone so early in the morning.

"Any interest in running tomorrow? If we left a bit before six, we could be back in time for a quick shower before meditation."

"I'd love to." Maggie's eyes light up. "Should we meet at the bottom of our tree houses, say 5:45?" she asks with a giggle. No doubt she, like I, has trouble with the concept of sleeping among the trees.

"Sounds like a plan." We say goodnight to Annie and Sophia, then head down the lit path toward our bedrooms in the sky.

***

I double-knot my running shoes before quietly shutting our door. I don't want to awaken Juliette. Maggie's waiting for me. Her long blonde hair is pulled into a ponytail, and she's wearing black running shorts with a pale pink sleeveless top. I suddenly wonder if I'll be able to keep pace with her.

However, moments later, I surprise myself, or she kindly slows her stride, as we comfortably jog, side by side, along the pristine white beach. Because the tide is out, there's a nice, flat surface beneath our feet. Maggie and I engage in small talk, asking each other questions about hometowns, family, occupations, and interests.

Within the first five minutes, I learn the basics about Maggie Carr. She works for a couple who owns a small architectural firm in downtown Pittsburgh. Born and raised in this city, Maggie attended Pitt—where she ultimately received a master's in architecture. Following graduation, she met Pete, a former Pittsburgh Penguins player. They've been dating for close to three years. However, when she spoke about Pete, the lightness in her voice faded. Perhaps she's second-guessing their relationship.

After she's done, I share my background and a bit about Tom and Patrick. While Maggie already knows how my three friends and I met, I fill her in on the rest of the story—mostly how my assignment for the *Inquirer* led me to reach out to holistic healers. "In fact, had I not gone through those experiences, I doubt I'd have trusted my intuition during our wild weekend in the Poconos."

"I'm still in awe about how you and Annie figured out the murderer's identity," Maggie says as she wipes the sweat from her brow.

"Don't forget—Juliette also played a big part." Breathing heavily, I further explain how Juliette picked up on clues while energetically working on Nicki. "It's funny, we rarely discuss that weekend. It's like it was some surreal experience. You know, since we've returned, I haven't heard Annie mention her clairvoyance." I pause. "And to be honest, my intuition hasn't been too active. Maybe it was merely meant for us to use that weekend … so we could figure out who killed Wyatt Bixby." I let out a small laugh, but is it funny?

"Well, your story is truly amazing. I wouldn't be surprised if both your intuition and Annie's clairvoyance resume this weekend."

I glance her way. "Really? You don't think it was only meant to help with the investigation?"

"Nope. I think it's for real. Those things may come and go, but they're rarely gone forever. Most likely you've been busy, you know, lost in the day-to-day, not paying attention," Maggie says with a smile. I return my gaze to the beach in front of me, wondering if she might be right.

Finally, I say, "I'd like to be able to rely on my intuition." I'm not sure who I'm speaking to at this moment. Something tells me these words are meant to be heard by someone or something besides Maggie.

"Then I suspect you will." Her tone is confident, optimistic.

"How can you be so sure?" It's then I wonder if she has any gifts of her own, ones she's not telling me about.

"Maybe ask yourself why you doubt this ability—or your gift as you call it." Maggie grins, but while her face is smiling, there is a sadness in her eyes. There's most definitely more to her story. I suspect she's intentionally holding back something. But we've just met. Why would she automatically open up to me? Besides, isn't that one of the cardinal rules to becoming friends … earning the other's trust?

***

Twenty minutes later—showered and dressed in yoga clothes— we're seated on our mats, ready for this morning's meditation session. Eduardo begins in a fashion similar to yesterday's practice. But this time, he incorporates breathwork into the class. While it's totally different from what Roberto did during our private session this past winter, I find Eduardo's guided breathing practice relaxing.

When we transition into meditation, I don't sense as much mental resistance. My body appears to be more cooperative. Could it be the breathwork, or might it be due to this morning's run? I'm just not sure.

However, what I do discover is practicing yoga after running is the perfect tonic for my body. Hamstrings, tight from years of road running as well as endless hours sitting in front of my laptop, begin to soften as Kali transitions us from one posture to another. Like meditation, yoga appears easier today, more natural. Again, I wonder about the cause, this time adding Kirtan to the list of possible reasons.

We head to breakfast as soon as class ends. My body craves the delicious food. There's definitely something special about this place. Even the water tastes differently here. Is it due to the natural ingredients, or could there be more?

While we've been here for less than two days, already shifts are occurring. Slowly, my body's unwinding, softening, expanding, causing me to wonder what might happen if I could finally allow myself to let go.

Dream all you like, but do you really think this week will change you?

The air leaves my chest. She's still here.

***

Seated at the same table as yesterday, I gaze at those in the room. There's a buzz. Individuals and duos who looked alone yesterday are now engaged with others. I suppose it's similar to how Maggie's joined us.

I pull the packet of information from my canvas bag—which functions as both my purse and tote—and scan the pages until I see the schedule for today.

Conor Kelly – Psychic/Intuitive Wisdom

No one's by the podium. In fact, the large front table, where Sonya spoke from yesterday, is vacant. Pausing to remember Saturday evening's welcome session, I clearly recall the sweet young man with the reddish-blond hair who's supposed to speak this morning. I wonder where he is and if everything's OK. I've never met a psychic unless you count Annie and her clairvoyance. But I think that's different. Besides, unless she's kept them to herself, she hasn't had any other "experiences" since our trip in February.

Seconds later, Conor comes rushing in. After apologizing for having to answer an emergency call from one of his regular clients, he takes a deep breath, shuts his eyes, and seems to center himself.

The room quickly quiets. People adjust their bodies before settling into their chairs. I turn toward Annie, curious as to how she'll respond to this workshop. Will Conor's story resonate with her?

"When people hear the word *psychic*, most envision an old woman staring into a crystal ball … with a black cat by her feet." I find myself laughing, as I, too, held this image prior to last February.

"The reality is, many people possess the ability to *see*. It's certainly not a magical power reserved for the 'special few.' I like to think that discovering your psychic ability is like finding a treasured heirloom in your attic. It's always been there, only you couldn't see it because it was surrounded by clutter."

Shifting my glance to Annie, I note she's perched on the edge of her seat. Annie's lips are slightly parted, as if she's inhaling his message, savoring every piece of it.

"Perhaps you're wondering how I first discovered my clairvoyance." Conor shakes his head and begins to blush, his face turning close to the hue of his hair. "It first happened when I was in dental school and living in Old City, a historic neighborhood in Philadelphia, Pennsylvania."

Hearing he's from our hometown causes me to perk up myself.

"Known for being home to the Liberty Bell, Independence Hall, and Betsy Ross's house, Old City is always busy … Tourists crowd the sidewalks while residents go about their business. The streets are packed, day and night." Conor, having perfectly described Old City, shakes his head, then glances at the floor for several moments.

"Five years ago, I was walking down one of these crowded streets when I spotted the most beautiful woman." His face shows the look of a man in love. "It was an afternoon in June, and I was on Chestnut Street. This woman stood outside of Amada, a Spanish restaurant, looking at the menu posted on the restaurant's glass door. At that exact moment, a strange sensation came over me." His face becomes serious.

"Being that this is a very old section of Philadelphia, there's constant construction. I guess there's a lot to repair." Conor casually shrugs his shoulders, suggesting this is a matter-of-fact statement. "On this day, there happened to be a renovation occurring next door to where this woman stood. While looking at her and thinking how stunning she was, I had this sudden vision of a piece of metal falling onto her, crushing her to the ground. Without even considering the consequences of my actions, I sprinted toward the woman, grabbed her, and pulled her from what I perceived to be harm's way." Conor pauses to clear his throat. Perhaps telling this story is still emotional for him.

"As you can imagine, she as well as the people around us panicked. They must have thought I was dangerous and intended to hurt this woman." I look around. Everyone in the room is captivated.

"And then it happened … A steel rod fell from the construction area and landed exactly where the woman had been standing."

A few people gasp, but the majority appeared to be mesmerized. Silently, we wait for Conor to continue his story.

"First, I felt a wave of relief, grateful she was OK. But then, when this gorgeous stranger looked up at me and asked, 'How did you know that steel rod was going to fall?' I froze, unable to respond because I had no idea what had occurred."

I imagine how confusing this must have been for everyone.

"As you might guess, I could not explain my actions. All I could mutter was, 'I have no idea.' It felt as though my body was taking instructions from somewhere else, but I couldn't pinpoint the source." He pauses, then scratches his forehead.

Now I'm totally hooked. Where is his story going? Why was he blushing earlier, or is that merely a nervous tendency?

"That was the beginning of, shall we say, a series of uncanny events. None were quite as dramatic as five hundred pounds of falling steel. Nevertheless, I quickly realized something about me had changed, or perhaps I was finally awakening to a gift I'd always had. Regardless, I was suddenly able to see, predict, and understand … things that were incomprehensible to me before that day." Conor pauses, runs his fingers through his thick strawberry-blond hair, then takes a sip from a mug on the table in front of him.

"Luckily for me"—he lets out a laugh—"this amazing woman named Janette seemed intrigued by what happened. In fact, she insisted on taking me to dinner that night, to thank me. Later that evening, we met at Buddakan, an Asian restaurant several blocks from where the steel rod fell. It was then Janette shared a secret … She, too, had intuitive experiences as a child. But no one believed her, so they went away."

That's exactly what happened to Annie! I turn to my right. Annie appears pale. Sophia, already anticipating a reaction, offers Annie a glass of water. After a few sips, Annie seems to settle. I return my attention to Conor.

"So here I am, at this amazing restaurant, sitting across from a beautiful woman who apparently also has—or had—this strange gift," he continues.

"Janette told me she's conducted quite a bit of research about psychic abilities and intuition. Slowly, I began to understand how Intuitive Wisdom shows up in a variety of ways. Some feel it in their gut, others visualize what was or will be, and then there are individuals who hear voices. Additionally, certain people just know without any physical sensation. It's unique to everyone."

It's then I remember reading about the "five clair senses"—clairvoyance, or clear seeing; clairaudience, or clear hearing; clairalience, or clear smelling; clairsentience, or clear feeling; and finally, claircognizance, or clear knowing.

Conor continues, sharing more examples of how his intuition led him on a new path, away from dentistry. "Believe me—I was hesitant, completely terrified to embark on this journey. After all, how could I justify leaving dental school to become a psychic? I knew my family and friends would never understand. Plus, there was the financial commitment I'd made to becoming a dentist. I guess I kept delaying what I knew was my calling." He takes a big swig from his mug before continuing.

"During my final year of dental school, Janette and I went to Maui over Christmas. One afternoon, while hiking to the crest of Haleakalā, a volcano, we both had the strangest experience. It started as a ringing in our ears. I now realize this was a signal for us to pay attention and listen. It was shortly afterward that we witnessed a purple glow around the volcano's rim." Again, Conor waits. But this time, he looks at those in the room, as if gauging whether or not we believe him.

"After a few minutes, the ring was gone. We both agreed this was some sort of sign. Of course, I had no idea what the purple ring meant, but I knew there was a message underneath.

That's when the dreams started, or at least I refer to them as dreams. I began to see my future, but it wasn't as a dentist. Instead, I was another kind of practitioner … a healer. I helped people figure out their purpose in life. And do you know the best part about it?" He smiles broadly as the twinkle returns to his eyes. "Janette was in all these dreams. I took *that* as a sign to propose, which I promptly did. And lucky for me, she said yes." Murmurs can be heard throughout the room.

"While I finished my final year of dental school and sat for the exams, instead of applying for typical positions in private practices, I chose a different route. After convincing my best friend, Steven, to join me, we wrote grants to open a small practice dedicated to providing dental care for people who are experiencing homelessness. Steven was a pro at obtaining financial support, so before long, we built our vision while ensuring we had an income source to fund both our practice and our personal needs. At the same time, Janette, who co-owned a boutique near Penn, began her Reiki certification. Together, we started researching holistic centers in the Philadelphia area, hoping to find a building for both of our practices."

I lean forward in my chair, knowing Elena, the massage and Reiki therapist who is now working with Sophia, would love this story.

"There was one healing center that resonated with both of us, so we applied for a space. In less than a month, we were setting up our new offices. It was perfect … I was able to work my schedule to have two afternoons off from the dental practice to do Intuitive Wisdom coaching. Of course, I wasn't sure exactly what an intuitive coach did, but somehow, I knew I'd figure it out." As he chuckles aloud, he reminds me of Patrick, with his *Don't worry, Mom, I've got it all covered* attitude.

"Fast forward, Janette is a respected Reiki practitioner, and I'm busier than ever." Conor grins, but then becomes serious.

"Perhaps you're wondering what exactly happens during an Intuitive Wisdom session." Again, a youthful expression comes over his face. "All I can say is each session is unique. We'll spend a few moments together talking. Getting to know you will help me tap in—*see* your aspirations as well as your concerns. But it's your time, so if you have anything you want to explore, discuss, or find answers to, I'll do my best to connect and provide you with the information."

Immediately I think about the weekend in the Poconos and how Juliette tapped into Nicki—and then picked up that Nicki was concerned about Wyatt. Is this similar to what Conor does? Juliette arranged for me to have a session with him on Thursday. What could I ask?

Conor offers to do a live demonstration and asks for volunteers. One of the women from Australia raises her hand.

"Thank you," he says as he walks toward the smaller of the two Australian women we'd seen in the bar the first night here. "What's your name?"

"Amelia," she says in the most delightful manner. It's then I remember that her sight isn't good. Apparently, Conor is aware of this, as he gently takes her arm and guides her to an empty chair by the table in the front of the room.

"Is there anything you feel comfortable asking?" Conor's tone shifts a bit, speaking in a smooth and soothing voice.

"Yes," she says, "I'd like to know why I am afraid of heights."

Conor smiles, takes her hands in his, and then looks deeply into her eyes. The room is still. After several minutes, Conor—who is now squinting—begins to speak: "I see you, not as yourself, but as another woman, walking along a path, up a steep mountain. You have several small children with you. One, who is quite young, is in a papoose on your back. But there are two other children ... a boy and a girl ... walking in front of you. They're playful, and you scold them, reminding them to be careful. But then, the boy tugs at his sister's arm. Instinctively, she pulls away ... to the right ... where there are loose stones on the path. The child slips, sliding closer to the edge of the mountain. You try to stop her, but it happens too quickly. She falls, tumbling down the mountain. Seconds later, the girl disappears. There is nothing you can do."

He stops speaking. I look at Amelia. Tears stream down her face, yet she seems at peace. Conor lets go of her hands and gently touches her shoulder, then whispers something in her ear. Several moments later, after he helps the woman return to her seat, he addresses the group.

"What we did was tap into a past life, one in which Amelia was a young woman, most likely Indigenous. She'd witnessed the death of her daughter, who fell off a narrow mountain path. I believe this subconscious soul memory from many lifetimes ago has stayed with Amelia, causing her to be afraid of heights.

"It makes so much sense," Sophia whispers to me. I nod my head in agreement.

Conor conducts two more one-on-ones in front of the group. Watching this makes me want to meet with Conor. But I need to think of several good questions, so I don't waste our time together.

As we leave this morning's workshop, I begin to feel butterflies in my stomach. I inhale deeply, accepting I can't control what will transpire later today with Francisco. As the air leaves my chest, I say a little prayer that all will be well, then follow the others out of the room.

Pray all you want, but is anyone listening?

***

Juliette announces that she and Maggie plan to grab a quick lunch before the jungle hike. "You know, we're going bungee jumping after hiking to the top of the mountain. Then we get to swim beneath the waterfalls." As usual, Juliette is over the top, floating in anticipation of the next activity. I'm glad Maggie's going with her. It's good for both of them.

While the youngest two of our group are off on their adventure, Sophia, Annie, and I have a quiet lunch on the second-floor patio, outside of the dining room. Afterward, they leave for a relaxing afternoon by the pool. But not me. I'm meeting with Francisco.

As directed, I arrive at the reception area at two o'clock. Francisco is already there, waiting for me, a big smile on his face.

"How was your lunch?" he asks in the gentlest of voices. The youthfulness I observed earlier seems to have vanished, and the gentleman in front of me appears wise, an elder of sorts.

"Delicious," I say, still staring at him. I see wrinkles I hadn't noticed before. The creases around his eyes appear quite deep. Maybe he didn't sleep well last night.

"Chef is quite masterful with how he prepares meals. After all, to do this deep work, you must also properly nourish the body." With that, he motions for me to follow him as he turns and walks toward the stairs.

We ascend three flights, to a floor I have not been on before.

"This is our private residence," he says as he holds a glass-clad door open for me to enter.

Once inside, I see that he, or more likely Dominque, has exquisite taste. The main living space is mostly white, accented with all of Earth's elements—rich mahogany wood, a dark stone fireplace, and plants ... lots of plants. While some are flowering, others have long tendrils that flow across shelves, ceramic bowls, and framed photographs. It's then I hear water. Turning to my left, I see an open-air balcony with a gorgeous metal waterfall feature. Underneath are succulents, embedded in mesmerizing rocks. But when I look closer, I realize they aren't rocks, *they're crystals*. And then I notice how the sunlight's reflection casts an enchanting rainbow off of them and onto the wall to my right.

"Welcome to our home," Francisco says, most likely aware of my awe.

Dominique appears. "Hello, Marlee. It is good to see you. Please, make yourself comfortable. May I offer you anything to drink?" The words flow from her mouth with ease, once again reminding me of Sophia.

"Thank you, Dominique, but I just finished lunch. Your home is amazing," I say as my eyes continue to jump from one gorgeous painting to another, then to the intriguing sculptures displayed throughout this naturally lit room.

"We love our apartment," she says as she gracefully sits on the white sofa. "There's something about this space I cannot explain. All I know is when I am here, the world outside seems to disappear … and I can go to places I normally cannot see." With that, she smiles but offers no more.

"Please, come this way to my office," Francisco says as his open palm gestures toward a hallway to the left. Dominique picks up a book sitting on the coffee table in front of her and opens it. I suspect bringing guests to their apartment for private sessions is merely part of their routine.

Halfway down the hall is an open door. As we approach, it's evident this is anything but a traditional office. While there is a gorgeous carved wooden desk in one corner, the rest of his "office" seems more like a meditation/healing room. A worn Persian rug lies atop the bamboo floor, anchoring the room in a grounding way. There are several different colored poufs, casually positioned in a circle. Underneath the window is a long, narrow raw-edge table laden with candles, gemstones, feathers, and a variety of musical instruments. And there's a large gong tucked into one of the corners of the room. But what surprises me most is the artwork—

tapestries that show depictions of a snake, an eagle, and a jaguar. Then I see the most delicate watercolor of a hummingbird. While I know it's only a painting, the hummingbird seems real, as if it might fly toward me.

Francisco smiles. "Feel free to sit anywhere that calls to you. Before we begin, do you have any questions?" His face is kind, fatherly.

I inhale deeply and say, "I'm concerned about what is going to happen. All I know is that Juliette said you will tell me a lot, and it will rock my world." Remaining standing, I feel my stomach muscles tighten. No longer are there butterflies. Instead, it feels like jaybirds battling one another.

Francisco chuckles, then turns serious. "Ah, Juliette, such a spirited soul. Remember what I said Saturday night. Each session is designed to meet what the *individual needs*. I will share what calls to be known—nothing more, nothing less. Do not fear, my child. Our time together is designed to help you find your purpose and overcome any obstacles holding you back from your soul's journey. It is not meant to frighten you or cause you pain."

Hearing this calms me a bit. Still, there's an uncertainty of what's about to transpire. What if this is like fortune-telling, and I don't like what's revealed? Francisco motions again for me to take a seat.

Choosing a purple-and-green pouf, I settle into a cross-legged position. Francisco sits opposite of me on a burgundy tufted cushion. Silence follows. I watch as he stands to pick up a bowl containing a lighter and what appears to be a bundle of sage. After lighting the dried parcel, he waves it around me. The swirling smoke creeps into my nostrils. Yes, this is most definitely sage.

After several moments, he places the bowl—and the smoking sage—on the table behind him, then resettles on his cushion. I watch in silence as he appears to transform. It's as if he leaves his physical body to go elsewhere … but to where, I have no idea.

He sways side to side then back and forth while softly chanting words my ears cannot decipher. Then he pulls out a feather that must have been tucked beside his cushion and begins to wave it in front of him. My heartbeat quickens. His chanting grows louder.

Do you really believe this "singing shaman" can help you? Can't you see it's all an act?

Damn you, Margaret. You're not welcome here … or any place that I am. Go away … now … and never come back! Squeezing my eyes shut, I imagine Margaret melting into fine particles … then slowly disappearing into space.

I refocus my attention on Francisco, ejecting all thoughts of Margaret from my mind.

Several moments later, Francisco stops chanting. After inhaling deeply, he regains his earlier demeanor, one that is calm and soothing. I feel my pulse slow in response to his shift. Or perhaps it's from me deporting Margaret into the unknown.

"My dear Marlee," he eventually says. "You have come here at a most appropriate time." Francisco's eyes widen as he gazes into mine. "You are at a crossroads, are you not?" He tilts his head, as if waiting for my response.

"A crossroads? I am not sure what you mean."

Francisco sits up a bit straighter, then looks even deeper into my eyes. "Is it true you are unsure of your next steps?"

Immediately my throat tightens and tears well in my eyes. I take big gulps of air, hoping to keep the tears from spilling past my lashes.

Francisco leans toward me and places his hand lightly on top of mine. "Do not be afraid, Marlee. All will be fine. But for you to fully release your fears, you must strengthen your faith in something higher than yourself … You must trust in God." Francisco sits back, as if waiting for me to speak. But words refuse to come forward, and I remain silent, frozen on top of my pouf.

I can't believe he said this. Does he know? Could he hear Margaret?

"But how do I know ... that God even exists?" My voice quivers as I finally ask the question I've always struggled with since I've been a little girl.

"Ah, how does one develop faith?" Francisco pauses, yet he continues to stare deep into my eyes.

I wait patiently, hoping he'll offer me sage advice to help me finally believe in what I've been told is real yet cannot see.

But instead of a simple phrase or a set of instructions, Francisco challenges me to consider the alternative. "Have you ever asked yourself what the purpose of this all would be"—he waves his hands through the air—"without something higher than ourselves?"

I sit in silence, trying to do what this shaman suggests. Taking several deep breaths, I ask myself, *What if there was no God?* How would that impact people, nature ... everything? I shut my eyes, imagining a world with no moral limitations, no thoughts of a life after death, nothing more than our mere limited existence here on Earth. Images of deceit, corruption, ill intent, and evil flood my brain, forcing me to quickly open my eyes to stop the visions.

"It would be horrible. There'd be no point."

"Exactly. God gives us hope. Believing in something greater than ourselves is what inspires us to make the higher decisions, to choose kindness, to listen to the voice of love ... not that of fear."

And it's at this moment the voice I long to hear suddenly speaks.

Trust in God ... He will help you to release your fears.

Everything around me becomes blurry. My hands begin to shake. Digging my fists into the pouf to better anchor myself, I pray this voice doesn't leave me—that it stays to offer me strength and provide me with guidance.

"And when you believe in God, new and exciting opportunities will come forth, often when you least expect them," Francisco says with a promising twinkle in his eyes. He then sits back. Turning toward the table behind him, he picks up the bowl of sage and relights the bundle. Slowly rising from his cushion, he stands by me, leaning down to fan the smoke around my midsection. Francisco chants again, but this time his voice sounds louder, with a darker, solemn tone.

As his words fill my ears, strange feelings begin to stir within. First, uncomfortable memories of my childhood surface—those of my older siblings cruelly teasing me, excluding me from their activities. My throat tightens in response. Suddenly, I feel the urge to cry. I'm unable to hold back these tears, and they freely fall from my eyes, over my cheeks, and onto my lap. Then, another image appears, but it's from my teenage years—those three "friends" who were anything but, who ridiculed me for wanting to fit in. With each teardrop that exits my body, something inside feels softer, more at peace.

The process continues. Eventually, thoughts arise from the not-so-distant past—fears of my cancer returning ... of Patrick leaving for college ... of Tom and I growing apart. My stomach clenches, then releases, almost in a rhythmic pattern. But, of course, these are the fears that haunt me the most, what I don't want to admit are possibilities.

Something within me swirls, but not gently. No, this intense sensation appears to be stirring up buried emotions, the parts of my life and pieces of myself I prefer not to revisit—my parents' funerals, the guilt I felt when breaking up with Travis, watching my hair fall out from the chemotherapy. The momentum increases ... almost to the point of pain. But when it finally slows, the discomfort dissipates. Could I finally be surrendering my past?

Simultaneously, Francisco's voice slows. When he stops chanting, I cautiously open my eyes only to find Francisco's sitting on his cushion in front of me, smiling.

Finally, Francisco speaks: "How are you?"

"Exhausted," I say. "What happened?"

Instead of answering my question, he asks me one. "Marlee, why did you come here?" His words are clear and direct.

"Because Juliette asked me to." My answer is automatic.

"True, but you had to have a reason of your own. Think. What might that be?"

Shutting my eyes, I repeat his question aloud: "Why did I come here?"

I allow myself time to consider these words, remembering Margaret told me to stay home.

It's then the other voice appears.

Believe.

My body begins to drift, almost float, in a most unusual way. It's as though I'm no longer in this room or connected to the pouf beneath me.

Instead, I find myself inside a cave. It's dark and cold. Yet, in the distance, there's a brilliant glow coming from a narrow gap at the far end of this cavern. It calls me. Slowly, I move toward it, proceeding cautiously until I'm able to peer out of the opening ... into an enchanted land.

Contrary to the darkness that surrounds me, the outside is glorious. As if to check myself and make sure I'm not dreaming, I turn around. Everything behind me is black, frigid, lifeless. My body craves the light and what's beyond. But how do I venture into this new world? There's no staircase. I feel trapped. Ahead of me is the life I want, but I have no idea how to obtain it.

This beautiful land beckons, calling my name in the most se-rene and tempting manner. Below, at the bottom of the canyon, are meadows filled with tranquil willow trees and vibrant wildflowers. There's a crystal-blue lake, and in the middle of it is a small island. At the far edge of the meadow, I see a quaint cottage, complete with a front porch and a vegetable garden behind it. A winding road continues to the far corner of the canyon, though I cannot discern what's beyond.

"I came here to find God... to understand the meaning behind it all ... why I am here on Earth ... discover what my next steps should be." The words escape my mouth without me being conscious of them even forming in my brain. "My life is good ... but I want it to be better. I just don't know how."

"Of course, you do." Francisco's tone is smooth, encouraging. I feel prompted to continue, so I do.

"I need to move forward ... want to ..." I feel a heaviness in my chest, and my breath becomes raspy. Admitting this induces a panicked state of sorts. "But I'm afraid."

"Have you asked God for His guidance?"

I smell sage. Gently opening my eyelids, I watch as Francisco waves the bundle around my head.

The floaty sensation subsides, and within a few seconds, I feel myself deeply rooted in my seat. Ask for guidance from God? I don't remember the last time I've really reached out to God. Sure, I pray, especially when it comes to Patrick. But that's different from having an actual conversation. And what if He doesn't respond? My mind reverts to my fear that God doesn't exist.

"How do I ask?" I am now the one searching into Francisco's eyes.

"It's quite simple. Quiet yourself and then go within. Ask for what you desire to know ... then pause. Listen for the slightest message. Whether it comes from God or your intuition does not matter. What is important is that you reach out and then wait for a response. If you hear a loud and booming voice, that is certainly not God, nor is it your inner guidance. That is your ego. God's voice and your intuition whisper. And neither will steer you in the wrong direction." He pauses, then leans closer toward me. "But you must believe, Marlee. Are you willing to trust in that which you cannot *see*?"

So much has happened these past several months. I've come so far, shifted many of my limiting thoughts. I want to believe, but can I trust in the unknown? I don't know.

"Trust ... let go ... believe. That is all that is required." His words, though simple, echo the question I've just asked myself. Could Francisco be reading my innermost thoughts? But then my mind shifts to what he is proposing ... Is this possible to do?

Immediately my biggest fears come to mind. First, I think of Patrick soon leaving for college, where I can do nothing to protect him. Then my mind shifts to the possibility of my cancer returning. And while my relationship with Tom has been amazing—better than ever—will it all change once Patrick's gone? Plus, what about the *Inquirer*? I feel as though working there has lost its allure. I used to look forward to Brad's emails, excited for the next assignment. But since writing about holistic healing, my work now feels empty. Soon I'll be forty-seven, and I have no idea what I want to do next. So much in my life is uncertain. It's as though I have no control over anything.

"But how do I trust? What will happen if I let go, surrender all control?"

"My dear, that is when you begin to fly."

MAGGIE
Tuesday, April 20

Unable to sleep, I stare at the swirling ceiling fan. Soon the sun will rise, and it will be time to run with Marlee. I stretch my legs, pressing my feet against the crisp white sheets snugly tucked under the mattress.

Deciding to capture the serenity of the moment, I turn on the light, then grab my journal and pen from the bedside table. Comfortably propped against the headboard, I begin to write. At first, the words come in bits and pieces. Yet, before long, they quickly fill the blank page.

> How could I not have been there when my mom passed? Maybe if I hadn't gone away that weekend, I could have done something ... given her CPR ... anything to save her. But the doctor insisted it would not have mattered if anyone else was in the house. He said, "It's just one of those things that sometimes happens."

Frustrated with myself—I cannot say how many times I've written these exact words—I pause, putting my pen down in the crease of my journal. Knowing I need and want to write about something new, I pick up my phone and tap the voice memo app to access the recording from yesterday's session with Sonya.

"Your natal chart reveals much about who you are as well as what you can become. Introspective, you require time alone to sit with your thoughts and regroup. Make sure you allow yourself this space. It is critical for you to have downtime, but remember not to become stuck in your head, as this will lead to feelings of loneliness even when you are with people.

"Maggie, you are meant to serve others. You are incredibly compassionate. Yet sometimes doing for others hinders what is best for you. So it is important you develop a balance, knowing when you must step away and take care of yourself.

"You're quite intelligent, and that will serve you well. Though you'd be wise to listen more instead of forming your response in your head while others are speaking. As a learner, you prefer reading information over listening to others and thrive through dialogue with your instructors.

"Be careful about negative self-talk and worry. You are a powerful woman and possess everything you need. Use your strength instead of fearing it. And it is critical that you remain in a state of high vibration. This will draw things *to you*. Do not worry about how others view you. Express your true self, and be who you are no matter where you are or who you are with. Stop trying to control people and situations. You do not require it, as you have the tools within to navigate your life. Surrender whatever you so tightly grip."

How could Sonya know so much about me?

"Your natural tendency is to be organized and maintain a healthy lifestyle. This, too, will serve you well, as you deplore chaos. Maintain these practices."

Once again, she's spot on.

"You feel things, physically, even small physical ailments that others may not notice. Some may think of you as a hypochondriac, but these are truly empathic sensations, as you pick up others' feelings and fears, as well as sensations from your environment. It is important for you to distinguish which emotions are yours as well as which are someone else's. Establish routines to protect yourself from others' negative energy. You may choose to wear or carry protective gemstones, envision you're surrounded within a protective bubble, or sage and ground yourself after being in the presence of others whose energy has adverse effects on you."

This truly resonates. I often pick up on people's feelings.

"You are extremely bright. Yet, while you are quick to see the big picture, you struggle with expressing your true emotions. When you were young, you did not talk a lot. Something traumatic may have happened to have impacted you. Regardless, you prefer to work in quiet spaces, away from chaos."

Ha!

"You love fully, and your love affairs are intense, filled with healthy passion. However, you treasure your freedom and independence. It will take a special person to satisfy your needs."

And that's not Pete …

"Be cautious of your pride; it can get you in trouble. You fear betrayal and hold onto your past, often yearning for the time of no responsibilities. But you are meant to embrace your responsibilities and collaborate with others."

She nailed that. For years, I've wondered about my father, as well as why he left my mom … and me.

"Your Rising sign is Pisces. While mostly shy and quiet, you may also appear quite passionate and verbal, confusing those around you, as they are not sure which version of you may show up. You view the world with rose-colored glasses, often hesitant to make firm and solid decisions. Restless by nature, you prefer to keep your options open. You act by feeling, not thinking."

There's that word *passion* again.

"You will do best in a relationship where your partner is grounded, to help counter the amount of time you spend in the clouds."

I turn off the recording and lean back against the bamboo headboard. Trying to grasp the meaning of everything Sonya said, I pick up my journal, then hit replay, listening once again while writing down those comments that most resonate.

I need time alone—but don't spend too much time in my head, or I will become lonely.
I am to serve others—but keep a balance and take care of myself.
Listen more—instead of formulating responses while others are speaking.
Watch out for negative self-talk and worrying.
Stay in high vibration.
Don't worry what others think of me.
Express as my true self.
Stop trying to control people and things. SURRENDER!!!
Empathic—which emotions are mine? Which are others?
Gemstones? Bubble up? Sage? Ground?
Didn't talk a lot as a child ... Traumatic experience!!!!
Special man to satisfy my needs????? Passion???
Pride will get me in trouble.
Fear betrayal???
Embrace responsibilities and collaborate.

Rose-colored glasses-hesitant to make
decisions-feel more than think???
Grounded partner.

When the recording stops, I once again place my pen into the crevice of the leather journal Mom gave me last Christmas. Staring at the quilt on top of me, that sensation returns, the one that has kept haunting me since my mother's death. It's as though I can feel her pain as she fell to the ground. But that's impossible. I wasn't even there to witness it. I only saw the aftermath.

Slowly, I shake my head, wanting to forever banish these thoughts from my mind. However, despite my best effort to shut down these devastating emotions, I cannot. They keep bubbling up.

Finally, I force myself to look down at the still-open journal resting on my lap. The summary of session notes stares back at me. I reread what I wrote—twice. Still, I can't help but wonder how Sonya knew so much about me. How could a person's time and place of birth reveal significant information about who they are? And what if we don't like what we hear? Can we change what is written in the stars? It's then I remember Sonya's final words from our session.

"*While this is what our natal charts tell us about ourselves and our path, we always have free will to change what's predicted.*"

Is what she told me who I want to be? So much made sense. It even explained my quirks, my habits, my preferences.

I shut my journal. It's too much information to process right now. While it's unsettling—as is that nagging feeling I've met Sonya before—it does fill in many missing pieces to my past. And looking back, our time together wasn't scary at all.

While I am somewhat apprehensive about this afternoon's session with Conor, I suspect none of these experiences will come close to what may occur when I meet with Francisco on Wednesday. I release a big sigh.

When I decided to come to this retreat, I hoped to find answers to questions I've had for so long … about my past … my parents … who I really am. But I didn't think it would be so difficult. I sigh again, accepting I must be brave and show up fully when I meet with these healers if I want to connect the dots from my past.

Rays of sun begin to stream through the bathroom window, filling the room with magnificent light, almost as if to suggest it's time to turn on my own light … to discover who I am and what I want.

My mind then drifts to the jungle hike with Juliette. Although nervous at the thought of jumping off a cliff, I did it. Afterward, I felt so proud. Of course, Juliette leapt without a moment's hesitation. That woman intrigues me. She's super accomplished, and she's not even thirty. Still, comparing myself to her—or anyone else for that matter—is never healthy. Juliette's witty and outspoken and seems to be on her way to awakening. I've just started, and from what I'm beginning to learn, it's a long journey, perhaps one without a definite destination.

Last night after dinner, I went to the dharma talk, "Living from a State of Compassion." Dominique and Jack Keeler, the doctor turned holistic practitioner, led the conversation. During the breakout session, I partnered up with Samantha, one of the two women from Australia. Jack instructed us to listen to the other person speak for three minutes, maintaining eye contact the entire time. And we couldn't interrupt, not even to affirm what the other person was saying. It was difficult to remain quiet and focused for so long. Immediately, I'm reminded of what Sonya said—how it will serve me well to listen to others without mentally rehearsing my response while they're speaking.

I bite down on my lip, amazed at the correlation. The sound of a knock on my door interrupts my thoughts.

I jump out of bed and answer the door in my pajamas.

"Good morning! I wanted to check if you were awake," Marlee says, looking ready to run.

I look at my watch. "Oh no! I was supposed to meet you five minutes ago. I'm sorry. Give me a sec to change," I say. While Marlee heads down the stairs, I grab my running clothes and quickly dress.

***

"How was your session with Francisco?" I ask Marlee as we begin running alongside the calm water. The sun casts its golden rays on top of the surf, causing a glistening effect.

"Amazing ... but kind of unsettling at the same time. It was as though he could see things inside of me that I've been blind to ... or denying. Do you know what I mean?" she asks as we begin to pick up the pace.

"Yes, I had a similar experience with Sonya. She told me aspects about myself that were true, and, well, some of them were almost too on target. I felt as if she could tap into my mind."

"Exactly," Marlee says, but she does not offer more. No doubt she, like me, is still processing the experience.

We remain silent until we reach the end of the cove. Running's always helped me better understand things. I guess you could call it my Zen time. But once we turn around to make our way back to the resort, we begin to talk, mostly about our jobs. Marlee's already shared she works part-time for the *Inquirer*, but this morning she goes into detail about some of her previous assignments. Then she admits she's not so sure she wants to continue to work at the paper. I refrain from responding and instead hold space for Marlee to express her hesitations. However, I can feel her confusion—there's a tug between her heart and her mind.

Marlee then asks me about my work. I share my job's responsibilities, what it's like to meet with clients, and how I do my best to anticipate what they need from me. But then I tell her about the offer my bosses made.

"I've never heard of Bend, Oregon," Marlee says. "But if you like your current job and the people you work with, it could be a great opportunity." There's a true sincerity in her voice. It's her next statement that causes me to pause. "You said you're from Pittsburgh. I'm guessing it would be difficult to leave family and friends." When she turns to look at me, her soft eyes convey genuine compassion at the thought of moving away from loved ones.

Do I go there with someone whom I've only met a few days ago? Though I'm hesitant at first, something within tells me it's safe to be open with Marlee.

And so I trust my instinct.

"Actually ... um ... it's only me. My mother passed away in February."

"Oh honey, I am so sorry," Marlee says as she comes to an abrupt stop and gently places both hands on my shoulders.

Determined not to cry, I continue to explain: "It was sudden. I had been away for the weekend ... skiing with friends. Early that Monday morning, I drove home to shower and change before work. I expected to find my mom sitting at the kitchen table, drinking coffee, and finishing the paper's sudoku puzzle. But when I arrived, our house was completely dark. Figuring Mom had overslept, I checked her room. But she wasn't there. After searching everywhere, I found her ... on the kitchen floor." I stop speaking, gathering the courage to continue. "The coroner's report said it was an aneurysm. Everyone told me there was nothing I could have done had I been there. Still ..." I sniff loudly, doing my best not to cry.

"How horrible this must be for you." But then Marlee pauses, as if offering me time to decide if I want to say more.

To my surprise, I do. "She was the only parent I ever knew." I swallow several times, unsure if I should expand upon this statement.

Again, Marlee doesn't probe. Instead, she stands next to me, head tilted, as if nothing else has any importance but me and my story.

I rub the sweat from my forehead. "No one ever mentioned my father. My mom raised me by herself … with help from her parents. But I guess what makes me the saddest is not knowing anything about my dad … who he is, his relationship with my mom, why he left. Whenever I would ask my mom or grandparents questions about him, they'd become sullen and tell me not to think about it." I heave out a big sigh. "Having no knowledge of my father, not even a photo of him, is what troubles me the most." By now I'm choking back the tears. "Why didn't he want me? And how come it was taboo to talk about him … like he never existed?"

Marlee remains quiet. Yet her eyes speak the words I've longed to hear. They tell me I'm safe. I'm loved. I matter. It wasn't my fault.

It's then I quickly realize what I'm doing—baring my soul to a stranger. But I wouldn't call Marlee *a stranger*. No. She's anything but. And so, without more than a moment's pause, I continue.

"And then there's Pete." I exhale loudly, feeling my shoulders slump forward. I momentarily shut my eyes, as though trying to erase any image of this kind, caring guy from my brain. "We've been together for a while. He's the *nicest* person I've ever known … but he's not *the one*. I mean, I care about him … it's just … I don't think I love him." I swallow several times as this guilt-ridden admittance seems to cause a choking sensation. "Pete keeps telling me how much he loves me and wants to take care of me. I'm afraid he's going to propose." As if on cue, I bite my lower lip.

It's my final statement that catches me off guard, causing me to burst into tears as I admit the very emotion I've tried to suppress. "I feel so alone."

Marlee gently takes me in her arms, allowing me to release my buried fears. As I sob uncontrollably, my tears mix with the salty sweat covering my face and Marlee's shoulders.

After several minutes, I step back, suddenly embarrassed by my meltdown.

Marlee doesn't say a word. Several moments later, as if sparked by an unspoken agreement, we both begin to run. Before long, we find ourselves back where we started. It's as though Marlee can read my mind when she asks, "Do you want to keep going?" She tilts her head toward the other end of the beach.

I nod yes. Marlee then begins to share how she lost her mom—and her dad—before she was twenty-four. Finally, *someone* who can relate to how I feel.

"I can't understand why Mom wouldn't tell me anything about my dad." Me saying this clearly unsettles Marlee. Without breaking stride, she reaches out and briefly puts her hand on my shoulder. Her touch feels maternal, filled with care and compassion.

By now we've come to a large rock formation, requiring us to turn around. I look at my watch, knowing I'll have to shower quickly if I hope to make it to meditation on time. But I don't care. It felt so good to share my story.

Once back, we take a moment to stretch our legs, pushing our hands against a palm tree as we alternate stepping each of our feet out behind us.

"I think you're one of the bravest people I've ever met. For you to come here alone … and so soon after your mom's death … to figure things out … well, that says so much about who you are … and who you are becoming." Marlee stops, but the look on her face makes it seem as though she wants to say more. I watch as a single tear rolls down her cheek. She clears her throat. "See you at meditation, OK?" I nod in response.

As I make my way up the wooden stairs and into the bathroom to shower, I wonder what propelled me to talk so openly with Marlee. I don't do things like that … not even with my closest friends.

But then I think back to what she said. Marlee called me *brave*. I'd never use that word to describe myself. Still, for someone who barely knows me and just learned my life's story to say that—well, maybe there *could* be a tiny bit of truth to it. I turn the shower nozzle to cold and embrace the frigid water cascading over my body.

***

Eduardo played singing bowls during our entire meditation. I felt corresponding vibrations in different areas of my body, specifically the second, third, and fourth chakras. Afterward, Kali led us in a power yoga sequence. Yesterday, she told us Tuesday's practice would be somewhat rigorous. Maybe that explains why there were some unoccupied mats. But I loved it. Despite the longer run this morning, my body seemed to crave the challenging movement.

And now, as I make my way up the stairs to learn about today's session—Sound Healing—I realize *how much* of my life I shared with Marlee this morning. I didn't mean to. It just came out naturally. But Marlee didn't exhibit pity. Instead, she seemed to embrace my situation and see me for who I am. Perhaps it's because she lost both parents at a young age and, unlike most people, can relate. Strangely, I do not feel embarrassed.

Lindsay Keeler reminds me of Carrie Bradshaw from *Sex and the City*. When I first saw her Saturday evening, she had her hair pulled back. But now, gorgeous long blonde curls frame her heart-shaped face. Dressed in a flowing batik-print skirt and powder-blue tank top, Lindsay appears taller than I recall.

"Good morning." Her voice is soft and tender. The room quiets as she captures everyone's attention. "I'm not sure if any of you have experienced Sound Healing, so I thought I'd spend a few minutes explaining what it is and how it helps us." She begins to fidget, as if standing in front of the group is uncomfortable for her.

Lindsay scrunches her slightly upturned nose and says, "This seems so formal. Do you mind if we push the chairs and tables aside? Then we can all sit on the floor."

Everyone gets up and begins shifting the furniture to the room's perimeter.

Now standing next to the closet located in the rear of the room, Lindsay says, "Please, come and grab whatever you need to make yourself comfortable for this morning's session. There are plenty of yoga mats, bolsters, and blankets." I sense a slight shift in her voice, as if changing our environment has helped put her at ease.

Lindsay places her mat in the front of the room, then encourages us to form lines, zigzagging ourselves to allow for more room between participants.

"Ahh, that's better," she says, looking more relaxed as she settles cross-legged on top of her bolster. With palms resting on her knees, she begins.

"Sound Healing is energy, plain and simple. It's merely another way of elevating ourselves as we activate our chakras and cleanse our body." She sits up taller, straightening her spine. A serene look comes across her slightly freckled face.

It's now apparent why she's rearranged the room. This is where she's at peace—seated on the floor, not standing in front of a captive audience. As I acknowledge her shift, I can feel a change within myself as well. This morning may be more interesting than I'd anticipated.

"Today I am going to play a variety of musical instruments for you. When sequenced in harmony with one another, they create an epiphany of sounds. The resulting vibration helps your muscles relax, your heart open, and energy move freely throughout your body."

She then goes on to explain the various instruments she will use and the individual chakras they'll impact. My curiosity piques when she rises and stands next to the two gongs behind her. "The gong is foundational in this practice. Listen, while I show you the range of sounds it can produce." Lindsay begins gently tapping on one, then both gongs. Slowly, the sound increases, creating deep vibrations inside my body. First the pulsation travels to my chest, then my ears, and finally my head. As she changes the manner and frequency in which she strikes these metal instruments, the sensations shift locations as well. Finally, she stops, but it takes several moments until the room becomes quiet, as the gongs' sound continues to reverberate.

"The sequence I will be performing this morning is designed to help you unearth some of your deeper emotions, perhaps aspects you've suppressed, intentionally or unintentionally." With this comment, a slight grin appears on her face. "It's natural to have a visceral response to Sound Healing. So please, don't be concerned with whatever comes up … or how your body reacts to it. Some people cry; others become agitated. And it's perfectly normal to feel nothing at all."

I swallow several times. The last thing I want to do is to cry or release any unknown anger amongst strangers. I'd already let go of enough tears in front of Marlee this morning. But then I remind myself why I am here—to figure things out. And if I must be swept up in an emotional frenzy while this woman plays musical instruments, then I guess I'm OK with it.

"Before we begin, we will do a few breathing exercises, and then I'll guide you through some subtle movements. Afterward, you'll lie down on your back, and I'll start playing the music, OK?"

Heads nod in agreement. I look at Marlee. She offers me a reassuring look. It feels nurturing … motherly. A lump forms in my throat as I wonder why being with Marlee invokes this reaction.

Lindsay guides us through alternate nostril breathing, instructing us to place our "peace fingers" on the bridge of our nose then use our thumb and ring finger to alternately close off our left and right nostril, so we only use one to inhale and one to exhale. Oddly, I find this practice calming.

After that, we do several Cat-Cow yoga movements, then seated twists and side bends. Lindsay instructs us to lie on our back and hug our knees to our chest. "Find a comfortable position on the mat, settling into stillness with both arms by your sides. Please use your blankets and other props to make yourself comfortable."

Several moments later, once the room becomes silent, she adds, "Shut your eyes and rest. Allow your mind to quiet. Focus on the music's vibrations." She then stops speaking.

The first sound I hear reminds me of ocean waves breaking on the shore. After several moments, I sense a swirling of sorts. While she demonstrated the various instruments earlier, I'm unsure which one she's now playing, as they all appear to combine forces to create the most beautiful sounds. But I do recognize when she moves to the gong. Its strong and deep vibration fills my body.

Lindsay alternates instruments, pace, and intensity. The entire time, my body follows her progression of symphonic movements. When I hear a clash of what I believe to be cymbals, my chest thrusts upward before it slowly sinks back into the mat. Although I'm expecting to feel tears, none surface. Instead, an edginess comes over me. My eyebrows furrow and my jaw tightens. There's a constriction in my throat, as if a vice is tightening around it. I thought this was supposed to help you release things, not hurt you. These powerful sensations move to my core. My stomach muscles tense, then begin to cramp. It's as though something's trying to come out of me, but I won't let go.

Pressure, tightness, compression ... I feel a sharp pain in my chest. Though only momentary, it causes me to arch my back in response to the intensity.

But then it's gone, as is the tightness in my stomach, brow, jaw, and throat. I'm no longer clenching. Instead, my body becomes limp, spent from the roller coaster ride of vibrational frequency.

Lindsay's still playing music, but it's softer, calmer, almost reminding me of walking through a misty summer rainfall. Cleansing, rejuvenating, yet restful ... that is how I feel ... at peace.

***

This afternoon's scheduled activity is horseback riding. Juliette's going, but Marlee and Sophia opted out, claiming they wanted to hang with Annie by the pool. As much as I'd love to go horseback riding along the ocean, my session with Conor is at two o'clock.

Sitting at lunch with my new friends, I feel my heartbeat quicken as I recall Conor's "readings" with those who volunteered during his workshop. I try to think of other things, like how delicious my salad is and whether I want the chocolate torte or the pecan cookies I saw on the dessert table. Nevertheless, I spend most of lunch preoccupied with creating possible questions for Conor. Marlee seems to notice my spaciness, as several times I catch her looking my way.

Unsure of where this session is meant to go, I contemplate asking if he contacts the deceased ... and if so, if he could tap into my mom. However, he didn't mention doing any of that, so maybe I should explore whether I should go with Sandy and Mark to Bend. Still, while that is certainly a critical decision with a looming deadline, there must be something better to inquire about during our time together. Then it hits me—why not ask Conor about my dad? For years, I considered buying the Ancestry test, but what was I going to do, start contacting men connected to my chart who were in their late forties to see if they possibly fathered a child twenty-eight years ago?

I pull the printed itinerary out of my bag. Checking the fine print, I see my session with Conor is in Yurt #7, located between the tree houses and the yoga/meditation studio. Hopefully, that's the lucky yurt, the one where people hear uplifting messages, not the place where their biggest nightmares are predicted.

Since I've been little, I've wondered about my dad. In fact, I became obsessed with knowing his identity around age thirteen. Yet, no matter how much I pleaded, my mom refused to share any information. All she said was, "I love you enough for two parents, so please, don't worry about this, Margaret."

Margaret—the name she always used when she was serious. Otherwise, it was Maggie, Mags, Magpie. But when I heard "Margaret," I knew I was either in trouble or we were about to have a big talk.

Because it's only 1:35, I opt to stroll around the property prior to my session with Conor. Admiring the blooming foliage, I wonder who designed these buildings. It's then I hear a soft rustling overhead. It's the monkeys. Being that it's midafternoon, they're quiet. I gaze toward the sky, intrigued by the interactions between the various-sized primates. Mother howlers are definitely the dominant parent. However, the males are clearly involved with their offspring. A heaviness comes over me. These little monkeys have more connection to their dads than I ever did. My fingers go to my jaws, realizing that oh-so-familiar tension has returned. I guess the benefits from this morning's Sound Healing session can't withstand my confusion about my father … whoever he is. Had he stayed with my mom … her entire life would have been different. She would have been happy … and maybe she'd still be alive.

Reluctantly acknowledging I cannot re-create the past, I begin walking toward Yurt #7. Maybe Conor can tell me something, anything, about my dad—who he is and why he was never there for me.

***

I sense Conor's down-to-earth energy as soon as I enter the yurt. He seems like someone I'd hang out with, not a psychic who's about to tell me something I may not want to hear.

"Hey, Maggie. How are you?" Seated at a small round table, Conor's dressed in khaki shorts and a maroon polo shirt. He then stands to greet me.

"Good, thanks, and you?" I ask, totally unsure of how an intuitive healing session begins.

"Awesome. I mean, being here, at this resort, does it get any better?"

After offering me a seat, he resettles into his chair. So far, this experience does not appear very woo-woo. In fact, when I signed up for a psychic healing session, I expected to meet with an older woman, one who's wrinkled and ripe with intuitive knowledge. But that's not the case. Instead, it's just the two of us, sitting on real chairs—not mats or cushions— around a small table. On top of the table are an empty notepad, a pen, and a box of tissues. It's the tissues that catch my attention.

"I like to begin sessions by asking my clients if there is anything on their minds—you know, an issue they'd like to explore. Some people have immediate questions. Others need time to consider what's been troubling them. And then there are those clients who only want me to do my thing and see what comes up." He sits back into his chair and crosses his right foot across his left knee. "How would you like to proceed, Maggie?"

I take a moment to consider his question.

"Well … I was wondering …" I stop talking, as once I ask the question, I cannot take it back, nor can I control the answer I receive. Still, I've been tormented for years not knowing. If I hope to have any peace, now is the time. "Can you tell me about my dad? What he's like? And well … maybe … why did he leave us?" The words fly from my mouth. In a strange way, just speaking them provides a bit of relief.

Conor leans closer, his head tilting to the right as he looks deeply into my eyes. He remains silent, but from the way his eyes are fluttering, I can tell his mind is going one hundred miles an hour. Still, he doesn't say a word.

Finally, Conor's eyes shut and remain closed for several minutes. Waiting for his response only causes my mouth to become dry and the muscles in the back of my neck to tighten. After what seems like an eternity, Conor opens his eyes.

"Are you ready?" he asks in a monotone, suggesting neither good nor bad news.

I gulp, then nod, suddenly terrified of what he'll say.

"Your dad is alive and lives quite close to you. But he doesn't know he's your dad. That's why you never heard from him. In fact, he's married … with children." The words flow from Conor's mouth without emotion, in a very matter-of-fact fashion.

"He … he never knew about me? He didn't … know my mom was pregnant?" I stutter the words, speaking in the softest of voices.

"No. Your mother never told him. How old was she when this happened?" He looks intently at me, as if trying to guess my age.

"Well, I'm twenty-eight, and I think my mom was seventeen when she became pregnant." I take a quick moment to check my math. "Yes, she was about to turn forty-six when she passed."

Conor's eyes widen before he says, "Her becoming pregnant at seventeen must have been quite traumatic." Then his face softens, and he lets out a slight chuckle. "And with the name Maggie Carr, I suspect you're as Irish Catholic as I am."

I nod my head vigorously. "My grandmother went to church every day. And my mom never missed Sunday mass."

Conor tilts his head before saying, "Then maybe you can understand the shame your mother felt and why she wouldn't tell you about your father ... or your father about you." He leans across the table, closer to me.

I look down at my lap and sigh. "I guess I get why she kept it a secret when I was little. But once I was old enough ... why didn't she tell me? Didn't I have a right to know? And what about him? Shouldn't he have known he had a daughter?" My pulse quickens as old feelings bubble up. But surprisingly, I'm feeling anger toward my mother.

"Ah ... shoulds and whys. These are certainly fair questions, but these were decisions your mother made a long time ago, most likely in fear. I wonder how her parents felt. Are they still living?" Why is he asking me this if he is a psychic? But then again, maybe he can only see certain things, which kind of makes sense.

"My grandparents were amazing. They took care of me while my mom was at work." I stop talking and hang my head as I stare at the floor, suddenly embarrassed by my accusations. "Only my grandfather is still alive. But he has Alzheimer's and is in a care unit outside of Pittsburgh." Sharing that information causes my heart to sink. My granddad has no idea his daughter died. I wanted to tell him, but his doctor claimed he'd never be able to process that information. Hearing Mom was gone would only cause him more distress.

"So, Maggie, now that you know your father is alive and living nearby, what do you plan to do with that information?"

"But how would I ever find him? I don't even know his name. And there's no one I can ask."

"Do you want to find out?" Again, Conor's look is neutral, neither persuading me to take him up on his offer nor encouraging me to refuse it.

Knowing it's now or never, I squeeze my eyes shut, then shake my head yes.

This time, Conor stands up and walks behind me, placing his hands on top of my head. I feel intense heat, though I'm not sure what this means.

Then, in an instant, the warm sensation dissipates. I open my eyes and see Conor returning to his chair. He picks up the pen and begins to write on the notepad. He then pushes the pad toward me.

John McIntyre.

I silently say this name to myself three times. My dad must be Irish … but of course. That makes perfect sense.

"So now what do I do?" I sheepishly ask. After years of wondering, I finally have a name and an understanding as to why my dad was never part of my life.

"That, Maggie, is totally up to you," Conor says, but this time, he's smiling, and I sense his twinkling green eyes are a signal to take a leap of faith and reach out to my father.

***

Once back in my room, I flop down on my bed and shut my eyes. This is too much to process. And how did Conor ever come up with that name? Maybe this John McIntyre doesn't even exist. Yet, despite my logical mind telling me how preposterous it all seems, deep down I know it to be true. But I'm too tired to think about it now. So instead of imagining how I'm going to reach out to *my father*, I choose to focus on my breath, eventually dozing off as I count my inhales and exhales.

When I wake up, the room is not as bright. I look out the window, realizing the sun is beginning to set. Glancing down at my watch, I see it's 6:15. I'd slept for over three hours. Damn.

Quickly, I brush my hair then change into fresh clothing. Tonight's the Full Moon Ceremony. We are supposed to come with our intention. But I forgot to write mine.

I grab the welcome packet we received during registration. There, inside of the front pocket, is a piece of ecru paper along with a felt-tipped pen and the sheet explaining the Full Moon Ceremony. After carefully reading the instructions, I take a deep breath, close my eyes, and try to decipher any intentions calling to me.

I will find my father.

These words come to me, reverberating in my ears, loud and clear, though I have no idea who or what spoke them. I don't think it was me, but then again, right now I'm not too sure about anything.

Taking my time, I neatly write my intention on the ecru paper, fold it in quarters, then tuck it inside my bra. My dress doesn't have pockets, and I don't want to bring a purse. Besides, it will be safe there, next to my heart.

MARLEE

Tuesday, April 20
Wednesday, April 21

Maggie joins us just as Juliette's finishing a five-minute monologue about her "amazing bareback ride along the fabulous beaches of Nosara." I turn toward Annie. "Are you looking forward to seeing the school tomorrow?"

"Yes!" Her eyes light up. "Camille promised to give me a full tour. At first there were only two classrooms, but now there's space for kindergarten through sixth grade!" Annie's grinning ear to ear as she shares this. Could it be my career-minded friend who never believed she could become pregnant is suddenly interested in elementary education? But then again, she specializes in adolescent psychology, so I suppose her enthusiasm could be work related. Yet something tells me this is personal.

As we're finishing dessert, Francisco rings a bell, summoning our attention. "It is time for the Full Moon Ceremony. Let us walk together to the beach. I hope you remembered to bring the slip of paper with your intention written on it."

Like ducklings, we follow our shaman down the steps, then out of the building, toward the ocean. Howler monkeys scream as they dance in the limbs above us. We pass our tree house, then Maggie's. Strangely, no one utters a sound. There's an unusual reverence in the air.

When we arrive at the beach, a fire, encircled by large pumice stones, blazes. Rows of driftwood, set up as our chairs, form a horseshoe around the roaring flames. Something's glistening on top of the wooden seats, though I can't tell the source. Yellow, pink, and orange petals have been strewn on top of the sand, forming a charming path that leads us to our seats. As we walk over the flowers, our feet lightly crush the delicate petals, creating a lovely fragrance of these native blossoms mixed with the surrounding salt air. Waves crash softly against the shore, providing a melodic background to this almost surreal scene. Though I've never been to a Full Moon Ceremony, I cannot imagine a better setting than this.

"Please … choose a seat and make yourself comfortable. We are about to begin." Francisco's voice is strong and in charge, a vastly different tone from the one he used when we met yesterday.

To my surprise, as I'm about to sit upon my piece of driftwood, I discover a gemstone on top of the log. That explains the sparkle I noticed earlier. I pick up the stone, closely inspecting it to determine the type of crystal. While the sky is darkening, the full moon combined with the fire's flames provide enough light for me to detect the stone's properties. It's deep blue, smooth, and cube-like. Could it be lapis lazuli—a fifth chakra gemstone? But of course … this is exactly *what I need*. I look toward Juliette, who is seated to my left. The stone she's holding is light pink. I believe it's rose quartz—a heart chakra stone. I suspect this is the chakra Juliette must heal. While she presents as incredibly confident, I believe she often finds it hard to express her true emotions.

Once everyone's situated, Vic lights bamboo torches strategically placed in the sand, adding one more magical element to our Full Moon Ceremony.

The ritual begins with Francisco calling in the four directions, then honoring the Earth, sun, moon, and stars. Each time, we energetically respond with, "Aho!" Though at first it feels awkward, I begin to relax and find it exhilarating to participate in this back-and-forth.

Francisco invites each of us, one by one, to join him by the fire to recite our intention aloud before tossing the paper into the flames. "Give your desire to the sacred fire. Feeding the flames with our intentions is what helps our wishes manifest."

When Francisco calls my name, I rise and slowly walk toward him. Once there, I pause and stare at what I've written before saying the words aloud. "May I have the courage to write as my true self."

With a bit of trepidation—as I know believing this is possible requires courage, vulnerability, and fortitude—I toss my intention into the bonfire, watching as flames engulf the paper. The ecru edges quickly blacken and curl. Within moments, my wish is reduced to ash, merging with the embers of others' intentions. I say a silent prayer, turn around, then slowly return to my log. But before I can sit down, *she* speaks.

It will take a lot more than tossing a piece of paper into a fire for you to find ... let alone write with ... your authentic voice.

No. She can't be here. She's not allowed. I thought I sent her away. But instead of ruminating on her words, I squeeze my eyes shut and envision myself writing at my laptop. I'm happy ... inspired ... unafraid to type what's on my mind. I then pause, expecting another derogatory comment from Margaret. But my mind is silent. She must be gone for now.

The ceremony does not take long. After everyone's offered their intention to the sacred fire, Francisco closes the ritual, this time thanking the serpent, jaguar, hummingbird, and eagle for their guidance.

As we walk back to the main building, I hear several people asking others if they want to meet at the bar for a drink.

"Anyone interested?" Maggie asks with a glimmer in her eyes once we arrive at our tree houses.

"Would you mind if I called it a night?" I ask, hoping not to offend Maggie. I didn't realize how tired I was, and the thought of bed sounds inviting.

"Yes, I think I should also get some rest," Annie adds.

"Likewise," Sophia says.

"I'll go with you," Juliette announces as she moves toward Maggie, grabs her hand, and winks. "Let's go celebrate this full moon."

"Have fun." I turn to Sophia and Annie. "See you tomorrow at meditation?"

Both nod, say goodnight, then walk toward the main building. As I climb the stairs to our tree house, gratitude fills me. I now realize Margaret was wrong. I belong here … There's work I must do … and there are individuals here to guide me. But can I really manifest my intention? Am I brave enough to write what's in my heart?

***

The next morning, I'm happy to see Maggie's outside and ready to go. I wasn't sure if she'd take a pass on this morning's run, as Juliette didn't return till after one thirty.

Maggie and I head down the beach, but she doesn't mention anything about last night. Instead, she asks about my time with Sonya. We compare notes, agreeing Sonya seems to be the real deal. I'm a Cancer, a natural nurturer. I love to create a warm home environment and take care of those close to me. Perhaps this explains my love of cooking and the joy I feel when I "feed" others. Maggie's an Aquarius, so her independent streak is to be expected.

Maggie then shares what happened during her session with Conor. Clearly, she's rattled by what he told her.

"Now that I have a name … and assuming I can find him … I mean how many *John McIntyres* can there be in Pittsburgh … will he even want to meet me?" Maggie's speaking in phrases, more like gasping strings of words as she runs. "What if discovering he has a daughter ruins his life? Maybe it was all meant to be a secret." There's an uncertainty in her voice I've never noticed before.

"What do *you* want to do?" I ask, hoping not to influence Maggie's decision.

"I guess I haven't thought about that," she says as she picks up the pace.

"Maybe that's what's most important. After all, there's no way to predict how this man might react. Who knows, maybe learning he has a daughter will bring him joy?" I pose the question, hoping she'll realize the possibility.

"Do you really think that's possible?" Maggie scrunches her nose, then suddenly stops running. "Is it OK if we sit down and talk about this?"

This is music to my ears, as Maggie's pace has been steadily increasing.

We sit on a large boulder at the edge of the beach. Palm fronds sway overhead as the cool wind dries the perspiration on my forehead.

"For my entire life, I've been consumed with knowing who my father is. Now that I have his name and understand he had no idea my mom was pregnant with *his* child, well, it kind of changes things. Suddenly, I'm not so angry ... but I'm ... I'm scared." She pauses, holding her head in her hands. "What if he doesn't want anything to do with me?" she asks, voice cracking.

I put my arm around Maggie's shoulders and pull her toward me. "It must be terrifying. Suddenly, a door ... one you've always searched for ... unexpectedly appears and opens right in front of you. And now you must decide whether or not to enter."

Maggie straightens up, tilts her head, and asks in an almost childlike manner, "What should I do?"

Before responding, I consider how Tom might feel if he were in this man's situation. Would my husband want to know he had fathered another child? After taking a moment to consider this, I conclude his answer would be yes. No doubt this would impact his world—our world—in many ways.

Unsure how to respond, I follow Francisco's advice—I shut my eyes and ask God for guidance. I pause, waiting for any sort of inspiration. It's then a voice inside speaks through me. "As long as you make your choice in love, you will have made the correct decision." Plain and simple, these concise words—which are not mine—come from my mouth.

Maggie nods her head. "That makes total sense. If I try to contact him because I'm angry, then it won't turn out well. But if I reach out to him from my heart ... to learn who he is, what he's like ... well, that's a totally different vibration."

My eyes well with tears. Any man would be lucky to discover Maggie is his daughter, even if she's the result of a casual relationship. Yet something tells me this was not a one-night stand.

"Should we head back?" I glance at my sports watch, suddenly realizing that meditation begins in twenty-five minutes.

Together we rise and begin to run back toward the resort. Our conversation is lighter, though Maggie does express a bit of concern regarding her session with Francisco tomorrow afternoon, which is understandable after the information she received from Conor. However, I assure her that it will be wonderful. "After discovering your dad—who never knew you even existed—lives nearby, how much more jarring could meeting with a shaman be?"

Before we part ways, something Maggie says concerns me. She mentions how thankful she is that she and Juliette didn't stay out late, sharing that they left after one glass of wine. Yet I clearly heard our door open at one thirty. If Juliette wasn't with Maggie, where was she?

***

Juliette never mentions anything about last night. In fact, when I returned to our room, she was dressed and ready for meditation, acting as if nothing out of the ordinary had occurred. During breakfast, she talked nonstop about Daniel Goodman, insisting we sit up front in order to have a clear view when he channels. So, like the good friends that we are, we arrive early and forgo our table tucked away in the back. Today we're front and center ... because that's what Juliette wants.

Interestingly, this morning begins differently from the last two workshops. Daniel doesn't talk about himself, nor does he share what to expect. Instead, Daniel silently sits in a chair situated to the right of the large table. When he finally speaks, it is in a soft voice, setting an intention for the safety and protection of all in the room. Everyone becomes still, as if anxiously waiting for what will happen next.

To my surprise, the intensity in his voice suddenly shifts, becoming distinctly different from his earlier tone. Words come quickly—pronounced with authority—flowing in a rhythmic fashion. The message is about recognizing the need to love, presenting as our true self, and honoring our connection to the Divine. The more Daniel channels, the more exhausted he appears. It's as though something has taken over his body. Daniel is no longer Daniel. He's become a vehicle for another, one he calls Zecheal.

Forty-five minutes later, Daniel falls silent. Apparently, the channeling is over. It takes a few moments, but I witness him slowly return to his former self. After taking a big swig of water, Daniel clears his throat several times. The room remains silent. All eyes are focused on our presenter. When Daniel finally addresses the group, he sounds nothing like the voice we had just heard. Daniel's now himself again.

Juliette, poised on the edge of her chair, looks mesmerized. The rest in the room also appear astonished. After a few more moments, most likely to collect himself, Daniel asks if there are any questions about what transpired.

I watch as a sea of hands go up. But what surprises me is when he calls on someone at our table. I turn to see it's Annie.

"Hello, Daniel. My name is Annie Thompson. I was wondering if you could help me understand something." She stops speaking and takes in a big inhale. Knowing Annie, she's mustering up the courage to ask what's on her mind.

"This past winter, mid-February to be exact … I had an *experience*." Annie swallows several times before continuing. "My friend, Juliette"—Annie points to Juliette, who radiates at the acknowledgment—"said I am clairvoyant … because I could *see* things that had occurred … to people I didn't know … at a place I'd never been. My description of a house was confirmed by a person quite intimate with the home." She stops, as though unsure whether she wants to continue. I watch as Sophia places her hand on Annie's shoulder and nods.

"Anyway, I was able to envision … a murder. I saw who the killer was and how the victim was killed."

Mumblings fill the room, causing Annie to turn bright red.

Daniel stands up and walks toward Annie. He begins to speak, not as Daniel, but as Zecheal. "What you saw was indeed what occurred. You have a gift. And with this gift comes great responsibility. Use it wisely. Do not utilize it to gain access to what is not yours. Rather, employ your gift to help others heal."

Daniel transitions once again, back to himself.

"Annie, having this experience was no doubt incredibly frightening for you. I remember the first time Zecheal came through me. It was as though I had been hit by a tidal wave. In fact, it took several days, if not weeks, to fully recover." Surprisingly, Daniel pauses to chuckle. "But the more times this 'process' occurred, the less it bothered me. Eventually, I realized I was supposed to be a conduit for Zecheal, and I suspect you were also chosen *to see* for a specific purpose. My advice is to go with it. Listen to the messages and take in the visions. Perhaps you can use it to benefit others." He offers a heartfelt smile, then returns to his chair, asking for another question.

As soon as the workshop is over, the five of us decide to have lunch at the pool. After finding five lounge chairs next to one another, we begin to unpack what occurred during this morning's session.

"Annie, what's it like to be clairvoyant?" Maggie asks.

"It's still new to me," Annie says, the uneasiness apparent in her voice. Perhaps she's still struggling with her gift.

"Has it happened again?" Maggie turns on her side to lean closer to Annie.

"Well, after that weekend, there have been several instances." Annie becomes quiet, then a little grin forms on her face.

"Annie! What didn't you tell us?" Juliette frowns, no doubt hurt Annie hadn't shared this information with her.

"Everyone's been fussing over me because I'm pregnant. The last thing I want is to call more attention to myself."

We pause when the server appears with glasses of cucumber water. Everyone orders salad, except for Annie, who opts for a grilled cheese with tomato—and a side of fries— claiming she's famished.

Juliette leans forward and says, "I told you Daniel was incredible, didn't I?" A somewhat smug look comes across her face, reminding me how much Juliette likes to be right. Yet maybe she's merely searching for validation.

"He certainly exceeded my expectations," Sophia says as she lifts her glass to take a sip of water.

"Well, I'm not so sure I get it," I admit. "Who exactly is Zecheal, and how can he speak through Daniel?"

"Zecheal is Daniel's Guide. Think of a Guide as a spiritual being who has ascended, meaning he ... or she ... may have once been human but now is a master of sorts. The name kind of explains it. He *guides* others, sometimes by speaking through them. Of course, Guides can also counsel individuals without channeling ... using intuition and other types of *knowing* ... like dreams, angels ... stuff like that." Juliette casually runs her fingers through her hair, as if what happened this morning was an everyday occurrence.

Daniel's Zecheal certainly caused me to wonder about Margaret, who I truly hope is now gone from my life. But while she's *spoken* to me for years, she's never *guided* me. Quite the opposite— Margaret's comments were critical and demanding, often demeaning, making me second guess myself.

"I thought Zecheal's message was beautiful. I most definitely believe we each have the Divine within us. Still, I find it challenging to witness this light in violent people, especially those who hurt children," says Sophia.

Her comment propels me to contemplate whether those I'd define as *bad people* could also possess a light within. Maybe their painful lifetime experiences are what keep them from shining, holding them hostage in the dark. But then a bigger realization hits me—who am I to label anyone as *good or bad?*

"Well, I can totally see how it's our small self, our ego, that causes all of our fear and pain. Yet I'd never heard it explained this way," Maggie says as the server arrives with our lunch.

During this back-and-forth, I remain silent, still confused by what transpired this morning.

"Yes," Sophia says as she takes a bite of arugula salad. "Release fear. Find love. It is so simple, yet we seem terrified by this concept. Perhaps it all begins with trust."

"And surrendering," Maggie chimes in. "Letting go is so hard for me. Whenever there's uncertainty, I try to control everything around me."

Listening to both Sophia and Maggie speak, I'm reminded of what Francisco said to me yesterday ... *Trust, let go, believe.* Instead of trusting what is, I, like Maggie, try to control everyone and everything. Maybe it's time to change. Francisco seemed to believe it is possible for me to do so.

As I continue listening to the others dissect Zecheal's message, I'm pleasantly surprised with how comfortable Maggie appears to be. Though she's opened up to me, that was while running—in a safe space, with just the two of us. But now, Maggie's freely sharing her thoughts and showing her vulnerabilities to Annie, Juliette, and Sophia. Perhaps she's beginning to trust others. Appearing more confident and calmer than the unsure young architect from Pittsburgh who climbed into the van on Saturday afternoon, it's as though Maggie's a caterpillar finding her way out of her tightly woven cocoon. And it's only Wednesday. If this transformation continues, who will she be when she leaves Nueva Vida?

***

It's almost two o'clock.

"Oh my gosh, I better get going. I have a session with Sabina ... for an Abhyanga massage."

Sabina's from Nepal, and she's an expert in Ayurveda. Apparently, she knows how to incorporate essential oils—based on a person's dosha—into her massage treatments. When I was contemplating which spa service to choose, I opted for this because I thought it might support my current Ayurvedic practices of tongue scraping, body brushing, and oil pulling—methods I learned this past January from Natalie, my friend who's been studying Ayurveda.

"I, too, must leave for my meeting with Francisco," Sophia says as she gently folds her cloth napkin and places it on top of the small table next to her chair. "If you will excuse me, I must go back to the room and change first."

"I'm scheduled for a private Sound Healing session with Lindsay at three o'clock," Maggie says, her voice light and upbeat, suggesting she's looking forward to this afternoon.

"I'm out too," Juliette says with a huge grin. "Last minute, I checked to see if Daniel was free this afternoon ... and he was." Juliette's eyes light up.

"Wow, that's awesome. I'd love to meet with him." It's Annie who speaks, surprising me once again with her interest in the channeler.

"Then why don't you come with me? I'm sure he won't mind. Besides, I'm fine with you hearing anything he has to say. I've got nothing to hide." Juliette stands, picks up her beach towel, then adds. "It's at two thirty. In the yurt next to the meditation room. Meet me there if you're interested." And with that, she turns and leaves.

"Are you going to do it?" I ask Annie, hoping she'll say yes.

"No, I can't. Remember, Camille is showing me the school."

"You know, it's only Wednesday. Why don't you check if Daniel has any other privates available? Are you free tomorrow?" Maggie asks, as apparently, she, too, thinks it might be good for Annie to meet with the channeler.

Annie doesn't respond right away, instead she stares down at the ground. "Tomorrow's my session with Francisco. But I *could* change that." Annie looks up and her voice inflects slightly as she offers this "solution," but I shake my head as I look at her with a *that's not a good idea* stare.

There's no way I want Annie to back out of meeting with Francisco. While it may scare her, when else will she have an opportunity to spend one-on-one time with a shaman? "Annie, why not ask if Daniel has any openings on Friday? I think you'd learn a lot by meeting with him. He seemed to relate to how you feel regarding your clairvoyance." I gently touch her arm and use my most supportive voice.

"First let me get through tomorrow." Annie pauses for a moment, then looks up at me with doe eyes. "Do you really think *I can do it*?" She tucks a strand of hair behind her ear—my signature move for when I'm nervous.

"Of course, you can." I take a seat at the bottom of her lounge chair. "I know you're afraid of what he might say, but trust that it will be fine. He reads people, so he'll know you're apprehensive. He would never do anything to upset you. In fact, what he told me was empowering." I pat her leg, then stand up. "I'll see you at dinner, OK? Have fun with Camille. And take some pictures of the school." I offer an encouraging smile before heading back to our room so I can take a quick shower before my massage.

***

Sabina is older than I expected. This small Nepalese woman, dressed in a white wrap dress, welcomes me with a cup of herbal tea, instructing me to drink it prior to the massage. After she leaves me alone in the room to undress, I sense something unique about the space. It's not at all sterile like many of the massage rooms I've been in before. Nor does it have a manufactured spa feeling. Instead, there's a soothing warmth present—natural, organic, calming. Perhaps it has to do with the tapestries hanging on the wall or the gorgeous woven rugs. However, when I see huge amethyst crystals underneath the massage table, I begin to wonder if it's the energy from the gemstones that's creating this sensation. Only then do I notice the other rocks placed throughout the room. Of course, she incorporates crystal healing in her treatments.

To the left of the sink, there's a long narrow table covered with amber-colored glass jars. I do not recognize the labels, as they appear to be written in another language. Beneath the table are bolsters and blankets. There's a wicker basket filled with instruments, some similar to those in Francisco's office.

Several minutes later, I'm lying on the table with my face comfortably resting in the attached neck cradle. I hear three quick knocks.

"Ready?"

"Yes." Something tells me this massage will be different from anything I've experienced.

"I will use a special oil to complement your dosha." Her English is quite good, causing me to wonder when she left Nepal.

"You are a Pitta with some Vata," she announces, confirming what Natalie shared when she first taught me about Ayurveda. "I must quiet the fire within you but ensure you remain grounded." I then hear lids being unscrewed, and I assume she's mixing ingredients from the amber jars into the massage oil.

"Next I will add herbs, grown here in our garden."

"What are they for?"

"Ah … this is the special sauce … the cherry … on top of the sundae." Speaking in a choppy manner, this tiny woman then cackles. I can't help but giggle in response, wondering how such harsh sounds could emanate from this little lady.

Sabina's hands begin to work my back and shoulders. Her strokes are smooth, even. Within seconds, she finds my tight spots. I hear a pop. Moments later, I feel the corresponding release. Ahh.

"Better?" she asks as she continues addressing other areas of constriction.

"Yes, thank you." Slowly, my body melts into the table.

As Sabina quietly works, I drift to another space, one that's foreign to me. It's as though I'm half awake, sensitive to my surroundings yet simultaneously somewhere else. While my body is on the table, my mind seems to be watching what's occurring from the upper corner of the room. This sensation is strange, but I like it.

Eventually, Sabina asks me to turn over. She then works on my quadriceps, shins, and feet before moving to my arms, clavicle, and neck. Sabina seems to focus on this area more than any of my previous massage therapists have.

"You are blocked here." When she says this, I become alarmed that something is physically wrong.

"What do you mean?" I ask, jolting from the happy place I'd been swimming in.

"No worries. I can fix it," she says before standing up and moving away from the table. I turn my head, watching her pull something out of a slow cooker that's sitting on the counter by the sink. Expecting to soon feel hot stones—I've had several of those massages—I'm surprised when she places a warm wet cloth on my neck. An intense smell causes my nostrils to flare. While not overly offensive, the smell is far from pleasing.

Within minutes, my shoulders drop closer to the table, and my entire spine seems to elongate.

"Your fifth chakra is beginning to open," Sabina says as she takes the cooled cloth from my neck, then adds new ones on each shoulder. "The restriction was caused by your second chakra," she pronounces, then pauses.

This doesn't make sense to me. The second chakra is below my belly button, not in my neck. "I don't understand," I say. "How can my second chakra impact my neck?"

"Ah, so you know about the chakras." Sabina momentarily leaves me, only to return with another magical hot hand towel. "The second chakra also lives in the back of your neck. It's where we hold shame and guilt. This is what keeps us from receiving ... a fifth chakra quality." She gently lifts my head and puts a towel under my neck. Immediately, my upper body relaxes as I contemplate how the second and fifth chakra are intricately connected.

"What's in the towel?" I ask, still trying to understand what's occurring.

"More special sauce ... to melt your shame and guilt ... help your fifth chakra open." Again, she cackles. Apparently, Sabina isn't going to reveal the herbs she uses in this concoction. It's no wonder that for hundreds of years people called female healers witches. Helping others by using herbs, oils, and extracts sounds intriguing today. However, in the past, this concept must have been unimaginable, perhaps even threatening. But lying here and experiencing firsthand the powers of these natural elements, I believe it to be pure magic.

Only then do I begin to wonder about the reason behind the guilt and shame Sabina claims to have found. While nothing immediately comes to mind, I spend the rest of the massage contemplating possible reasons for these emotions.

Racking my brain, I can't remember anything I've specifically done that would make me feel overly guilty or shameful. Sure, there are those little lies and unkind acts, but nothing to warrant a significant blockage. But then I begin to wonder ... what if this is not about what I've done to others ... but perhaps it's the judgmental thoughts and critical mindset I've had toward myself.

Could years of believing Margaret's negative verbiage be the root cause? Taking a moment to consider this possibility, I conclude it makes perfect sense. After all, listening to the internal reprimanding about my appearance, beliefs, behaviors, and decisions must have negatively affected me. And if I can finally release Margaret from my head, might the shame and guilt also go away?

Thirty minutes later, I'm dressed and on my way to our room. I wonder if Juliette's back from her session with Daniel. If so, I'm sure I'll hear all about it. But it's Maggie I'm most curious about. She's been through so much. And with what Conor revealed yesterday, I hope her time with Lindsay went well.

This morning, Maggie sounded conflicted about contacting her dad. However, reaching out to him may help her resolve the missing pieces of her past. Regardless of how he reacts, it would provide closure. Plus, maybe he'd embrace discovering he has a twenty-eight-year-old daughter. Stranger things have happened.

***

Juliette's not back, so I take the opportunity to call Tom.

"Hey, I've missed you." I feel my heart warm when he answers the phone.

"I've missed you too. It's so quiet around here."

"How's Patrick?" I ask, remembering he had a chemistry exam yesterday. "Did he mention anything about his chem test?"

"Now that is the last thing that you should be thinking of," Tom chides me. But worrying about our son is one habit that's difficult to let go of. "I'm sure it went well. At least, he didn't mention anything for me to think it didn't," Tom adds, perhaps to provide me with a bit of comfort.

I doubt Patrick ever mentioned his chem test. But maybe that's for the best. This is their guys' week, and while a part of me wants them to maintain our normal family schedule, secretly I hope they're having fun doing what they want to do, stuff they wouldn't do when I'm around.

"How's the retreat?" Tom asks, sounding genuinely interested.

"It's amazing. The presenters are incredible. Kinda wish I had a follow-up article to write because I'm learning so much." I decide not to discuss any of my sessions. There's still a lot to unpack before I can properly explain the takeaways. Plus, I have a hunch that

when I meet with Conor tomorrow, he may help me better understand Francisco's message.

"Maybe pitch the idea to Brad. Who knows, he might be open
to you creating some kind of spiritual column?" Tom suggests, then
chuckles, making me wonder if there's anything serious about his
idea or if he's merely teasing me.

Tom asks about Annie. I assure him she's fine, suggesting he
let Jonathon know this week has been good for her. Then Tom tells
me he invited Jonathon, Michael, and Jared, Sophia's husband, to
come over Thursday night to watch the Sixers game on TV.

After saying goodbye and telling Tom how much I love him,
I stretch out on my bed and let out a big sigh as my mind replays
the past days' sessions. Flashes come through of me sitting in
Francisco's office, him saying, "... *new and exciting opportunities
will come forth, often when you least expect them.*" I wonder what
he meant by that. Could this be another job? Or maybe it's merely
a new assignment.

Next, I go to my session with Sonya. What she said pretty
much confirmed how I see myself. I am a true Cancer. Sonya used
the words *loyal*, *protective*, and *intuitive*. She also told me I can be
overprotective at times. Immediately, I think of Patrick playing the
goalie position on his soccer team and how for years I'd cover my
eyes whenever an opponent approached the net.

I was surprised when she shared my Rising sign was Pisces,
suggesting I may be very emotional and can easily be taken advantage of or seen as vulnerable. "Feeling detached" and "overactive
imagination" were other descriptions that resonated with me. And
the one word Sonya used—*chameleon*—perfectly described how I
acted for years. It wasn't until recently that I've begun to use my
voice and speak up for myself. She also commented on how sensitive I can be as well as my tendency to want to escape when things
become too overwhelming. In essence, she described me to a T.

And when Sabina said my fifth chakra was blocked, well, that pretty much explains everything. I've spent years trying to be who I thought others wanted me to be. Plus, I find it challenging to express as my real self, using *my* true voice. Perhaps the guilt and shame could be attributed to Margaret's relentless negative comments. But Sabina said she was unblocking this chakra, and it certainly felt that way. Hopefully this will help me become open to whatever new opportunities Francisco predicted.

Juliette walks through the door.

"Oh my God, Marlee," she says, throwing her beach bag down on one of the chairs next to the small table. "Daniel is incredible! I want to channel. It's amazing."

I prop myself up against the bamboo headboard, knowing this is going to be a long one-sided conversation. But I don't mind. It's good to see Juliette happy.

"He's been hearing from his Guide for almost eight years. But it took nearly two for Daniel to embrace what he was being called to do. Which, of course, makes total sense. I mean, he was an accountant at a major firm in Chicago. Besides making a lot of money, Daniel had such a *traditional* job … and a wife and daughter. Can you imagine the courage it took for him to leave his career so he could follow this spiritual calling? How many men do you know who would do that?"

She has a point. Imagine if Tom suddenly heard voices in his head. I don't believe he'd ever stop being a surgeon to do whatever it is Daniel does.

"And Daniel's so accomplished. He's written six books. Actually, *written* is not the correct word, as his Guide does all the talking. Still, the words Daniel says are translated into texts. Even though Zecheal is speaking through him, I guess Daniel is the author, in a weird kind of way.

"What did you do during your session?" I'm extremely curious about this. Impressed with how Daniel interacted with Annie during the workshop, I can only imagine what Juliette may have learned.

"Well, I wanted to know how my dad's doing. It's been seven years since he passed over ... I guess I needed to make sure he's OK." Juliette's face softens and her voice mellows when she mentions her father.

"Was Daniel able to connect?" Unsure whether *connect* is the proper word, I assume Juliette will know what I mean.

"Yes." Juliette flops down on the bed and stares at the caramel-colored ceiling. Uncharacteristically, she becomes silent.

When she still hadn't spoken after several moments, I ask, "Are you comfortable sharing what he said, or would you prefer to keep it to yourself?" I try not to be intrusive, but I'm dying to know what Daniel's capable of doing. Plus, I'm sure Juliette would be relieved to know her father is OK, wherever he is.

Juliette turns on her side to face me. Tears fall down her cheeks, but she does not appear sad. "Daniel said my father is so proud of me ... how I went to India ... and Yale ... then opened my own yoga studio. Oh, and he thinks Michael is awesome ... *perfect for me* were the exact words Daniel used." She pauses to smile. "My dad loves how spirited I am ... committed and totally determined. But ..." The smile on Juliette's face suddenly disappears.

Confused at this dramatic shift, I sit up, plant my feet on the floor, and lean toward her. "But what?"

"*He thinks* I should see my mom."

"Who thinks you should see your mom ... Daniel or your dad?" I am so confused.

"My dad ... Daniel is the vehicle for my dad's thoughts." She scrunches her nose when she says this, as if understanding how channeling works is common knowledge.

"How do you feel about it? Do *you* want to see your mom?" I try to remain neutral, but I distinctly remember Juliette sharing how her mom left her and her dad. I believe her exact words were, "*She chose gin over me.*" Having an alcoholic mother must have been excruciatingly difficult. I exhale, remembering how kind and loving my mother was.

"No ... I don't. In fact, I'd be fine if I never saw her again. It's like she's dead to me," Juliette vents, but then she softens. "But the point is ... *my dad* wants me to see her ... and try to reconcile. I'm just not so sure I can do that." This time, Juliette sounds like a little girl, uncertain and afraid.

I get up and take a seat on Juliette's bed next to her. In response, she wraps her arms around me, a rare and unexpected reaction. Slowly, I feel her dissolve in my embrace. It's then I understand how much Juliette *needs* a mother. Maybe not *her* mother, but a nurturer, someone who puts Juliette's needs before her own. No doubt her dad did his best to fill this void. But I suspect he could only do so much. And besides, he's been gone for seven years.

"What do I do?" Juliette finally asks, as she falls back onto the bed, once again resembling a helpless child.

"I wish I had the perfect answer for you," I say. "But I don't think there is one. What does your heart say?" I wait to see if she responds, but she doesn't. So I continue talking: "I know you want to honor your father. And maybe reaching out to your mom is what's best." I pause, hoping for God or my intuition to guide me, like it did with Maggie earlier this morning. "Or, perhaps, this is all too much to ask." Sitting up straighter, I prop myself up with my elbows. "Do souls who have passed know what's best for another? Or do they still have their own interests at heart?"

After heaving out a sigh, Juliette turns on her side and says, "That's a good question." Becoming more composed, she rises from the bed and heads into the bathroom. "I've decided I don't want to think about it now. I won't let this spoil my week. Too much good is happening for me to become upset over this. Besides, it's almost five. We all agreed to meet at five thirty. I need to shower, but then I'll be ready to go." Within seconds, she's transformed back to her independent self, pretending she is perfectly fine and needs no one.

And with that, Juliette disappears into the bathroom, shutting the door behind her. How can she so casually brush this off? For a moment, I felt as though she was letting me in. But Juliette creates a barrier around her, protecting herself from becoming vulnerable. However, she was finally beginning to trust me. The only other time I felt so close to her was in the Poconos.

I sigh, resigned that Juliette is one tough nut to crack. She too easily returned to being on top of the world, in charge of everything and everyone. Still, something tells me that's only a facade. Despite how "awakened" she appears, inside is a hurt little girl who's avoiding many unresolved issues.

***

While drinking herbal teas and sampling vegetarian appetizers, we share our afternoon experiences.

"The children are so sweet," Annie says, her face glowing, though I doubt it's all due to being pregnant. She's bubbly and animated, eager to tell us about this innovative school for elementary students. "Camille's in charge of creating the curriculum and hiring the teachers. Her husband, Trevor, oversees the building's construction and works to ensure fundraising ... not only to guarantee they can purchase supplies and pay their teachers, but also to add a classroom each year. You should see the playground. It's amazing. They've done an excellent job integrating the natural surroundings with progressive play equipment. And the classrooms ... there aren't any chairs … The kids use those round balls … It keeps them more engaged in what they're learning, *and* it helps them develop stabilizing muscles." Annie's wide-eyed, sounding in awe of what she's experienced.

"Sophia, how was your day?" I ask, knowing she met with Francisco. During lunch, Sophia divulged her hope that this session would provide guidance regarding her recent decision to add holistic methods into her practice. "Did you receive the information you desired?" I add, assuming she had.

Sophia demurely smiles, and her gorgeous eyelashes flutter a bit. "Yes. I feel *much* better about the situation."

I place my hand on top of hers, thrilled she's found clarity.

"Francisco stated I must trust my intuitive ability." As Sophia speaks, she blushes, a rare response from my Italian-born friend.

"We all told you the same thing, but I guess you had to hear it from a shaman," I say, happy she's discovering her path.

"Apparently so." Her eyes narrow as she slightly twitches her nose.

***

"You're going to love this." Juliette, back to her old self, leads the four of us into the yoga studio. "Yoga Nidra is amazing! Seriously, a forty-five-minute class is equivalent to several hours of sleep. If you like it, I can text you links to classes I've recorded so you can do this practice at home."

While I've never heard of Yoga Nidra, I love yoga—and sleep—so it's bound to be wonderful. When we arrive, lit candles line the walls of the studio. Kali is seated on her mat, front and center. Crystal singing bowls, as well as more candles, encircle her.

"Welcome. Please find a space." She greets us with a serene voice. Instead of wearing her traditional yoga garb, Kali's dressed in black silk pants and a gray sleeveless tunic. A string of gorgeous black beads hangs from her neck.

"Her necklace is so cool," Maggie whispers to Juliette.

"That's a mala necklace … and I bet it's made from black tourmaline. Malas are kind of like a rosary, but not the same. There are 108 beads … and that's the number of times you repeat your mantra. *Mala* is a Sanskrit word for 'garland.'" Juliette settles onto her mat, places her legs across the bolster, then puts a blanket under her head. She leaves the second blanket folded by her side.

The rest of us mimic how Juliette sets up for tonight's practice. We lie there, waiting for Kali to begin.

"*Yoga Nidra* translates to 'yoga sleep.' So all you need to do is lie still, relax, and listen to Kali," Juliette shares before shutting her eyes.

"Finally, a yoga practice that will be easy," Annie says in a less-than-quiet voice. From my position in the middle of the group, I catch Juliette lift her head, turn, then frown at Annie. No doubt Annie didn't realize her comment might offend Juliette, as the three of us have been going to Juliette's Wednesday night restorative yoga class for the past two months.

Kali speaks in a soft and calming tone: "Welcome. Tonight, I will be guiding you through Yoga Nidra. Before we begin, I invite you to make yourself comfortable. Perhaps place a blanket over you, as your body will cool off as you begin to relax."

There's a bit of commotion in the room as people reach for their blankets. However, everyone quickly becomes quiet.

Kali continues speaking, but not in her usual manner. I lift my head to look and see she's reading from a paper sitting on the floor in front of her.

"Close your eyes and settle onto your mat. Allow your knees to rest across the bolster and your hands to relax by your side. During Yoga Nidra, I will guide you to a place between wakefulness and sleeping. Try to remain awake as you listen to my voice. Tell yourself you will not fall asleep.

"Become conscious of any sounds you hear ... the noises you hear outside of this building ... the noises you hear inside of this room. With your eyes remaining shut, visualize this space, the four walls, the floor, the candles. See yourself lying on the floor. Imagine your hair, your clothing ... Know that your body is lying on this floor.

"Feel the coolness of the air as it enters your nostrils, then sense its warmth as it exits. Breathe in for four counts ... hold ... then exhale for five counts. Repeat this four times at your own pace, focusing on longer exhales than inhales."

I hear several people clear their throats, perhaps trying to lengthen their exhales.

"Yoga Nidra is about to begin. Decide on a sankalpa ... a positive phrase such as 'I am letting go' or 'I see beauty all around me.' Say your sankalpa to yourself three times, followed with 'I am practicing Yoga Nidra, and I am relaxed but will not fall asleep.'"

Naturally, I choose "I am letting go" as my sankalpa.

Kali then guides us to feel our fingers, our hands, our arms, our shoulders ... all the way down to our toes. Next, she moves to the back of our body, starting at our scalp and ending at the soles of our feet. She encourages us to release any stress or strain in these areas. Kali tells us to feel heaviness, then lightness, then warmth, and finally cold. One might think following her directions would be difficult, but I find this exercise completely natural, even soothing.

Transitioning to visualization exercises, she asks us to imagine a red feather, a full moon, a field of flowers, and other images. We are to repeat our sankalpa. I doze off but quickly feel myself return, hearing her say to be aware of our breath, the clothes on our body, our skin.

Before I know it, she says, "The practice of Yoga Nidra is now complete."

Slowly, she guides us to roll on our side before sitting cross-legged with our hands folded at our hearts. After several moments, people rise and begin to mingle, no doubt discussing their experiences.

"What did you think?" I ask Sophia, who's been particularly quiet this evening, perhaps preoccupied with whatever happened during her session with Francisco.

"It was beautiful. Did you find it peaceful, Marlee?" she asks, her emerald eyes aglow, reflecting the flickering candlelight.

"Yes, I thought it was amazing. And I was surprised with how easily I could follow Kali. I didn't think I'd be able to, though I may have fallen asleep for a few seconds," I admit.

"Often, I play Yoga Nidra meditations at night to help me sleep. Jared also finds this practice calming." Once again, Sophia surprises me by sharing something about her personal life that I'd never expect. I'm reminded of how dangerous assumptions can be.

Curious as to how Annie feels, I turn toward her. She, Juliette, and Maggie are deep in discussion.

"What did you think?" I repeat my question to the three of them.

Annie becomes quiet, and Maggie's eyes shift between Annie and Juliette. I wonder what's up.

"Annie had visions," Juliette says. But she's not announcing this like she has in the past. Her expression shows a seriousness I haven't observed before.

"What visions did you have, Annie?" Sophia asks with concern in her voice.

Wide-eyed, Annie takes in a big breath. "It was of my baby. First, when she was born, and then as she grew older."

"It's a girl? That's wonderful," I say, thinking how a little girl would be perfect for her.

"It wasn't that wonderful," Annie says, then sniffs as her eyes become moist.

"What did you see?" Sophia moves closer to Annie then places her hands on Annie's shoulders.

"My daughter ..." Annie pauses. "She's ... she's like me ... clairvoyant ... but so much more than that."

I stare at her, then glance toward Juliette, who's seriously scaring me. Juliette's biting her lower lip, and her face appears pale despite the amount of time she's spent in the sun.

"Like her dad, she becomes a surgeon ... but not the same kind of surgeon ... a psychic surgeon ... She doesn't do regular surgery ... She uses energetic incisions ... and she is able to heal the terminally ill."

MAGGIE
Thursday, April 22

"**D**o you think it's true, what Annie saw?" I blurt out as soon as Marlee descends the stairs of her tree house. "I kept waking up in the middle of the night, rehashing what she said. But I don't get it. How exactly does Annie *see* these things? And could it only have been her imagination this time? After all, I'm sure she has many concerns about soon becoming a mom."

"I know, it's hard to fathom Annie's visions are the real deal. I can probably accept it more easily because of our experience in the Poconos." Marlee lets out a loud exhale as she shakes her head. "There was absolutely no way for her to have known any of those details she *saw* that weekend. And that information is what allowed us to figure out who killed Wyatt. Without it, there's no way the chief of police could have arrested Caroline Rhimes."

I sigh, accepting I may never truly *get it*.

"How was your Sound Healing session with Lindsay? I don't think you said much about it yesterday." Marlee changes the subject as we begin to jog toward the beach.

"I liked it … a lot. Having a private session with Lindsay is kinda like what we did as a group, except being the only participant magnified everything, and lying next to the gong was incredibly powerful. The vibrations were super intense up close. Before we began, Lindsay asked if there was anything on my mind. So I told her about my session with Conor and how I wasn't sure what to do. She said she could create a sequence of sounds to strengthen my confidence so I could make my decision from a position of love and power, not fear and uncertainty. I think working with Lindsay helped me better process and release some of the emotions I was experiencing. At least I feel calmer today." I pause, thinking back to my tearful release at the end of the session.

"That's wonderful," Marlee says. "Suddenly finding out your father's lived near you all these years but never knew about you—well, that's a ton to process." Marlee turns toward me, and without saying another thing, she gives me an understanding look.

"I don't think I fully grasped the implications of what Conor told me. But I'm now beginning to realize that if I reach out to John McIntyre, then the ball's in his court. I have absolutely no control of whether he'll be open to any sort of relationship."

"That's true," Marlee says between heavy breaths. "But whether or not *you choose* to contact him ... and regardless of how he responds ... you'll no longer wonder about your dad's identity and why he wasn't there for you." Marlee's pace increases, as if she's not only challenging me to keep up with her but also to consider her point. "Do you feel some peace knowing he was unaware your mother was pregnant?"

I nod. "Lindsay and I talked about that as well. She's so easy to relate to. Lindsay told me her parents divorced when she was five, and even though she spent weekends with her dad, she still felt abandoned at times. And not just by her dad but also by her mom. She wanted both of her parents to attend games and events. But the way the custody was set up, it was either one or the other." I momentarily stop talking and turn toward the crashing waves. "I guess growing up with divorced parents isn't necessarily better than my childhood. Even though my dad had no idea I existed, I was raised by a loving mom and devoted grandparents. So, in a way, I am kind of lucky."

Marlee smiles. "It sounds like your mom ... and grandparents ... adored you. Having people who truly care about you is better than living in a family that *looks good* but is dysfunctional."

Marlee's words resonate. "I did have an incredible grandfather who did his best to fill in the gaps. He was the one who taught me how to drive. And I remember him helping me move into my freshman dorm. He lugged all my stuff up five flights of stairs, on a day that was humid and ninety-five degrees." I shake my head in awe of my grandfather's stamina before he became sick.

"He sounds like a special man. It must be so difficult to witness his decline."

"Yes ... I hate going to that memory care unit. It hurts to watch him sitting there ... staring. He has no idea who I am. He didn't even know my mom, and she'd visit him every day after work." I sigh, hoping our decision to not tell Granddad about Mom was for the best.

"He may not be able to show he recognizes you," Marlee says as we move closer to the surf where the sand is firmer, "but I believe deep down, he senses your presence and can feel your love."

"I hope so," I say, staring at the stretch of beach ahead of us.

***

The large crystal singing bowls from last night are still there. But today, Eduardo's rearranged the mats in more of a horseshoe shape. Perhaps he'll use the bowls during meditation.

Marlee and Juliette come in several minutes later. Juliette sits to my left, while Marlee takes the free mat on my right. However, there's no sign of either Sophia or Annie.

"Do you think they overslept?" I ask Marlee and Juliette.

"When I got back from our run, Sophia texted to say Annie didn't sleep well last night. The vision she had during Yoga Nidra really upset her," Marlee says.

"That's certainly understandable." I can't imagine how I'd feel if that happened to me.

"You know, the more I think about it," Juliette chimes in, "the more I realize how amazing this baby will be. I mean, seriously … if this kid grows up with the ability to do psychic surgery and save people, she'll be one of the most renowned healers ever."

"But would you want that for *your* child?" Marlee asks.

"Of course." Juliette's quick to respond, but then, I watch as her eyebrows scrunch together, and a look of confusion comes across her face. "What *she could do* would be pretty freakin' spectacular, but I guess there would be a price for her to pay."

"Exactly," Marlee says. "Sure, I want Patrick to be successful, but not if it comes at a high cost to him personally. Maybe it's just a mom thing, but I think Annie wants her child to have a happy and healthy life … a normal existence. I don't think she wants her to be *freakin' spectacular.*"

Listening to Marlee and Juliette speak, I take in both perspectives. While I tend to agree with Marlee, I've never seriously thought about having a child, so I find it hard to relate.

Our conversation is interrupted by the soft resonance of the singing bowls. Others must also be aware, as the room becomes quiet and everyone either sits on a bolster or lies down on their mat. Similar to yesterday, I feel the soothing sounds connect to various parts of my body. Most of the pulsations are in my lower belly, the sacral chakra. My yoga teacher in Pittsburgh shared that this is the center for passion, creativity, intimacy, and intuition. Suddenly, I'm jolted by the word *passion*. I distinctly remember Sonya's exact words about passion when she read my birth chart.

"You love fully, and your love affairs are intense, filled with healthy passion. However, you treasure your freedom and independence. It will take a special person to satisfy your needs."

Could my second chakra be blocked? Because I certainly don't have any strong feelings of passion. Sure, I have feelings for Pete, but they're not exactly passionate. I assumed I was incapable of such emotions.

It's then I remember my conversation with Lindsay. We talked about how a blocked second chakra can present as secrets, repression, and a lack of intimacy. I think I'm guilty of all three. For years, I wouldn't tell anyone about my dad. In fact, I avoided the topic at all costs. And intimacy, true intimacy, is something I can't even imagine. When I'm with Pete, I guess I kind of pretend. Honestly, I can't go there. No doubt I'm a bit of a loner, detached, and anxious at times. I just thought that is who I am. I exhale and attempt to quiet my mind to allow the vibrations from the singing bowls to flow through my body.

But within moments, my thoughts are once again swimming around my head. Lindsay explained how this can also be due to an underactive—or blocked—second chakra. After the Sound Healing, she shared ways for me to help open my sacral area. She suggested I carry carnelian, an orange gemstone, and use certain essential oils like ylang-ylang and orange essence on my belly. Lindsay gave me several affirmations to say every morning, one being "I am enough," claiming that reprogramming my thoughts will do wonders. And she told me it's vital to adopt a morning routine—which she called a toolbox—to help me start the day off on a high vibrational note. Maybe I should take her advice. I guess it wouldn't be too hard to begin each morning with meditation, affirmations, and journaling.

Eduardo rings the bell, signaling meditation has ended. How could it already have been thirty minutes? The time passed by so quickly.

Kali then surprises us with a restorative yoga class. Holding the supported poses for an extended period allows my tight hamstrings and quads to release. It's really a shame Annie and Sophia aren't here. I think Annie would have liked this practice. I hope she'll feel up to coming to today's workshop, though there's no way she'll be able to take part in the sweat lodge afterward.

***

Annie and Sophia are already seated at our old table in the back of the room when Marlee, Juliette, and I arrive. But I'm still thinking about today's yoga practice, not this morning's workshop. I can't wait to try out a restorative class at my yoga studio. But it's then I'm reminded of my job predicament—will I be staying in Pittsburgh and looking for a new job? Or will I commit to joining Sandy and Mark in Bend and searching for a new yoga studio?

Francisco begins speaking, allowing me to momentarily dismiss these confusing thoughts.

"Good morning. Today is indeed a very special day. While some retreats begin the week with a cleansing ceremony, I believe it is best to conduct this ritual toward the end of our time together. I suspect each of you has released quite a bit of 'unexpected toxic emotions' during the past few days." He raises his eyebrows in a knowing fashion.

Many in the room respond to this with a light chuckle or a slight nod of the head.

"This is our day of cleansing. All week you've been uncovering what has been holding you back and keeping you stuck. Now it is time to sweep it all away to create an open space for beautiful new opportunities to arise. For some, this cleanse may feel more like a strong suctioning rather than a light dusting. But remember, we each receive what we require … and we are always able to handle whatever comes our way." Francisco pauses and smiles, taking a moment to look at each table before continuing. "I would now like to introduce Anahata. Born in Houston, Texas, as Mary Jane Braxon, she became Anahata after spending three years at an ashram in India."

"Oh my God! I wonder which one she went to. How cool would that be if we were at the same place?" Juliette's practically popping out of her seat.

"When she returned, she traveled across the globe, studying with various healers. Then, seven years ago, she and her partner settled in Costa Rica, right here in Nosara. And it is incredibly lucky for us that they did. Before we begin, I ask for your help in moving the tables and chairs to the sides of the room."

Following Francisco's request, everyone pushes the furniture out of the way.

"Please, everyone, gather in a circle," Francisco says as Anahata enters the room wearing geometric palazzo pants and a sheer wrap over a sleeveless top. This intriguing woman with long gray hair appears younger than she probably is. While her body is fit, her skin shows years of experience. My best guess has her at sixty-five.

Anahata sets a large woven tote on the front table with a loud thud. "This morning we will cleanse your body and your soul, dismissing what is no longer necessary for your evolution." Her voice is direct, monotone. She doesn't express any emotions when she speaks, nor does she reveal a particular accent. Instead, she appears to communicate through her penetrating steel-blue eyes.

This woman reaches into her bag and reveals a metal bowl, which she places on the table. Next to it, she puts a glass vase. Taking a bottle of water from her tote, Anahata fills the vase and then removes some sort of plant material—I believe it's a kind of herb— from the metal bowl, adding it to the vase. Afterward, she takes out several bundles of sage, two large shells filled with sand, two pieces of wood, and an industrial yellow lighter—which looks quite odd when mixed in with the other items.

"First we cleanse you." After lighting two bunches of sage, she hands one to Francisco.

They walk toward us. Anahata moves to the left, while Francisco goes to the right side of the circle. I watch as they direct individuals to take a step forward, hold out their arms in a T, and widen their stance. Very methodically, they run the sage around the outline of the person's body, ensuring the white smoke hits all areas. Afterward, they motion for the individual to turn around and then conduct the same routine on the back of the person's body.

Juliette turns to her right, whispering to the four of us. "They're smudging everyone. It's a Native American practice to clear negative energy."

When Anahata comes to me and instructs me to step forward, I note her face is expressionless, almost vacuous. It's as though she is not in her body as she completes these robotic procedures on each of us.

I like the smell of sage and have tried smudging before. Pete never understood what I was doing, but he's not into this kind of stuff.

My eyes follow the smoke as it swirls all about. Somehow the sage manages to envelop every inch of my body. It seems strange a smoke would be used to cleanse—I always thought it made things dirty. Automatically, my mind goes to Pittsburgh's abandoned steel mills and their large smokestacks. No doubt these buildings didn't cleanse anything. Quite the opposite, they caused a great deal of pollution and illness.

When they finish, Anahata sages Francisco, then he does the same for her. Each places their bundle in a shell filled with sand.

"We are now ready to begin," Anahata says as she reaches into her bag and grabs a large feather.

I hear a slight gasp, causing me to turn to my right. Annie, who is sandwiched between Sophia and me, looks terrified. I noted her hesitancy when Anahata told her to step forward to be smudged. No doubt this cleansing ritual is only adding to Annie's apprehensive state.

Anahata picks up one of the pieces of wood, lights it, then fans the flame with the feather, causing the most intriguing-smelling smoke to appear. With ease and grace, she begins to weave in and out of the circle, moving between the participants as she chants in an unfamiliar language.

"That's palo santo," I hear Juliette whisper to Marlee, who is standing to my left. "The Incans used it a lot. But now, there's all sorts of controversy around it … because it's a sacred tree from South America, and people want to make sure it isn't overharvested …. like white sage has been."

As Juliette speaks, I catch Francisco looking in our direction and raising his eyebrows, no doubt a signal for us to stop talking. However, Anahata does not seem to notice. She's somewhere else; her eyes stare but not at us, rather through us.

Anahata stops chanting, and the room becomes silent. She places the feather in the bowl and puts the palo santo next to the bundle of sage, on top of one of the shells filled with sand. She then removes the herbs from the vase—holding them in her left hand while pouring the water into the metal bowl with her right. She walks toward the far corner of the circle, dips the herbs into the bowl, and then flicks water from the stems onto those standing in front of her. She repeats this process until she hits everyone with droplets of water. This brings me back to my childhood when priests would bless the parishioners with holy water during mass.

Several minutes later, Anahata speaks: "The ceremony is complete."

That's it. No thanking God or acknowledging Mother Earth. Without another word, Anahata turns and exits the room.

I look around and everyone seems as confused as I am.

"Please, let me explain what occurred." Francisco offers as he moves to the front of the room, obviously aware of the perplexed faces in front of him.

"Anahata is a woman of few words but revered by many. She is known as a priestess of sorts. Anahata's studied with healers who are held in the highest esteem. What just occurred may not appear to have been significant, but because *she* conducted this cleansing ritual, it is as though you received communion from the Pope himself." With that, he smiles and gives us a slight wink.

"We will continue the purification process by proceeding to the sweat lodge. However, if you are claustrophobic or have any medical issues, I advise you not to participate. Perhaps you might choose to take a dip in the ocean or spend time in a cool shower to complete the cleansing."

"I'm out," Annie says in a voice that's a bit too loud.

"No worries, Annie. I will stay with you," Sophia offers.

Yet something inside of me thinks Sophia would love this. But just as I'm about to volunteer to stay with Annie, Juliette speaks up.

"You go, Sophia. I've done this a ton of times."

"Thank you, Juliette." I detect Sophia's genuine appreciation in her voice. "I would love to participate."

"No one needs to babysit me," Annie says, looking a bit embarrassed.

"Oh, Annie, I'm not babysitting you. I want to hang by the pool … you know … work on my tan." Juliette pauses. "Besides, I have a session with Anahata. Apparently, she only does one private session each week." With that, Juliette tosses her head, stands up, and says, "Let's go, Annie. I have my bathing suit with me, so we can head straight to the pool once you've changed."

As soon as Juliette and Annie leave, I say, "Well, I'm glad the three of us can do the sweat lodge together. Are either of you claustrophobic?" I pause to wonder how I'll react to the small space and intense heat.

"Not that I am aware," Sophia says, tilting her head as she awaits Marlee's response.

"I don't think I am," Marlee says. "Actually, I'm trying to recall the last time I was in a tight space."

"Last night, I read about this ceremony in the welcome packet. We're supposed to wear bathing suits, but nothing metal. So make sure you take off all your jewelry," I say.

"Even my wedding ring?" Marlee asks, a look of concern coming over her face.

"It is probably best. Otherwise, the metal may burn your finger," Sophia says. By Marlee's reaction, I sense there's more meaning behind her concern.

"I've never taken it off before," Marlee admits as we walk back to our rooms.

***

Marlee and I meet Sophia on the patio outside of the main building.

"I believe the sweat lodge is this way, near the vegetable garden. I remember seeing it when we had the tour on Sunday," Marlee says as she leads us up the small path toward the jungle.

Five minutes later, we're standing in front of a small hut, no more than five feet tall at its highest point. Using my trained eye, I suspect its diameter is fourteen feet, perhaps a few inches less. There's an opening on the side that's covered by a thick woven blanket. About three yards in front of the hut, a man tends a large fire.

"We're here for the sweat lodge," Marlee says, though the man only grins, shaking his head yes.

"I do not think he speaks English," Sophia says.

Slowly, more people arrive, looking as confused as we must. Then, from an obscure trail leading to the jungle, Francisco suddenly appears. He's shirtless and dressed in gray pants cinched above the ankles.

"I am so happy you have chosen to participate. This is a most beautiful cleansing ceremony. Yet it is not for the faint of heart. The heat is intense. If you think you may feel overwhelmed,

I suggest you sit near the door." Francisco points to the hut's covered entrance.

After grounding us and completing a brief opening ceremony, Francisco says, "Please, follow me. It is important to enter on the left side of the door, moving in a clockwise fashion until we are all seated. You must crawl into the hut. The ceiling is low, and you do not want to hit your head."

As directed, we form a line behind Francisco, getting down on hands and knees as we awkwardly enter this man-made clay dome. It's dark inside. The only light comes from the makeshift door and a small hole in the ceiling. I count eleven of us, plus Francisco. He passes a wicker basket around.

"Please, take an instrument. During the chanting, you may enjoy focusing on a rattle or drum to free your mind from the heat."

When it's my turn to pick, I choose a small drum.

"The ceremony will take almost two hours. There are four stages. At the beginning of each, our 'keeper of the fire' ... the man you saw outside ... will add hot rocks to the center of the sweat lodge." Francisco motions toward an empty circle that is in the middle of the hut. "Each time, you will feel a greater intensity of heat. However, in between, we will open the door to allow fresh air to circulate."

I take a gulp and look toward Marlee. She seems a bit nervous, and I catch her grasping her knees with her hands. However, Sophia sits regally with her spine erect, reminding me of a queen of sorts, but in a good way.

What happens next is difficult to describe. The heat in the sweat lodge quickly rises when the firekeeper adds the first hot stones to the center of the dark, sandy hut. The lava rocks radiate an eerie red glow. Then Francisco throws cedar on the fire, which immediately creates a pungent odor. Next, he takes a ladle from a bowl and tosses water on top. Steam rises, making the air thick.

It becomes difficult to breathe. During this entire process, he is chanting—in English—to Mother Earth, the ground beneath us. He shakes his rattle, and we join along. The heat permeates my pores, traveling deep into my body. But just when I think I can no longer handle the intensity, Francisco calls for the firekeeper to push aside the heavy blanket. Cool air rushes through the doorway.

I look toward Marlee, who's covered in sweat. I can only imagine what I look like. Even Sophia seems impacted by the extreme heat. Sand from the floor sticks to the bottom of my legs. I adjust my seat, crisscrossing my stiff legs in the opposite direction.

But as I'm beginning to feel somewhat comfortable, Francisco repeats the process. The firekeeper adds more rocks, then Francisco tosses tobacco on top before dousing the hot stones with water. As he chants, this time to Father Sky, it becomes even hotter than before. I hit the drum more vigorously, as if doing so will cool me off. But it doesn't. I try to see how others are responding, but it's too dark to make out their expressions. I can only sense Marlee's and Sophia's reactions, as I sit between them. They seem OK, but their eyes are shut. So I tell myself to calm down. I am safe. It will be alright.

When Francisco calls for the firekeeper to open the door, I find myself gasping for fresh air. A woman awkwardly crawls over us to leave the hut. No doubt it's become too much for her. Francisco pauses the process to go outside and check on her. Several moments later, he and the woman return. Francisco instructs her to sit by the door. Again, he tells the group we can leave at any time. She's insistent she wants to stay.

We begin the second half of the ceremony, and I know the challenge to remain will only become more difficult. Relax. This is all part of the process—it is supposed to be hard. As the smell of the sweetgrass, which Francisco just added to the center stones, swirls in my head, an internal unwinding begins to occur. Almost impossible to explain, it feels as if part of me is uncoiling, slowly leaving the lower part of my body, my second chakra. I sense resistance, as if I'm afraid to let go. Hunching over, hoping the air below will be a bit less stifling, I do my best to inhale through my nose and exhale the stale air through my mouth. Still focused on the area under my belly button, I notice something's shifted ... There appears to be more space. It's then Francisco calls for the door to be opened. Fresh air floods the sweat lodge, allowing new life to enter.

After the fourth and final round of glowing stones, verbal offerings, sage, water, and chants, we finally finish the cleansing ceremony. Covered in sweat and sand, I crawl around the small hut—exiting through of the other side of the doorway.

Francisco has us form a horseshoe before explaining what has transpired. "What you endured was no easy feat. But in the process, not only have you detoxified the physical body, but you have also shed many emotional and energetic impurities. This ritual, coupled with this morning's ceremony, has helped you release much of what you've stirred up this week. Now you are ready for new possibilities and adventures. In essence, this was a spring cleaning ... like none you've ever had," he says as he grins, showing his immaculate white teeth.

"Now go, jump into the beautiful ocean, and wash off any remaining residue from the release. Have fun. Play. Laugh. Do not worry about a thing. Tomorrow, I will be conducting the morning workshop. We will discuss how to transition back to daily life—your family, friends, job. After six days of focusing on our individual paths, it can be a challenge to return home. But there are ways to make the assimilation easier. I will share methods to maintain the energetic vibrations you've gained this week. Tomorrow afternoon is the guided paddleboarding excursion at one of our beautiful rivers. If you would like to participate, please meet in the lobby at one thirty. We will return by four thirty, allowing ample time to prepare for our closing ceremony prior to dinner." Francisco's suddenly glowing, as if this is his favorite part of the retreat. "But tonight, we celebrate. After dinner, Dominique and I will be hosting a party on the pool patio."

I look toward Marlee and Sophia, hoping they want to attend. Both nod. It's then I realize how lucky I am to be "adopted" by these women. I can't imagine how different this week would have been had I not met these special ladies and was *on my own*. These heavy words remind me what will happen when I return to Pittsburgh. But instead of allowing this thought to dampen my mood, I acknowledge the uncertainty that lies ahead and tell myself, "I am here now," one of the affirmations Lindsay recommended I use.

"Come on. Let's wash off," Marlee says.

Following the others, we make our way down to the ocean. The cool water laps over my thighs as I walk into the surf. When fully immersed, with only my head above the water, I begin to think about what transpired. Could I have sweated away the pain, confusion, and sadness? There have been so many emotions—almost too many—for me to process. While I don't have any answers, I do feel lighter, more buoyant. Sure, part of it is the salt water's effect on my body, but it is so much more than that. It's as though I'm in a neutral position, one where I can start over and make decisions for myself—not for my mom, nor for Pete, but for me. I tilt my head back and let my body sink into the ocean, allowing the salt water to fully cover my face, rinsing off any final remnants of dirt from the sweat lodge. Maybe my second chakra did release. And if so, could I possibly ever become that passionate being Sonya described? Or is that too much to hope for?

When I return to the beach, it's as though I'm walking in my true body for the first time. It feels oddly comfortable. I look around. No one seems to be mingling. Instead, everyone appears to be having a similar reaction, almost as if lost in self-contemplation.

The warm sun quickly dries the ocean's water, creating a thin salty layer on top of my skin. I smile at Marlee and Sophia, telling them I'm going back to the room and will see them at lunch. But I note something's shifted in them too. It's as though a huge burden has been lifted from each of these women. There's a sense of peace in their faces, their walks, their presence. Both appear younger, as though they haven't a care in the world. But isn't that how I also feel? Yes, I am aware of what decisions lie ahead. But I will deal with that later. For now … in this moment … I can just be.

***

To my surprise, I'm no longer nervous to meet with Francisco. Maybe it's because of the sweat lodge ceremony. Or perhaps the more time I spend around him, the less "shaman-like" he seems. Still, I'm unable to place a finger on the exact words to describe how Francisco makes me feel.

"Hello, Maggie." I hear Francisco's voice before I see him.

When we arrive at his and Dominique's apartment, I pause, cognizant our session is finally happening. Is it possible Francisco will help me learn more about myself and what I should do when I return to Pittsburgh? If this session is anything like the one with Conor, I may experience major breakthroughs. I release a slight sigh, not wanting to get my hopes up.

Francisco leads me into his office and offers me a seat of my choice. I settle onto a sea-green pouf, pulling my knees closely into my chest. My heart begins to palpitate, but in anticipation, not fear. He lowers the light, creating a calming yet serious atmosphere. Our shaman then conducts a cleansing, like he did with Marlee.

"My dear Maggie, you have been struggling, have you not?" Francisco asks after placing the bowl of sage on the floor and settling onto a small cushion directly across from me.

I nod. Suddenly, the back of my throat feels tight.

"There has been a lot of pain and loss in your life. But now you are at a point where you must make decisions. Is that true?"

Again, I nod, noting the constricting feeling's becoming stronger.

"But this is an opportunity, is it not? You have a new sense of freedom, and I am not so sure you understand all that means."

"Freedom?" I ask, confused.

"From the responsibility and duty ... the life you thought you *should* live. Yet that path no longer lies ahead of you. Instead, you are at a junction. It is time for you to decide what *you* want." As Francisco shares this, he tilts his head, then leans closer, as if to emphasize it is my turn to speak.

"I don't know. I haven't really let myself think about it." Which is the truth, as I keep asking the question but never allow ample time to consider the possibilities.

Francisco's eyes begin to glow, creating an amber quality I hadn't noticed before. "Losing your mom in such a tragic way takes time to heal."

I gasp, wondering how he knew this information about Mom. But then I remembered the questionnaire we received before coming on the retreat. I'd shared that information under the question, *What is your current struggle?*

"If only I had been there. Maybe I could have prevented ... her death." As I say these words, tears uncontrollably stream down my face.

Francisco reaches toward me, placing his hand on my arm. Instantly, it calms me.

"My dear, there was nothing you could have done. It was your mother's time ... and her choice. She'd made that agreement before she incarnated."

While I'd read about soul contracts, I'd never discussed this concept with anyone. "Is that what really happens? We get to choose when and how?"

"I'm not so sure we have input on all of the details." Francisco's words are soft and slow, almost soothing as we discuss this morbid topic. "But we do agree to a time line of sorts." He pauses, and then a seriousness comes over him. "Would you like to contact your mother? To see if she is all right?"

"You can do that?"

"We can try, that is … if you wish."

Without taking the time to fully consider his question, I say yes, then tightly shut my eyes as if to seal the commitment to reach out to Mom on the other side.

Francisco becomes eerily still. His breathing slows and then his eyes flutter. After several moments, he opens them, though they now appear to be a pale blue. There's care yet worry in his face. It's when he speaks that I recognize who now sits across from me.

"Magpie. I am so sorry. I didn't mean to leave you alone, all by yourself. You have worried about me since you've been a little girl." His face softens a bit. "There were moments I thought you were the mother, and I was the child. But that responsibility is no longer yours. Be who you are meant to become. Discover love … Find your joy and happiness." And then he stops talking and his expression and the hue of his eyes return to normal—what is his, not my mom's.

Francisco does not speak. Instead, he watches, perhaps waiting for me to take the next step.

"You were her?" I ask, bewildered at what occurred.

"I asked that she enter my body, to speak to you. I sensed she wanted to reach out and let you know she was fine."

"You said 'Magpie.' How did you know she called me that?" I swallow hard as I try to process everything. I know I did not use that word in the questionnaire.

"*I* did not know a thing. It was *she* who was speaking." Francisco sits up a bit straighter. "Your mother had a clear and direct message for you. Would you like to discuss it?"

I tuck my chin to my chest, lowering my forehead onto my knees. Can he offer me guidance? If so, then now is the time to ask for help.

"I don't know what to do. My bosses, who own the architectural firm where I work, are moving to Oregon ... and they want me to come with them. But I've never lived anywhere but Pittsburgh. And my granddad is in a memory care facility nearby ... He has Alzheimer's ... He doesn't know me ... but I'm the only one he has left. And then there's Pete. He's been amazing ... so kind to me ... especially after Mom died. But I think he wants to get married ... settle down ... I love him as a human, but not in *that way* ... how you're supposed to when you commit to someone ... I'm so confused." After frantically spitting out these phrases, I melt, becoming a puddle of desperation in the middle of the shaman's office. Unable to contain my fear, pain, and confusion, I totally surrender and allow what is still inside to release.

Francisco stands, then moves to sit next to me, gently wrapping his arm over my shoulder. Careful not to pull me too close to him, he whispers softly: "You must learn to nurture yourself. You have the ability within to do so. It is time for you to be Maggie, not Magpie, not Pete's girlfriend, nor the young woman who does what others expect her to do and be. This is the moment you are being called to step into your own power and take hold of your life. Ask what *you want*." Francisco pauses, perhaps for emphasis.

"You have a gift. It is how you relate to others ... You can feel people's energy ... read their emotions. Maggie, you are empathic. But you already knew that, didn't you?"

While I have not officially claimed myself as such, what he says makes total sense. In fact, it explains those strong sensations I often encounter when I am around others. Maybe that's why I have trouble knowing which emotions are mine. I frequently confuse others' as my own. And sometimes it's almost impossible to distinguish between the two.

"Do not be afraid. Your empathic abilities will help you guide others to better understand what is *underneath* their feelings and actions ... so they may live a fulfilling life. And you will learn how to keep yourself safe by establishing energetic boundaries. You can do so without sacrificing your capacity to sense another's emotions. While this gift is wonderful and part of your life purpose, it is not designed to hold you back or keep you from living *your* dharma. You are ready. It is time to take the first step."

He removes his arm, gently touches my cheek, then walks to a large bureau. I watch as he opens a cabinet door, but I'm unable to see what he is doing as his back is to me.

While I wait, I begin to contemplate what this first step might be.

He returns, takes a seat on his cushion, and then reveals what is in his hands. It's a book. He hands it to me. The mottled brown cover is worn. I cannot make out the title nor the author.

Francisco must see me squinting. "Yes, I'm afraid it is a bit old." He smiles before continuing: "The book is titled *Truths of the Night Sky*. A dear friend gave it to me, and I've referenced it frequently, especially when struggling with looming decisions. As Sonya so eloquently shared, astrology *can* show us the way—that is, if we accurately decipher the messages from the planetary movements and interactions. While I've enjoyed this book immensely, something tells me it is now meant for you."

"Thank you." I carefully open the book and begin to leaf through its pages. "How did you know this would interest me?" I believe my voice sounds almost childlike, filled with awe.

"My dear Maggie, I see your potential, even if you cannot recognize it in yourself. You have an untapped gift for reading people and helping them discover their path. *This* is why you are here ... to shine your light so others can find theirs. My hope is this book will help you do so," he says as his eyes travel to the book I now hold tightly to my chest.

"I am meant to understand astrology?"

"Most certainly ... and I suspect once you master this subject, you will use astrology to benefit others." He smiles, then says, "I am not suggesting you quit your job as an architect. Not in the least. But perhaps see the connection between the two."

What could he possibly mean? How could astrology and architecture be connected?

It's then Francisco rises, as if to suggest our time together has ended. But I want to know more. I don't want our session to be over.

"You are a blessing. Your mother knew it. And I suspect that your father will as well ... in case you choose to reach out to him." He gives me a subtle wink.

How did he know that? Did Conor say anything to him? Eyes wide, I utter, "But ... how do you ..."

"Remember, we all have gifts." With that, he smiles as he walks toward the door.

***

Strings of sparkle lights hang overhead. Lit tiki torches surround the pool illuminated by floating candles. To my right is a table covered with bowls of lemons, oranges, limes, and other fruits. Alana smiles and waves as she prepares pitchers of beverages.

Taking in this spectacular scene, I now realize how much has transpired the past several days. Not only have I met four amazing women, learned I am meant to study astrology, and discovered my dad never knew about me *and* practically lives in my back-yard, but I've also released buried aspects of my second chakra. Still, there's more. Through Francisco, I felt my mom's presence and *heard her* tell me it was time to live *my life*. And after today's cleansing ceremonies, I feel renewed, almost as if I've been gifted a chance to start over. But this time, I get to choose ... I no longer feel the need to do what I think I *should*. Feeling blessed, I return my focus to my friends.

"Conor is amazing," Marlee says as we pull together several lounge chairs so we can sit down and chat. "He sees me writing, but in a different way. I'm still not sure what that means, but I'm trying to be open, you know, consider opportunities I'd never have entertained before. Oh, and he also mentioned that cooking will play a key role."

"Cooking and writing?" Annie looks toward Marlee, sounding confused. "But you write for the *Inquirer*. Do you think it means you'll quit and maybe work for a food magazine?"

"I have no idea," Marlee says with a shrug of her shoulders. Tonight, my older friend has a different presence to her. Though I cannot identify what's shifted, something's definitely changed. I suppose Marlee seems more relaxed, almost as if she's OK with not knowing what's next.

"I can't begin to describe my session with Anahata. She's like Yoda." Juliette leans in closer and raises her eyebrows. "As you know, I've done all sorts of healings, soul retrievals, delved into past lives ... shit like that. But what she was able to tell and do ... well, it was at a totally new level."

"Anahata most certainly possesses a mystical air to her. Not only is it the way she carries herself, but it is also as if she's not fully here, on Earth. I sensed that she is from another dimension." It's Sophia who says this.

"Another dimension?" I ask.

Juliette jumps in to answer my question. "There are multiple dimensions, but most of us are not aware of them. We live in the third dimension—you know, 3D. It's all about being in our physical bodies. But there's a density and a low vibration to this dimension." She pauses as she sits up and pulls her shoulders back in a command-ing way. "With the higher dimensions" —she juts her chin out as she says this—"vibrations increase. We can all access these levels, but not everyone is willing to go there. The fourth dimension operates as a sort of portal to the fifth. And the fifth dimension ..." Juliette pauses as she takes a huge inhale. "Well, that's where the magic happens. It's where our hearts see the oneness in all. We are no longer stuck in our physical limitations. Instead, we manifest our true selves' desires." She exhales, and a serene look comes over her.

"So we live in the third dimension, but we can go to the fourth and fifth—that is, if we are open and willing?" I ask, trying to cement this notion in my mind.

"Exactly." Juliette crosses one leg over the other. "Some peo-ple have a knack for it and can do this on their own. Others re-quire guidance. And there are those who cannot comprehend, let alone become open to the frequencies in these higher dimensions. I doubt they'll ever travel there during this lifetime."

"So what happened with Anahata?" Marlee asks, returning to the original conversation.

"Well, as you might guess, she didn't say a lot. It was the way she helped me visit worlds I've never seen ... or imagined."

"Where did you go?" Annie asks, her eyebrows furrowing in confusion.

"Other galaxies, places that are inhabited by beings who are not like us."

"Were you scared?" Annie's eyes widen and her jaw drops.

"Not at all." Juliette waves her hand in a dismissive manner. "These beings were beautiful souls. So much more evolved than we are. They had different systems on their planets; none of them were based on greed or lack. Instead, there was a connection, a beautiful symbiotic relationship between the actual planet and those who live there." Juliette seemingly floats away, as if returning to her experience with Anahata.

"That sounds beautiful, Juliette," Sophia says. "I can only imagine how incredible your session was." Surprisingly, Juliette only nods and doesn't say another word. Perhaps she's momentarily reliving what transpired earlier this afternoon.

There's a pause, and I take this as an opportunity to share a bit of my experience with Francisco. Sophia's, Juliette's, and Annie's eyes widen as I repeat some of what Francisco said. I keep a few details to myself but reveal enough so they can understand. I then add how Conor told me the name of my father—and that my dad was alive and living close by.

Juliette blurts out, "Holy shit! That is a ton to process, Maggie. How are you handling it?"

"I'm not sure. I'm kind of numb. But Francisco, well, his message was inspirational. And knowing I possess the power to choose for myself and no longer need to make decisions based on what others need from me ... well ... it's liberating ... in a strange way."

"It saddens me that you have experienced such sorrow ... losing your mother so recently." Sophia pauses, looking down at the stone patio, shaking her head.

Becoming a bit uncomfortable with this attention, I ask Annie about her time with Francisco, as I believe she met with him right before I did.

Annie puts her elbow on her thigh, then rests her chin in her cupped palm. "He is incredible. I've never experienced anything like it." She pauses, then turns to look at each of us, as if to reinforce her statement. "He helped me ... you know ... with the vision I had."

"Thank God," Juliette said. "I know how much that was troubling you. Of course, if I heard that about my kid, I'd be super psyched." Juliette smirks.

I watch as Sophia gives Juliette a slight glare.

"Oh, but I totally get why the thought would be upsetting to most people." Juliette attempts to pull her foot out of her mouth.

"What did he tell you?" Marlee asks, turning her chair slightly to the right toward Annie.

"Francisco shared that my vision was only meant to prepare me for the fact that this child will be exceptional. I don't mean to sound like a gloating parent ... it's just that she ... and he said the baby is a girl ... will possess gifts like mine. And she will fully utilize them for a higher purpose." Annie sits up tall, as if proud of her unborn child's prophecy. "If she wants to be a psychic surgeon, I am totally OK with that. It's her life, and I will support my child in all her endeavors." With this proclamation, Annie heaves out a huge sigh.

Marlee places her arm around Annie and pulls her in for a brief hug. She then asks Sophia what she did today. "I don't remember you mentioning a session. Did you go to the pool or get a massage?"

"I met with Jack Keeler." Her voice becomes serious. "Yesterday, during my session with Francisco, we spent most of our time discussing my shift from solely relying on traditional medicine to including a holistic, naturopathic approach. I told him of my concerns, and he assured me I was ready but needed to trust my intuition. Francisco was emphatic about me developing faith in my ability to diagnose and treat my patients ... when to use traditional methods and when to opt for more holistic ways. He said that if I did not believe in my abilities, I would revert to how I previously practiced, afraid to trust my inner-knowing."

I think this may be the most words I've ever heard Sophia speak. But she's not done.

"Francisco felt I would benefit from speaking with Jack. When I agreed, Francisco arranged for us to meet."

"How did it go? What's he like? Is he as nice as his wife, Lindsay?" Juliette's firing off questions without a breath in between.

"Well. Brilliant. Yes." Sophia offers a demure grin, a playful move I didn't expect from her. "Jack shared his personal journey, and we discussed potential roadblocks while transitioning my practice. However, it appears as though *I* have created most of these barriers. Jack reinforced Francisco's message ... I must release my fear of misdiagnosis or prescribing the wrong treatment if I wish to become the doctor I hope to be." Sophia tilts her head as if to accentuate this point.

After a distinct pause, she continues: "I believe I now understand what I must surrender. Perhaps today's cleansing ceremonies have already assisted with this process." Sophia blinks her eyes several times. "There is one more thing." She pauses, and a Cheshire grin comes over her face. "Jack asked me if I would like to do an internship with him. Of course, the majority of it would be remote. But I also would return here, to Nosara, to work directly with him."

"You said yes?" Annie asks, eyes bulging in anticipation of Sophia's response.

Sophia gracefully nods. "We are meeting tomorrow afternoon to finalize the details. I will begin working with him as soon as I return home." Sophia's eyes glisten, the light from a nearby torch adding an additional gleam to them.

"I'm so happy for you," I say, though I am not quite aware of Sophia's history or the reasons she desires this transition. However, after asking a few clarifying questions, I better understand what a big step this is for Sophia.

Alana approaches us, carrying a tray of champagne flutes. Half are filled with champagne and berries; the others are pomegranate juice and seltzer.

"So this week is really panning out for all of us," Marlee says, taking a glass of champagne.

"I believe it is," Sophia says, then adds, "I would like to propose a toast … to Juliette … for asking us to join her on this retreat." We all raise our glasses to Juliette, though I am kind of the odd one out.

It's then Marlee speaks up: "And to Maggie. For sharing this very special week of self-discovery with us." The four then toast me, and as our glasses clink, it's as though my heart cracks open a bit. A warmth fills the empty space within my fourth chakra. But it doesn't stop there. The sensation continues through my core, my limbs, my head. I feel heard … trusted … even after I allowed my vulnerabilities to surface. No doubt I'm changing. But will I be able to sustain this transformation once I return to Pittsburgh … or move to Bend?

MARLEE
Friday, April 23

Today's the final day, and I want to make the most of it.

As much as I miss Tom and Patrick, a part of me is not ready for the week to end. I let out a slight laugh, remembering my hesitation about coming, afraid I might change *inside and out*.

Elevar has been transformational on multiple levels. Growth from the workshops, private sessions, and the aha moments would have been enough. But there's been more. It's the people who've made this experience like no other. I slip my feet into my running shoes, then tie them snugly.

Still, I have more questions to ask and crave additional time with these master healers. And my gratitude for this time away lies beyond exploring my personal path … I've loved witnessing my friends' evolutions. Maybe female friendships mean more to me than I've been willing to admit. And meeting Maggie—though she's much younger—well, there's a special connection. It's as though we're filling an empty void for one another.

I can't deny my urge to mother her. If I ever did have a daughter, I'd want her to be just like Maggie. This is in no way a slight to Juliette. I have a definite soft spot for her. Plus, Juliette keeps me on my toes. God knows she challenges me to leave my comfort zone.

Yet Maggie's different from Juliette. As much as Juliette *needs* a mother figure, she fights it. Instead, she's determined to appear strong, independent, impenetrable. But Juliette's as vulnerable as the rest of us, though she rarely shows it, probably because she's afraid to.

Now Maggie, *she's* open to support. But she doesn't want to ask for help for fear of being a burden. Maybe I see a bit of my younger self in Maggie. Still, my intuition—if I can call it that—tells me to nurture her.

Juliette's sitting on the balcony in a Lotus position, meditating before our meditation class. Or perhaps she's mentally preparing for her session with Francisco. But isn't she exhausted? It was after midnight when I heard her come in last night.

As I descend the stairs, I see Maggie stretching, balancing on one leg as she pulls the other behind her to stretch her quad.

"How late did you guys stay out?" I lightheartedly ask. However, as soon as the words leave my lips, I become concerned I might be sounding more like a parent than a friend.

"Oh, I didn't make it much longer than you did. I think I was in bed by nine thirty."

Something does not calculate. If Maggie was back long before midnight, who was Juliette with? Sophia and Annie left the party when I did. A part of me wants to ask, but I know it's not my business. Besides, if Juliette wants to tell me, she will. I turn my focus to Maggie.

"I guess this is our final run." As I say this, unexpected tears well in my eyes. I've come to look forward to this morning routine. Our conversations have been special. They make me feel useful, perhaps even needed.

"I know. I was thinking that exact thing," Maggie says as she offers me a crooked smile.

Slowly, we head toward the beach.

"Marlee," Maggie says once we begin running, only to pause, waiting several moments before continuing. "What do you think I should do when I get back to Pittsburgh?" She turns and looks at me, biting her lower lip.

Unsure if there is a correct answer, I wait a moment before offering any thoughts. "I think it all depends on what *you* want." I pump my arms and ask for help. God ... I could really use some guidance right now. I then wait for several moments before speaking.

"It seems as though your life is like an empty canvas. Now you get to decide what colors you want to use to paint *your picture.*" I offer a smile, trying to be optimistic. However, I realize the dilemmas she's facing are gigantic, and whatever she decides will significantly impact her future.

Maggie, who is staring straight ahead, says, "The way I look at it, I have three decisions ahead of me. First, do I take Sandy and Mark's offer and move to Oregon? This is the most time sensitive because I promised to tell them on Monday." Her voice quivers with her last comment.

I nod, trying to remain quiet so she can talk this out on her own.

"Then there is the issue with my father. I don't need to decide now, but if I choose Bend over Pittsburgh, and if I don't reach out to him *right away*, then I probably never will."

"True," I say, gasping a bit for air. Maggie's increased the pace as she's contemplating what awaits when she returns.

"My third issue is Pete. I mean, do I *really* want to stay with him?" Her shoulders slump as she sighs. "Sure, he's super sweet ... and he's been by my side this entire time. He even offered to come on the retreat with me, which is kind of funny because there is nothing spiritual about the guy." Maggie shakes her head as she softly laughs.

"But he would have done it for you?" I ask, already knowing the answer.

"That's the problem. He'll do anything I ask." The next few moments are silent. The only sounds are the surf and our sneakers striking the sand.

"I know, there are many women who want that in a man. But not me. I need a challenge. Not that I want a male chauvinist or anything." She rolls her eyes as she makes this comment. "But I want a partner, one that prompts me to be my best, not someone who drops whatever they're doing to meet my needs … or treats me like a princess." Her voice grows louder, and I can sense her frustration.

"I agree. There needs to be a balance."

"But there's more." Maggie stops dead in her tracks, causing me to take a few steps back to meet her where she stands. "I want passion." Her voice is loud. "I now realize I *need* passion. At least that's what Sonya told me." Her entire face blushes as she reveals what's lacking in her relationship with Pete.

"You can't ignore that," I say, hoping I'm not influencing her decision. Still, I can't resist adding, "Because if it is not there now, don't think it's going to suddenly appear."

"Exactly!" Her eyes widen as her voice inflects.

"So what are you going to do?" I finally ask, raising my eyebrows.

Maggie doesn't speak, but instead starts to run. I suppose she requires more time to answer my question. Doing my best to keep up with her pace, I patiently wait for her response.

"I am going to break up with Pete, tell Sandy and Mark I've decided to move to Bend, and then … before I move … I will reach out to my father."

Wow. I didn't expect her to answer all three questions. But I suppose Maggie's been in nonstop analysis regarding her next steps since she's arrived. Suddenly, a warmth fills my chest. I'm proud of Maggie for making this strong pronouncement. However, before I can properly respond to her triple resolution, she continues.

"This way, if my dad doesn't want to acknowledge I exist, it really won't matter … because I will soon be in Oregon."

"And what if he wants to establish a relationship?" I can't help but pose what I think is the most likely outcome.

"Well ..." She pauses, looking confused about this possibility occurring. "While I doubt he'll want anything to do with me ... *if* he would ..." She becomes silent for several moments. "I guess we could make it work. Maybe talk on the phone ... email ... text ... stuff like that." She turns toward me and once again stops running. "Marlee, do you really think he might... *could* he actually want to get to know me?"

It's then I realize Maggie's convinced her father will reject her. It's as though she cannot release the pain she's held her entire life.

"I do," I say as I gently touch her cheek. "Sure, the news may come as a shock. I can only imagine how my husband would react if he suddenly discovered he had a daughter from a past relationship." I swallow and say a short prayer this never occurs. "But I truly believe he'd want to do the right thing ... get to know his child." I tilt my head, locking my eyes on Maggie. "You know, he never chose not to be there for you. He had no idea you ever existed."

Maggie swallows, then slowly nods, blinking back tears. "I know."

"Give your dad a chance. Reach out to him as soon as you get back. And then wait and see what happens. This way, if he reacts as I suspect he will, you'll have some time together ... before you move."

Maggie nods as she bites down on her lower lip. After a few moments, she says, "Thank you, Marlee." Once again, my heart swells. But it's not only because I'm proud of Maggie; it's mostly due to my deep affection for her.

"How about we finish this run strong?" And with that, she takes off. I do my best to keep stride with Maggie. But she's flying— her feet graze the sand as she propels her body forward. It's as though a huge weight has lifted off her shoulders ... She's finally free.

***

When we enter the meditation room, Eduardo's seated on his cushion. Upon seeing us, he places his finger to his lips, indicating we are to remain silent. I watch him repeat this behavior as others come into the building. Confused, people merely settle onto their mats, attempting to prepare for today's final meditation. While no one speaks, many glance around at others, as if wondering what's going on.

At exactly seven o'clock, Eduardo gives three strikes to a bronze metal bowl that's sitting in front of him. Meditation has begun. But this time, there are no crystal singing bowls, no music, no words to guide us. Instead, the room's completely silent. Slowly, I sense myself sink into the abyss of nothingness, where there are no thoughts, no agendas, nothing to contemplate, no decisions to make. There's only room *to be.*

Another three strikes of the bronze bowl startle me out of my trance-like state. Never before have I experienced anything like this. The solitude, the depth, the quiet, the peace. This must be what true meditation is about. Slowly, I wiggle my fingers and begin to crack open my eyes, noting Kali's entered the room and is heading toward the closet.

"I suspect many of you have never sat for thirty minutes in silence," Eduardo says. "While the concept can be daunting, I venture to guess you found it rewarding, no?"

People nod; some smile.

"Celebrate your meditation practice and how it has grown during our time together. Taming the mind is no easy feat." He pauses before adding, "And please, do not stop sitting on your cushion once you've returned to your homes. This week, I've offered you several different ways to meditate. Remember which resonated most with you, and then try to continue that practice at least four days a week. If you do, you will witness profound changes." He sits taller, as if to emphasize his last comment.

I turn to Annie. There's a huge smile on her face, and she's placed both hands on her belly. I wonder if the baby was kicking again. Maybe her baby senses the calmness Annie feels while meditating. Actually, it makes a lot of sense. But there's more to Annie's expression. She seems happy. Dare I say *at peace*? This week's been amazing for her. I'm incredibly thankful she didn't back out of coming on the retreat, something Margaret told me to do. Funny, I haven't heard a peep from *her*. Could it be ... but that's too much to hope for.

We then transition to our final yoga practice. Kali passes out blocks, sharing this morning's sequence will be more vigorous than yesterday's restorative class, but not as challenging as the power class we had on Tuesday. She turns on the music, and we begin to move. My body flows with ease, which truly surprises me because of all the running—as well as my need to increase my pace to keep up with Maggie. Normally, I only run three days a week. But running on sand is supposed to be easier on the joints. Plus, this week, I've been more relaxed, away from the everyday stress. I then begin to wonder whether Maggie made running easier. Could there have been a purpose behind our runs?

It's only after we say our final namastes that I realize how famished I am. After thanking Kali and Eduardo, we head to the main building for breakfast. One of the things I will miss most about this week is René's cooking. However, I can't wait to try to replicate some of his dishes. Sure, accessing all the ingredients may be challenging, but I can be crafty when it comes to re-creating recipes.

René stops at our table, making it a point to say goodbye to each of us. "You leave tomorrow, early?" he asks in his thick French accent.

"Yes, we have a seven-thirty shuttle to the airport," I respond, but his eyes are on Juliette. Yet this time she's looking back at him, and not in an annoyed manner.

"Well then, it is goodbye ... until next time?" But instead of his usual arrogant boldness, René's eyes narrow and his lips form a solemn line.

He walks over to Juliette, takes her hand, and gently kisses the top of it. "I hope you will not wait too long to return." His words seem incredibly genuine, almost humble. Could there be something between Juliette and René? She glances at me briefly before shifting her eyes to the floor.

No one seems to pick up on Juliette's behavior. However, I don't think anyone else knows she was out twice this week ... past midnight ... without any of us.

Juliette's eyes lift, meeting mine, looking desperate, as if pleading, *Please, not now.*

And so I remain silent. If Juliette wants to talk about it, she will.

As Annie returns from the buffet with her second freshly baked blueberry muffin and more scrambled eggs, she says, "I'm beginning to worry."

"What do you mean?" a nervous Sophia quickly asks.

"How am I going to lose all of this pregnancy weight so I can fit into my bridesmaid dress?" With that, she spreads a big dollop of butter onto half of the muffin and takes a bite.

Unable to restrain myself, I laugh aloud. "Well, maybe watch how much nonbaby weight you put on." I remember how I struggled to lose those extra pounds after Patrick was born.

"Oh, Annie, we'll just get you a larger dress," Juliette says, with a wave of her hand, like it is the last thing in the world to be concerned about. "I'm just happy you're going to be part of the wedding."

But Juliette doesn't sound particularly happy. Instead, I note a twinge in her voice and how her shoulders seem to hunch forward when she mentions getting married.

Luckily, no one else seems to be aware. In fact, I'm surprised by what next comes out of her mouth.

"Maggie, I know we've only just met. But, well, the five of us really seem to have a special bond." Juliette clears her throat and sits up a bit straighter. "As Annie said, she, Sophia, and Marlee are all my bridesmaids. I was wondering … if you … would you consider being one too?" Juliette's voice softens, almost as if she's afraid of Maggie's response.

"Really? You want me to be in your wedding?" Maggie's eyes widen with gratitude. "I've never been in a wedding before … Yes! Thank you … This is such an honor." Maggie, who's jumped out of her chair to hug Juliette, is grinning ear to ear. I don't think I've ever seen her this elated. I wish I could say the same for Juliette.

"Then it's settled. I'm now having four amazing bridesmaids. I'll let Michael know he needs one more groomsman." Juliette smiles, though her expression does not seem genuine. Something's up. It's as if she's convincing herself that this wedding is going to be fabulous, yet a part of her doesn't seem to be on board. Maybe there is something between Juliette and René. While I'd like to think Juliette would never cheat on Michael, I'm not so sure she wouldn't. She's one complex woman, and despite her advanced spiritual practices, she seems to hold a great deal inside. Plus, she's dealing with a lot this week. But then again, aren't we all?

***

"I hope our time together has met your expectations," Francisco says, his eyes moving from one table to the next. "Perhaps you've learned more about yourself … your desires … your dreams. Or maybe you have let go of something you no longer require." He pauses, allowing us a moment to consider his words. "Even though I have yet to meet with several of you, I feel confident in saying each person in this room has made tremendous strides on their path."

I turn to my left and spot Samantha and Amelia, the lovely couple from Australia. Both have their eyes fixed on Francisco while their heads bob up and down, nodding in agreement.

But am I further on my path? Francisco knew I was at a crossroads of sorts, that I want more from life, though I'm not so sure what it could be. He said new and exciting opportunities would present themselves. But first I had to trust, let go, and believe in God.

I'm still trying to piece together his cryptic message. And can I really deepen my faith, trust in the unknown? I remember Francisco told me that God and my intuition whisper. Anything loud is only my ego. Could the voice that spoke so clearly to me while I was in the Poconos be my intuition? And if my fifth chakra is blocked, must I first clear it if I hope to fully connect to this voice?

Maybe Daniel will have some insight when I meet with him today. Then another idea pops into my head, one that's been troubling me for some time. I wonder if Daniel can provide any information about the connection between Caroline Rhimes and Wyatt Bixby. I can't help but believe there was a reason he chose her as his realtor. More importantly, did they have a history that might shed additional light on why she murdered him?

Francisco pulls me back to the present moment.

"Because many of you have signed up for the paddleboarding excursion, today's workshop will end by eleven. I want to make sure you have ample time to attend any private sessions and then have lunch before departing for the river."

As Francisco carefully explains this morning's game plan, my mind returns to the meeting with Conor, who told me that he saw me writing, but in a different way. And it involved cooking. Although

I'm racking my brain to understand what he envisioned, I'm at a complete loss to make sense of it all. Am I writing a cookbook? I guess I could do that, but it seems kind of boring.

I pause when I hear Francisco loudly clear his throat, as if he's calling me back because he's about to say something important. After all, most of what this shaman says has significance.

"While your time at Nueva Vida has taught you many things, it is for naught if you do not incorporate these experiences into your daily life. Attending retreats can rejuvenate the soul and show us aspects of ourselves we never envisioned. However, the true work begins when we return home ... to our spouses ... our children ... our jobs ... our friends ... all the joys and responsibilities in our life. Can we take the insights"—he pauses to smile—"the aha moments, the connecting of dots ... and incorporate these deeper understandings into how we think, act, and behave?" Again, he stops talking, tilts his head, then scans the room. "Because if we are not aware, it is very easy to fall into the ways of our past."

"This week, not only have you learned a great deal, but you've also *unlearned*. I am referring to old operating systems that no longer serve you. Your eyes have been opened to what is possible, what is available ... but is accessible only *when we believe*. This, my dear friends, is how we elevate."

Francisco then begins to pass packets of stapled papers to those in the room. "Please look at the second page. I would like you to consider these questions and then create a plan for when you return home." As he gives each participant a handout, my thoughts go to what I've learned and perhaps unlearned this week. I've heard him use the term *operating systems* before, but I hadn't truly considered what it means. I supposed it's how I went about my day, my practices, habits, and thought processes. So what do I want to change once I'm home? What no longer serves me?

Francisco is now at our table. The first page of the packet says "Elevar." I flip to the next. There, at the top of the paper, are the exact questions I just asked myself. How did this happen? Did I know what was in the packet, or was it a mere coincidence?

He instructs us to answer these questions:

What do I want to change in my life?

What no longer serves my best interest?

I look around to see everyone's begun writing. I reach into my tote to find my favorite felt-tipped pen, take off the cap, and begin pondering the words in front of me.

First, what do I want to change in my life? Taking a huge inhale, I shut my eyes and begin to think about the ramifications of any changes I might make. A bit overwhelmed, I decide to skip the first question.

What no longer serves my best interest?

Without consciously thinking, my hand begins to write.

Worrying
Being fearful or anxious
Judging others
Being critical of myself
"Shoulding" myself
Pleasing others
Wearing masks
Trying to control things, people, situations

While I am sure there are many more things I could add to this list, I suppose this is a good start. But now I must return to *What do I want to change in my life?* This is more difficult to answer, so I take some time and go within, trying to connect what no longer serves me to what I've learned this week. I think about those aha moments Francisco referred to. Finally, I pick up my pen and begin.

What do I want to change in my life?

Stop writing what I think others expect to read.
Stop putting others' needs in front of mine.
Stop worrying; instead know when concern is appropriate and when it is not.

I pause, realizing I've begun each sentence with "Stop." Is there a better way to phrase how I want to change things in my life? What if I wrote in the positive, almost as if they were affirmations?

I will write as my authentic self regardless of what others may expect from me.
I will be kind and compassionate, but not say yes when I mean no.
I will accept myself and others as they are, without the need to judge or criticize.
I will do my best to stay positive and remain in a high vibrational state.
I will show up as my true self, regardless of where I am or who I am with.
I will trust, let go, and allow.
I will believe in my intuitive abilities and that I have the answers within.
I will have faith in God knowing He has my back.

I add the last two because they're important. If I hope my intuition will return, I must believe I'll be able to trust its messages. And it's clear I cannot do this alone. This will require faith.

Francisco speaks: "Let's stop for now. Of course, you can return to this section and add more thoughts later. In fact, I encourage you to do so, as additional ideas will naturally come to mind as you complete the rest of this packet." He takes a sip from the mug in front of him. "Please … turn to the next page. Now I would like for you to add actual habits and practices you would like to incorporate into your day. What can you *do* to help facilitate the changes you desire?"

Samantha raises her hand.

"Do you mean like practice yoga, meditate, eat cleanly?"

"Those are excellent example—that is, if you believe they will help you achieve your goals. Perhaps incorporate smudging into your daily routine, listen to healing music, or take walks in nature. There are no right or wrong answers. It truly depends on what you require."

Those words again—*what you require*. I exhale, knowing there's a meaning to it all. What do I want in my toolbox? Already, I've incorporated several Ayurvedic practices into my daily routine. Plus, I'm doing yoga once a week, but I guess I could practice more frequently. Knowing there are endless possibilities, I turn the page and begin responding.

Habits and practices to add to my day:

> Meditate for twenty minutes in the morning
> Journal daily
> Walk outdoors

I stop, put my pen down, then lift my eyes upward, as if the answers might be printed on the ceiling overhead. What else?

My hand reaches for my pen and begins writing, yet I do not feel as though the words are coming from me.

Begin writing for myself, not the paper. Explore what I want to share.
Allow myself time to read for pleasure.
Plan date nights with Tom.
Practice breathing whenever I feel unsettled.
Be a true friend.

Again, Francisco speaks, interrupting my train of thought. He's ready to go on to the next page. But I'm still here, excited to complete this section. Nevertheless, I flip to see what's next in his packet.

"For your final task this morning, I would like you to write a letter to yourself. But first, I want you to read how you responded to the questionnaire, the one you completed prior to arriving."

Suddenly, there are murmurs throughout the room.

"We were supposed to make a copy and bring it with us?" Annie asks what all of us are thinking.

However, Francisco addresses our concerns. "Please, there is no need to worry. You see, I printed your responses *but never read them.*"

It is then I hear Maggie gasp. All color drains from her face. She looks at me and whispers, "If he didn't read our questionnaires … how did he *know so much about us?*"

It's at this exact moment I realize why I'm here … to be guided by Francisco … a mystically gifted shaman. Unsure what he told Maggie to cause her to believe he'd read her questionnaire, I merely shrug my shoulders, then offer my own impish smile to her before returning my attention to our shaman.

"This exercise was meant to prepare you for our journey together. Most of you sent this survey in weeks ago, and perhaps some of your answers would have changed had you waited till later to respond. Regardless, read what you wrote and then write a letter to yourself. Did you gain what you had hoped from this experience?

Or perhaps you grew in unanticipated ways … areas you had no idea required expansion."

Francisco's eyes exude compassion mixed with wisdom. It's as though he knows we've exceeded any expectations we had for this retreat. While I don't remember exactly what I wrote, I suspect it addressed surface-level concerns, truly insignificant when compared to the deep discoveries I've made these past few days.

After looking at his watch, Francisco says, "It is now 10:35. Please take as long as you like, but when you are finished … or are at a point where you are ready to pause … I encourage you to go on with your day. We still have much to explore. If you do not have additional sessions or will not be joining the paddleboarding excursion, perhaps you wish to spend time relaxing to incorporate all that's transpired this week. No doubt you've taken in quite a bit *and* released a great deal as well." He clears his throat before continuing.

"Tonight is our closing ceremony. We'll meet at six o'clock on the beach, just before the sun sets. Afterward will be our celebratory dinner. Chef René, Vic, Alana, and others will provide you with a magnificent ocean-side buffet. We have much to be thankful for. I am extremely grateful each of you chose to come to Nueva Vida to elevate yourself, your life, your future." Francisco sets his mug on the table, then begins to pass out envelopes that contain our questionnaires.

I can't help but look at Juliette, who appears to be in a different space—she seems confused, perhaps even remorseful.

When Francisco arrives at our table, he hands each of us a white legal-sized envelope with our name printed on the front. Everyone is silent. Juliette rips hers open, quickly leafing through the stapled pages. But the rest of us carefully unseal the envelope before we pull out our questionnaires.

The room is silent as people read what they'd written prior to coming on this retreat. I hear several chuckles, a few sniffs, and lots of clearing of throats. Slowly, one by one, people put down their questionnaires, turn to the next page of their packets, and begin writing. I find myself doing the same.

I search for the appropriate way to describe this week but fall short. Mere words cannot properly capture what's transpired—the discoveries and understanding, as well as the subsequent questions that have surfaced. Still, I begin.

> The experiences in themselves have been incredible, especially the sweat lodge. And each workshop and private session exceeded all expectations. My horizon has broadened, as I now know there's so much more available to discover. It's all waiting for me. I only need to say YES.
>
> I think I'm ready.
>
> Trust, let go, believe ... Have faith in God and my intuition. That seems to be a central theme, especially the "letting go" part. And I will be tested as Patrick gets ready to leave for college. That's a big piece of the surrendering that's ahead of me. Yet what is it without trust and believing? There's now an even stronger knowing, that once this happens, Tom and I will have more time to grow in our love, a most definite silver lining to our son leaving for school.
>
> But it is not only about Patrick and Tom. My reason for coming was to find clarity, discover what's next in my life. I wanted to know the path to fulfillment as well as my purpose.

While I don't have definite answers, I now have direction. I am meant to write ... authentically ... as my true self. Unsure what I will write or where it will appear, I'm convinced this is my next step.

And friends ... not only has this week strengthened my relationship with Annie, Sophia, and Juliette, but it's also brought a new person into my life—Maggie. No doubt we have a definite connection, one I hope will continue, regardless of whether she moves to Oregon or stays in Pittsburgh. I feel as though I have something to offer her, as she does for me. We've formed a bond, though it is difficult to describe ...

I stop. A thought's come into my mind. Why didn't I realize this before?

Maggie is short for Margaret. And Margaret is the voice inside of my head that's criticized and judged my thoughts, beliefs, and actions. I now understand Margaret represents my ego's desire to keep me safe. But I believe I sent Margaret a message this week. She no longer needs to speak. I can now take care of myself.

Is it possible Margaret—who kept me small—is now gone and replaced by Maggie, a sweet, gentle soul who I can nurture, and no doubt nurtures me in her unique way? With us, there is no judgment or criticism. Only concern, care, and compassion.

While it's not complete, I feel compelled to stop. I've stumbled onto something. Maggie and I do have a connection, one deeper than I can explain. I turn toward where she's sitting. Pen in hand, she's furiously writing. Several moments later, she pauses, lifts her head, and looks at me. Her mouth moves, and I can detect her silent words.

"Thank you."

Her glistening eyes show a fortitude in her I've yet to witness. I believe she's committed to moving forward. No, I know she has. My intuition confirms any doubt.

***

My final session of the week is about to begin. It's with Daniel.

I'm not sure why Juliette signed me up to meet with a channeler. Sure, I find the concept fascinating, but how does channeling relate to me and my personal development? However, I suspect there is a reason. There always is.

Shy but kind, Daniel motions for me to join him. He's seated at a large round table in a small conference room located on the second floor of the main building. The room is plain yet inviting, kind of like Daniel. There's a vase of calla lilies on the table, which warms my heart as those were the flowers I chose for my bridal bouquet.

"I hope you're having a good day, Marlee," Daniel says. His soft and tender voice sounds nothing at all like it did when he spoke to the group as Zecheal. I suppose this man prefers one-on-one sessions. He doesn't appear to be the type who thrives in the spotlight. However, as he shared on Wednesday, this is not something he sought to do. His Guide chose him, so now he shows up to receive Zecheal's transmissions.

"Is there something in particular I can help you with, or would you like for me to tap in and see what my Guide has to say?"

he asks as his mouth slightly curves upward. It's not a full smile, but I believe this is a generous gesture for Daniel.

Knowing he's asking me what everyone else seems to inquire—*what do you need, Marlee?*—I pause and reflect before speaking. There are two options: I can ask a specific question, or I can allow him to offer me whatever insight his Guide might have. While I'm tempted to choose the latter, I then remember my confusion over what Conor and Francisco had told me during our sessions. Plus, I don't want to forget to ask if he can tap in and see if there was anything between Wyatt and Caroline, besides her being his realtor.

"Actually, I have a few questions. First, I was hoping you could offer some clarity about something that happened this past February." I take a few moments to expand upon our weekend in the Poconos, the murder, Annie's clairvoyance, and how I found the incriminating evidence against Caroline Rhimes.

"But there had to be more to their relationship. I wish I could understand why Wyatt picked Caroline as his realtor. Was it merely a coincidence or something more?" There, I've said it. It's off my chest.

"So you'd like me to tap into Wyatt … and see if he has any deeper connection to Caroline?"

"Can you do that?" I'm practically pleading, hoping Daniel can finally put this mystery to rest.

"I'll try." Daniel smiles and shuts his eyes. Suddenly, his face begins to morph, almost as though it's becoming elongated, more chiseled—he's turning into Wyatt!

"I've known Caroline for quite some time." Daniel's voice is now crisp, direct, authoritative. "She is Patricia's child. Aunt Patricia is my mother's youngest sister, making Caroline my cousin, though Caroline is twenty years younger than I. When Patricia was sixteen, she became pregnant with Caroline. Of course, my grandparents were horrified. They would not permit my aunt to keep the baby. Instead, they sent her to upstate New

York ... where young girls went to have their babies before giving them up for adoption."

"Years later, Caroline found Patricia and confronted her. The scene was quite ugly. I distinctly remember how upset my aunt was because I was there when it happened. Patricia was more a friend than my aunt, considering how close we were in age. Regardless, I heard it all—the accusations, the blame, the tears. Naturally, I felt extreme sympathy for both women."

"I kept in touch with Caroline. She seemed to need guidance. Of course, that ended up being me helping her out of problems, paying her debts, and doing whatever I could to protect my aunt from having to come to the rescue of the child she gave away. She already dealt with huge amounts of guilt. Had she known how Caroline turned out, Patricia would only have blamed herself." Daniel—speaking as Wyatt—exhales loudly. I watch as his shoulders drop down his back.

"So Caroline was Wyatt's younger cousin?" I ask, totally dumbfounded. "Is there anything else you can tell me? Was there more to why she killed him, besides him threatening to expose her activities?"

Daniel returns to being Wyatt. "At first, she wanted money. But later, when I hired a private detective to discover what she was up to, well, Caroline feared I would tell her mother what she had done. My aunt is a successful prosecutor, and her distinguished legal career made her quite wealthy. Patricia never married, so Caroline is her only offspring, making her the sole recipient of her inheritance. Caroline panicked that Patricia would cut her out of the will if she knew about her prostitution charge, among the *other things* she did."

"Oh my God. That explains everything. Thank you!" Finally—closure to what's been weighing on my mind since Presidents' weekend. I can't wait to tell the others.

"You said you had more than one question," Daniel says, now back to his true self. "What is it you would like to know?"

I take in a big breath and try to center myself before I proceed. "This isn't as easy as the last question."

Daniel smiles, tilting his head as he gazes into my eyes.

"It's about what I learned through earlier sessions this week. You see, when I met with Francisco, he said I would soon come upon new opportunities, but first I had to trust, let go, and strengthen my belief in God." I clear my throat. "And then during a massage with Sabina, she shared that my fifth chakra was blocked. She used her 'special sauce' to help clear it, but I'm not sure if this chakra is fully opened," I say, though I have no idea what an open chakra looks like. "But there's more. Conor told me that I'd be writing, but in a new way. And it has to do with cooking." I let out a big sigh.

"Daniel, I'm confused. I know these gifted individuals have offered me insights about my life purpose. However, I can't seem to put it all together. I don't want to do the wrong thing. Can you help me?"

Now Daniel's smile grows, and there's a glimmer in his eyes I hadn't detected before. Perhaps he likes challenging requests, hoping he—or his Guide—can help.

"OK." Daniel sits up straighter in his chair. "Let's see what I hear," he says before he shuts his eyes. Intently, I watch his mouth move and his eyes flutter beneath their lids. After several moments, he begins to speak—not as himself, but as Zecheal.

"You ask what you are to do with all the information you have received this past week. The choice is always yours ... You can integrate these wise words to learn why you are here and what you are meant to do ... or you can choose not to. There is nothing wrong with returning to your life as it is. But if you want to connect the dots of this week's discoveries, it is quite simple." Daniel pauses to catch his breath.

"You have a gift, Marlee. It is your ability to shine your light through your writing as your authentic self. You do not have to do anything with this gift, but if you desire to do so, the sky is the limit regarding what you can share with the world. Now is the time to decide. Again, there is no right or wrong answer, though some choices are higher in vibration than others. And if you wish to travel the higher path, it will require you to trust and believe in yourself and your abilities. This includes your intuition ... and God. It is critical for you to have faith that something higher has a Divine plan for you. It is there. It always has been. However, you have been choosing in fear, not love. That is why you must trust and believe. Only then will you find your true voice, for you will no longer be afraid of how others will view you. Your true voice knows what you are meant to share."

Again, Daniel stops, taking a break. I watch his facial muscles twitch a bit, as if he's resetting for the next bit of information to come in. "You asked about cooking and how it correlates to writing. The answer is however you wish. Perhaps ponder what you know about the subject that others may not. This is not to say how to clarify butter or ways in which to create a rich venison stew. Rather, it is what you bring when you step into the kitchen. What makes your approach unique? It is in the process, not the product."

Silence. After several moments, Daniel returns.

"I hope that was helpful," he says in *his* voice.

I nod as my eyes begin to blink. Trying to take it all in, I want to remember exactly what was said, as I'm convinced it holds truth and wisdom.

"It was. I believe I am supposed to continue writing, but not as a part-time journalist for the newspaper I've been working for." I pause, as if cementing this declaration into my head. "But there's more ... It's *how* I write and *what* I write that will change."

Daniel nods, confirming I'm properly interpreting the message from his Guide.

"I am to trust my voice ... believe I have the ability to write something meaningful, though I do not yet know what that is."

"Did you understand the message about the cooking component?" he asks, tilting his head almost like a teacher might do to ensure his student comprehends the lesson.

"That still confuses me. I think I'm supposed to reflect on what's different about the way I approach cooking. It's not merely measuring and following recipes. I guess I'm not writing a cookbook," I say with a brief laugh.

"Exactly. There seems to be something different about your relationship with cooking, though it is not my place to tell you what that is. Look within. Spend some time with this concept. Perhaps meditate on it—ask your Guides."

"My Guides?" I ask. "I don't have Guides," I say with a wave of my hand.

"But, of course, you do. We all do. You merely need to learn how to tap into them."

"But how do I even begin?" My eyes become wide with confusion, truly unsure of what he's suggesting.

"Would you like to try now?" Daniel asks with a small smirk on his face.

The more time I spend with this man, the more I realize he's not how I first imagined. He's deep, curious, and filled with knowledge about life and the supernatural.

Though I am not sure where this is heading, when will I be sitting across from a channeler again? What if he *can* show me one of my Guides—if they even exist? I can't *not* take him up on his offer. "OK. Let's do this." I sit up tall, push my shoulders down my back, and shut my eyes.

Daniel begins mumbling some words, though I cannot understand what they are. Perhaps he is speaking directly to his Guide, requesting that he help me find mine. I wait, though not patiently, preoccupied with whether I'll have a vision or if words will come through my mouth. But nothing happens.

Several moments later, I hear Daniel clear his throat. I open my eyes, only to see that he's gotten up from his chair to retrieve something from a leather briefcase that's leaning against the far wall. He returns, placing a pad of paper and a pen on the table in front of me.

"Here you go," he says, offering nothing else.

"Is there some information you'd like me to write down for you?" I ask, wondering what he wants.

Daniel grins, shaking his head. "Pick up the pen. See what happens."

Following his instructions, I place the pen in my right hand and move the notepad directly in front of me. Inhaling deeply, I shut my eyes and ask, "What am I to know?" I do my best to believe and trust. Then, before opening my eyes, I ask God for His guidance. I exhale loudly, then begin to write.

While working at the Inquirer has taught me a great deal, it is now time for me to branch out, leave what is comfortable to explore my true voice. This could present itself in many fashions. I could write for another venue, or I could create my own path, finding a unique way to share what I want to say. And there is so much to share.

No longer do I want to write about news, the negative information that creates fear and lowers our vibration. Like the article I wrote this winter, I desire to show readers another way, share practices available to help alleviate the stresses of everyday life. I now know I am meant to nurture people, to help them find their peace.

I stop writing. But it wasn't me who was writing—it was someone else. Unable to explain what happened, I place the pen down on the table, then read what I've written.

Are these words mine? I don't think so. They don't exactly sound like me. But then again, how do I sound? What is my true voice? I feel a strange sensation in my throat. However, it's not the typical constriction that so often occurs when I write. Instead, it's different, almost as if there is more space, breadth, length.

"Do you understand what happened?"

"That wasn't me who wrote this," I stammer.

"Exactly. It was your Guide channeling through you." Daniel has a proud look, as if he's made his point.

"But my Guide doesn't speak like yours does. It comes through my writing instead?" I ask, trying to make sense of what's happened.

"Correct." Daniel leans back and crosses his left ankle over his right knee. "Have you heard of individuals who channel their writing?"

"No. Until I signed up for this retreat, I'd never even heard of channeling."

"I suggest you do some research on it. It may help you better understand and settle into your gift." He's not telling me; instead, he's challenging me to own it.

"But what about the cooking?"

Daniel uncrosses his leg, then leans closer to me and says, "Why don't you ask?"

Without a moment of hesitation, I repeat what I'd done before. I shut my eyes and ask, "What am I to know?"

Several minutes later, pen in hand, I receive my answer.

This is not about recipes. It's about the love you bring to whatever you make. It is how you take care of others ... the nourishing meals you prepare from your heart. It's the way you choose your ingredients, the grace and intention with which you chop, dice, baste, and blend. This is the difference. It is your purpose, your intent, the reason you cook. You can do the same through your writing.

The pen falls from my hand. "What the hell just happened?" I ask, my voice trembling as my hand shakes.

"You are learning how to connect," Daniel says simply, as if it's the most natural thing in the world.

"Connect?"

"Yes, that's what channelers do when they wish to receive information from their Guides." As he leans back in his chair, his eyes drift toward the ceiling. "There are many techniques you can employ to help you with this process." He stops, adjusting himself in his seat before continuing: "Some people have a ritual they follow to invoke the conversation. For example, I've seen people sage, light candles, or play meditative music. Then again, if it calls to you, you could say a prayer of sorts, setting the stage for what is to come."

"I like the last one ... saying a prayer." Of course, I would. Prayer is something I'm comfortable with.

"Well then, I suggest you create something that feels natural to you. Maybe begin with an intention, stating what you hope will occur during the transmission."

"Does your Guide always show up?" I ask, wondering if I'll be ghosted.

"Mostly, though at the beginning, I remember times when it was difficult to connect." Daniel pauses, resting his chin in his cupped left hand. "But come to think of it, I don't believe it was Zecheal who was resistant. Rather, I believe I was not in the proper state of mind to receive the incoming information."

"That makes total sense. If your focus is elsewhere, how could you possibly hear your Guide?"

Daniel looks at his watch. "How are you feeling about all of this, Marlee? Learning you can channel is a lot to take in."

I release a small laugh. "I'm still not sure I believe it."

"Ah ... trust ... let go ... believe. Perhaps those words ring a bell," he says with a wink.

Why, of course, they do. That is exactly what Francisco said. Instead of being freaked out by the synchronicity, I feel a strange comfort knowing the messages from this past week are coming together like puzzle pieces creating a magnificent landscape.

"You're right," I say, then inhale deeply before tucking a strand of hair behind my ear.

"I hope our time together has been helpful. I believe my next session is with a friend of yours." There's a mischievous spark in Daniel's eyes as the corners of his mouth turn upward.

Who could that be? Juliette already met with Daniel. Besides, today's her session with Francisco. And Maggie mentioned how much she was looking forward to her massage. It's not Sophia because she is scheduled for an Ayurvedic treatment with Sabina.

"Annie's seeing you?" I ask, a tone of amusement in my voice.

"Why, yes." Daniel offers no more information. I assume holistic healers follow similar privacy rules as medical practitioners.

"I'm glad she is meeting with you," I offer, knowing Daniel cannot respond. "As you know, Annie's clairvoyant, though she struggles with her gift. Maybe you can help her better accept this ability."

"Have you accepted yours?" His grin is a mile wide. Yes, this man sitting across from me is totally different than he first appeared. There's a veneer he's built for self-protection. Yet, underneath, he exudes warmth, kindness, and a quirky sense of humor. I like Daniel. Tremendously.

***

Carlos stands by a large van, ready to drive twelve of us to a nearby river. Annie stayed behind. Not only does she have her session with Daniel, but I also remember her saying she's meeting with Camille afterward. Perhaps she has more questions about the school. During the drive, I share what I learned about the connection between Wyatt and Caroline.

"That totally makes sense. People kill for money all the time," Juliette says.

Maggie adds, "You must feel so much better knowing. I mean, finally there's closure."

"Yes, there is. And maybe now I can let it go. Do you think I should tell Travis ... and the chief of police? But would either believe me? Perhaps it's best to leave things as they are." I suppose I've answered my own question.

Twenty-five minutes later, we turn off the main road and proceed down a narrow dirt path. Large branches hang overhead, smacking the top of the van. Suddenly, the jungle stops, and I see a beach ahead. Carlos parks.

In front of us is the river. Actually, I think it's an estuary, as the water from this river flows into the ocean.

Carlos approaches two men whom he later introduces as Ricardo and Juan. Juan appears to be in his midtwenties; however, Ricardo seems much older. Both look to be Costa Rican. The younger man speaks in a shy manner, though I note he frequently glances in Maggie's direction. The elder of the two possesses a bit of mischief in his eyes, as if he holds the secrets of this sacred river. I hope Ricardo's my guide.

"Please, follow us. We will show you to the boards," Ricardo says as he motions for us to walk toward the river's bank. He's missing a front tooth, but his smile is beautiful nonetheless.

The wide beach suggests low tide. After each of us chooses a paddleboard, Juan distributes the paddles. He blushes when he gets to Maggie.

"This half"—Ricardo points to Sophia, me, the two women from Australia, and a couple from Ohio—"come." I awkwardly pick up my board, ensuring I do not drop my paddle, and fall in line behind Sophia. Turning around, I mouth "good luck" to Juliette and Maggie as we part ways.

Ricardo stops, then gathers us around him. He instructs us on how to mount our boards. Afterward, he tells us to get into the water and try for ourselves. Once we're all safely kneeling on our boards, he gives us a quick "what to do" as well as "what not to do" speech. While we each signed a waiver before we left the resort, he emphasizes specific precautions we must take. Still, I've paddled before. It's not that difficult.

After we find our balance, he tells us to stand and paddle in a large circle, then switch directions once we are comfortable

"Everyone looks good! Let's begin!" As he joins us in the water, a wild grin emerges on his face. It's then he starts to sing. Although I cannot understand the words, I adore the sound of his voice. Ricardo's fun and upbeat, and it's as though his song's inviting us into a new world—perhaps his world—the river.

As we make our first turn, Ricardo points to the bank on my right. "See … a mama crocodile. Please, move to the left. We do not want to disturb her."

"No one mentioned crocodiles," Sophia says, carefully navigating her board toward the opposite shore.

"Crocodiles! How fantastic!" It's Samantha, the woman from Australia. I turn toward her and see she's holding her phone over-head, taking pictures of this gigantic reptile.

"Please," Ricardo says, "let's all be safe."

With that, she tucks the phone into the back pocket of her shorts that cover her one-piece bathing suit and picks up the oar she'd placed by her feet. Finally, after another admonishment from Ricardo, she begins paddling, moving away from the mama croc.

For the next ninety minutes, we slowly navigate the winding river. The mangroves' thick branches narrow our passageway. Large, unusual insects crawl about the foliage. Thankfully, they ignore us. Sophia, graceful as ever, carves her oar through the water as though it's second nature. I never thought of her as athletic, but there is a distinct fluidness to the way she moves.

Ricardo leads us back the way we came. Finally, I see the ocean in the distance, indicating we're almost done. However, the tide must have come in, as less beach is visible. When we get close to our starting point, I look to my left and see the large crocodile has not budged. At least ten feet long, this reptile's eyes appear to be shut, though I doubt she's sleeping. It's then, out of the corner of my eye, I see Samantha veer left, toward the crocodile. She seems to be videotaping this creature and is definitely not looking where she's going.

"Samantha!" I yell, as I make three strong strokes toward her. "Stay away!" I cannot help but worry. She could get hurt. Of course, she doesn't listen.

Thankfully, Ricardo steps in, as I certainly didn't know what I was going to do to stop her. "My dear lady, you must turn around. It is not safe for you to be so close."

Only then do I realize how fast I'm going—toward the wrong bank, the one with the crocodile. The current's picked up, most likely from the incoming tide. Luckily, I see a large piece of still driftwood ahead. It's not moving, so I guess it must be imbedded in the river's floor.

My mind flashes back to summers in the Poconos. Having spent years grabbing docks and other objects to stop my rowboat when it was moving too quickly, I reach for the driftwood. However, I am not in a rowboat, safely held within its aluminum sides. Instead, I am standing on a paddleboard—a completely different situation. My body stops at the driftwood, but my board propels ahead.

Splash!

Pure terror overcomes me, knowing the sound of me falling in could jolt the mama croc into the water and toward me. Within seconds, another thought comes to mind—there is rarely only one crocodile. What if there are others nearby, underwater?

I surface, lifting my head to search for my board. Upon spotting it, I swim as fast as possible, clumsily hoisting my body on top of it. There's no thought as to whether my bikini top—or bottom—has come along with me. Honestly, right now, I don't care.

Ricardo paddles over to me.

"You are safe. Do not worry."

Lying on my belly, I quickly glance at my chest, ensuring I'm not topless. But my bathing suit's there, mostly in place.

I'm breathing heavily, still panicked about what could have happened. Sophia's now a few feet from me.

"Are you alright, Marlee?" she asks as she kneels, stabilizing her board against mine.

I swallow, then nod. "What was I thinking?" I don't even realize I've said this aloud.

"You were concerned for Samantha and wanted to ensure she was safe." Sophia tilts her head in the most compassionate way. "That is who you are … You think of others before yourself."

Do I? But don't all mothers do that naturally? Isn't that part of the assignment once we agree to parenthood? And it doesn't merely apply to our offspring. It becomes part of our DNA. We become protectors, fixers, mama bears.

Once I've caught my breath, I adjust my bathing suit, then carefully stand up before paddling back to the beach. When we arrive, I spot Juliette and Maggie huddled together, laughing. It's good to see Juliette connecting with a woman her age.

***

I pull my favorite dress off the hanger, slip it over my head, then head to the bathroom to apply a bit of makeup. Tonight's the final celebration, and I want to look my best.

According to my watch, Annie and Sophia won't be here for another thirty minutes.

When I come out of the bathroom, Juliette's all ready, dressed in a long raspberry-pink sari. "You look stunning!"

"I bought this in India," she quietly says. "It's for special occasions."

I'm not used to Juliette speaking in a soft voice. I turn toward her, only to see her cheeks are damp.

"What's wrong?" I ask. As soon as I move toward her, she begins to shake and tears pour from her eyes.

"Can … I … talk … to you?" she stammers before collapsing into my arms.

Sensing fear in Juliette's unusual outburst, I stammer, "Of course …"

She sniffs several times before saying, "I messed up … I didn't mean to … It just happened."

Her words confirm what I'd suspected. She was with René. But instead of asking questions, I hold her, allowing her time to proceed when she's ready.

"It was so wrong … unfair to Michael. I'd kill him if he cheated on me." She swallows several times, then pulls back and stares at me—wide-eyed—as if to gauge whether I'm judging her.

Although I want to ask why, the answer seems obvious. Juliette's always been jealous of other women around Michael. So she did the exact thing she feared Michael would do … She cheated on him … before *he* could hurt *her*.

I guide Juliette to the edge of her bed and take a seat next to her.

"What do I do?" Juliette asks, then hides her face with her hands.

"Are you unsure about marrying Michael … or was there another reason you were with René?"

Juliette sniffs, then looks up, and for the first time ever, I sense her fear. "How did you know it was René?"

I just tilt my head and look at her.

"And what makes you think Michael would ever want to marry me … after what I've done?"

"But I asked if *you* were questioning this marriage."

Softly, she whispers, "I want to be with him … but I'm afraid."

I place my hand on her shoulder. "What are you afraid of, Juliette?"

"That he'll leave … like my mother left my dad and me."

Plain and simple, Juliette has a fear of abandonment. Her mother deserted her, and then her father died, leaving her all alone. Remembering my earlier hunch, I feel compelled to say it aloud.

"Perhaps you thought that if you cheated on Michael, then if he ever decided to cheat on you … or leave you … you'd be *even*?" While I don't like that word, I cannot find anything better. "What I mean is, if you hurt him first, then he couldn't hurt you any more than you hurt him."

Returning to tears, Juliette slowly nods her head up and down.

"I see," is all I say as I take a moment to consider what's ahead for this couple. After several minutes of silence, I say a quick prayer, asking God to give me some sage advice to offer Juliette.

I pause, shut my eyes, take a deep breath, and then allow the words to flow. "If you are sure that you still want to marry Michael, it is important to explain what happened and why it happened and assure Michael it will never happen again. This must be done in the most humble and genuine manner. Show your vulnerability, who you are inside the protective armor that shields your true self. It won't be easy. And by doing so, you risk losing him. But … if this marriage is meant to be … and if you are truly sorry and committed to Michael … then what occurred may only be the impetus that helps your relationship transition to a higher, purer, and more truthful level." I pause, open my eyes, then add, "This is going to force you to get real with him, bare your soul, and let him see the scared child you pretend does not exist." This last bit of advice is truly mine.

Juliette stares at me. I'm not sure if she's shocked by my words or if she's searching for a maternal figure to tell her it will all be OK. And so that is exactly what I do.

"You know, even if Michael decides to call off the wedding, this happened for a reason. It's part of your path, helping you to grow into your higher self." Once again, Juliette sniffs and nods her head yes.

"I was so stupid." Juliette swallows several times as she wipes her tears with the back of her hand.

I look at her. Her normally perfect makeup is smeared all over her face, and the crystal-blue eyes that light up every room she enters are now cloudy and bloodshot. I can't help but notice her gorgeous sari is stained with teardrops.

"Yeah, you were," I acknowledge with both a grimace and a lightness in my voice. The last thing she needs is for me to judge her. "Does Maggie know?"

"She has no idea." Juliette hangs her head. "All week long, René's been pursuing me. On Monday, he asked for my cell. Then he started texting … nonstop." She looks down. "But I responded, played the game." Her voice quivers as her eyes stay fixed on the floor. After several moments, she continues.

"After the Full Moon Ceremony, Maggie and I had a margarita at the bar. René saw us and came over to talk. When Maggie said she was tired, I told her I'd walk back with her but wanted to spend some time by the beach … to meditate." Juliette momentarily glances at me, tears streaming down her cheeks. "She didn't suspect anything when I headed to the ocean. But what I didn't tell her was that René was waiting for me … and not to meditate." Her shame-filled eyes turn away from me, no doubt embarrassed by her actions. "But I didn't sleep with him. We just kissed."

"And last night?" I softly ask, recalling what Maggie had shared this morning.

Juliette's eyes return to the floor. "I told her the same lie … that I wanted to meditate on the beach. It was all I could think of." She shakes her head. "I'm such an idiot." She again dissolves into tears.

I hold this stubborn, overly confident yet emotionally fragile young woman, slowly rocking her. We remain this way for several minutes.

Then gently, I pull back, lightly gripping her shoulders as I ask, "So where are things with René?" I recall their tender goodbye earlier today.

"I told him it couldn't continue … that I was engaged … and what happened was wrong." Juliette begins crying again.

I nod my head before saying, "Michael loves you, and you love him. Don't be afraid to share your truth. Otherwise, your marriage will be built on a lie." I believe someone above is helping me, as these words seem unnatural to me.

"I promise. I'll tell him as soon as we get back."

"Juliette, you don't need to promise me a thing … You owe it to yourself … and Michael … to be honest." With that, I smile and sit up a bit, releasing Juliette's shoulders. "I think another dress may be in order," I say before looking at my watch. "Annie and Sophia should soon be here."

"I don't want them … or Maggie … to know," she quickly says.

"Don't worry. I won't say a thing, not to them, or anyone else. Not even Tom." I lean toward Juliette and give her a kiss on her forehead and say, "This may be one of the hardest things you'll ever have to do … baring your soul to Michael, knowing he very well may leave you after you do so. But if that isn't pure, vulnerable love, then I'm not sure what is." I pause, take a deep breath, then add, "And knowing Michael, he'll be pissed, but I think he'll forgive you. And if he does … then *you know* you were meant to be together … and your future will be brighter than you ever imagined."

***

"Are you afraid to sleep here at night?" Annie asks, wide-eyed when she sees there is no lock on the door or secure covers for the windows.

"Not in the least. The sounds are soothing. It's one of the things I'm going to miss when we return." Surprisingly, it's me who says this.

"I'm going to miss the food," Annie says. "It's been amazing."

"It most certainly has," Sophia says, then turns toward me. "Did you ask Chef Moreau for his recipes?"

Before I can answer, Maggie arrives, looking absolutely stunning in a strapless cream-colored dress that falls just above her ankles.

"Wow, you clean up good," Juliette, perfectly put together, says as she comes from the bathroom. Her eyes once again sparkle as she teases Maggie.

While I'm unsure how Michael will react to Juliette's confession, deep down, I know Juliette will be fine. It won't be easy.

However, dealing with her fear of abandonment may be exactly what she must do to move forward.

"Annie, how was your time with Daniel?" I ask, hoping she had a positive experience.

"It was … um … fabulous." Her eyes begin to dance.

"What did he say?" Juliette asks, shifting her focus from Maggie to Annie.

"Lots of things." Annie pauses, sits down on my bed, then flops back, resting her head on my pillow. "He told me that when it first happened to him, he was terrified." She stares straight at the ceiling. "But that after a while, it became second nature and didn't scare him anymore."

"Did he tap into his Guide to help you understand your gift?" I ask, wondering if our sessions were similar.

"At the end he did, but mostly we just talked … like real people."

"It must have felt wonderful to spend time with someone who has learned how to accept his abilities … and then utilize them to help others," Sophia says as she sits next to Annie on the bed.

Annie springs up. "Yes! Finally, I could talk to somebody who's gone through a similar experience. And Daniel told me not to worry … It keeps getting easier, more natural. Eventually, it will seem like I've always been able to do it." There's a peace to Annie I've never seen before.

"Are you comfortable sharing what his Guide said to you?" I ask, incredibly curious.

"Zecheal said I'm here for a reason … to use my gift to help with my practice. When I heard that, it all made sense. In fact, I'd already been doing it, I just didn't know what was *underneath* my actions. And now that I do, well, I can't wait to get home and meet with my patients."

Shocked with what's coming from Annie's mouth, I can only imagine Jonathon's reaction when his wife arrives home.

"But there was one more thing ... something I had to ask." Annie becomes serious as she leans back against the headboard.

"What was it?" Sophia asks, placing her hand on Annie's.

"I asked how my parents will react to the baby."

Sophia takes in a big breath, then looks toward me as she exhales. I, too, have been wondering if this was a concern for Annie. After all, since Annie married Jonathon, her parents have been quite distant.

It's then I see the confusion on Maggie's face. "I don't understand," she begins. "Who wouldn't welcome a grandchild?"

Annie turns toward Maggie. "My parents never accepted the fact that I married Jonathon. They're ... well ... stuck in their ways." Annie frowns as she shares this, avoiding the word *prejudice*. "Jonathon's Black."

"My family's Irish Catholic ... and growing up, some of them had little tolerance for those of other faiths or backgrounds." Maggie exhales loudly. "It always drove me nuts. I couldn't understand their reasoning." She shakes her head.

"I've struggled too," Annie says. "In essence, my parents forced me to decide between them and Jonathon. There was no doubt in my mind ... I chose my husband."

"So what did Daniel say? How will your parents react to the baby?" I ask, taking a seat on the bed next to Annie.

Annie's eyes light up as she replies, "Apparently, this baby is what brings us back together. She'll be a bridge of sorts. Of course, it won't be easy ... or happen overnight. But Daniel assured me that over time, things will change."

"Thank God," Sophia says as she releases a long sigh.

After an uncomfortable pause, Juliette shifts gears. "I don't know about you, but I can't wait for the closing ceremony. The last time I was here, it was magical. But now that I'm here with all of you, I can only imagine how great it's going to be!" Her eyes sparkle as she makes this pronouncement. Thankfully, Juliette has returned to her old self. A part of me feared she'd break down in front of the others.

One by one, we file out of our room, down the steps, and toward the beach. Unsure of what's ahead, all I know is this ceremony will provide a closure of sorts—or maybe the start of something new.

Still, I can't help but wonder about Juliette and Michael. I'd never say this aloud, but I give their relationship a 50 percent chance. To my knowledge, no woman has ever cheated on Michael. I'm not sure how his ego will take the news. Regardless, if Juliette cannot be honest with him now, then it may be best they part ways.

MAGGIE

Friday, April 23
Saturday, April 24

Wooden folding chairs form a circle around the unlit bonfire. There's a large rectangular table several feet in front of the calm surf. It is covered with bouquets of flowers as well as various objects, though I cannot decipher what they are. Francisco and Dominique stand by the table. He's dressed in dark gray linen trousers with a long sleeve white cotton shirt, the first few buttons undone, revealing his tanned chest. Dominique's lavender dress flows gracefully in the warm breeze. The sun's last rays bounce off her stunning silver pendant earrings.

After everyone's arrived, Francisco steps toward the center of the circle.

"This week together has exceeded all expectations. Our talented speakers have outdone themselves, sharing their knowledge and gifts during our morning workshops. Perhaps these sessions have helped you move forward on your path?" Francisco asks as he stands a bit taller. "And I would be remiss if I did not mention how much I enjoyed our one-on-one sessions." He smiles, turning to those seated around him. "Each one of you possesses a magnificent essence meant to carry you far in life. It is my greatest hope I was able to offer you *something* to make your journey here on Earth a bit easier. If I provided you with an ounce of clarity regarding your next steps, then *mission accomplished.*" He grins before giving us one of his classic winks.

"I suspect some of you are like rocket ships, ready to take off." A few in the group giggle. "Others, I assume, will require time to assimilate all you have learned. There is no right or wrong way to leave Nueva Vida. Yet know each of you has elevated, grown, and discovered aspects of yourself you had no idea existed."

He walks toward Dominique, who is standing in front of the long table, and takes her hand. "Before we begin our closing ceremony, I'd like to share a bit more about my journey to becoming a shaman." A devilish grin appears on his face. "Perhaps some of you are curious?"

Juliette sits straight up in her chair, her full attention on Francisco.

"Had I told you this story when you first arrived, I fear some may have headed back to the airport," he says with a laugh.

A gleam returns to his eyes. In a rare moment of public display, he kisses Dominique gently on the cheek, then begins to speak with ease, his words elegantly flowing. Francisco first recounts pieces of what he told us Saturday evening. But no longer is he setting the stage for how Nueva Vida began. Instead, he is sharing *his* anguish after losing his first wife, *his* anger toward "modern" medicine, and *his* fear of leaving the life he knew to follow an unknown path.

"I was an anomaly. Not many wealthy men from Santiago travel to the jungle in search of a shaman to teach them *the ways*. At first, those I sought for guidance were leery, misreading me and my intentions. Or perhaps their intent was merely to test how determined I was to *unlearn*.

"Unlike most who venture down this path, I did not come from a bloodline of shamans. Nor did I experience dreams announcing this as my calling. I had no idea what an icaro was, and I lacked any understanding of plant medicine. However, deep inside, I yearned *to know* how shamans heal, as my medical education, while helpful in some ways, lacked all the answers. I could treat symptoms, yet I could not always identify or cure the cause." He momentarily pauses, taking several breaths before continuing.

"Eventually I met Don Miguel. Of course, he demanded I prove myself, show my commitment and willingness to sacrifice the comforts of my former life to live in the jungle. At the time, I figured I'd lost everything important to me, so it was not difficult to accept a new way. In fact, I welcomed the simplicity ... the solitude ... the ancient methods."

All eyes are locked on Francisco. The only noise comes from the waves lapping over the sand.

"I adopted their dieta ... gave up red meat, oils, sugar, alcohol, caffeine ... even sex." Francisco laughs heartily as he shakes his head, then glances at Dominique, who is now blushing. "After mastering the icaros—the healing songs sung during rituals—I learned about the sacred plants and how to make ayahuasca, a ceremonial drink used to help discover your soul's journey. Once I had this knowledge, I received the Munay-ki Rites and visited local villages, doing my best to heal the people."

Francisco pauses, runs his fingers through his hair, then smiles. "Pardon me, I usually don't explain this process to others. Surely, I am using words that are new to you. *Munay* stands for universal love, and *ki* is Japanese for healing. These rites are about healing through the universal love that surrounds us."

He spends the next several minutes discussing the nine separate rites, or passages, he underwent during his initiation into shamanism. The first is the Bands of Power, where he received five separate bands of energy: one each for earth, air, fire, water, and pure light. Immediately my mind jumps to the band Earth, Wind & Fire. Could there be a deeper meaning to their name?

Next, he explains the Healer's Rite. Apparently, this is meant to heal the healer. The third rite, the Harmony Rite, involves the seven chakras and corresponding archetypes. Obtained as "seeds" that must be nurtured through a flame of a fire, Francisco tells us of the serpent, jaguar, hummingbird, and eagle, each repressing our first through fourth chakras. By now, I'm on the edge of my seat. Since I understand the chakra system, I can finally relate to what he's saying. The fifth, sixth, and seventh archetypes have Indian-sounding names. Their purpose is to clear the energy centers, allowing the recipient to emanate a rainbow-like glow of pure energy.

"Being a shaman is about healing others' wounds while increasing their energetic fields. But our purpose is not only to fix what is wrong. Shamanic healing also helps our body's systems repair as we age." I wonder if that is why Francisco looks so young. While I do not know his exact age, from the stories he has shared this week, he must be at least seventy.

Several minutes later, after explaining the remaining rites— many of which are a bit too complicated for me to comprehend— Francisco pauses and says, "I have given you a textbook version of shamanism. But like so much, it is not the *what* but the *how*."

Annie, who is seated to my right, nudges her elbow against mine. Equally confused, I shrug my shoulders, having no idea where this is headed.

"While I am trained in plant medicine, it is not something I typically offer those who come to see me." Francisco really hasn't explained what ayahuasca is or its purpose. But, from the little I know about this concoction, it's not something I'm rushing to try.

"Instead, my goal this week has been to help you release the pain your energetic body's been carrying. Of course, I am not referring to physical pain, though I can assist in this area. Instead, I prefer to focus on the traumas we each hold, what is often called 'the issues in our tissues.' We all have them." With outreached hands, he grins ear to ear. "It is so very important we let go of these pains we hold deep inside. For if we ignore them or push them down further into the recesses of our being, eventually they will fester, manifesting in fears, anger, anxiety, or even dis-ease." Francisco stops to look around the circle, a very familiar behavior. I guess that's his way to make a point.

I turn toward Juliette, whose earlier exuberance has subsided. No doubt he's hit a chord with her. Come to think of it, she's been a bit off the past two days. I'm not sure what is occurring, but I feel as though she's carrying a heavy burden. However, I quickly dismiss this thought, returning my attention to Francisco.

"And now, I hope you have a better understanding of what I do as well as my role here at Nueva Vida. My goal when creating Elevar was to provide you with a breadth of experiences to assist in healing your body, releasing your pain, and guiding you toward your soul's purpose." In a regal manner, he takes a bow before continuing: "I believe it's time to begin our ceremony."

Francisco, with Dominique now by his side, begins chanting the most beautiful song. Dominique shakes a pearl-colored rattle in beat with Francisco's rhythm. Their harmony sounds like a blessing, an invocation of sorts. I suppose he is asking for the spirits to join us during our final night together. As his chanting grows in intensity, he removes a box of matches from his pants pocket, strikes one, then tosses it into the unlit bonfire in front of him. Immediately, flames flare against the early evening sky. Moments later, I sense the fire's warmth on my skin.

I stare into the crackling bonfire, mesmerized by the colors of the dancing flames. Suddenly, Francisco stops singing, and Dominque shakes the gourd three final times.

"I want to thank each of you for being part of Elevar. As you may suspect, no two retreats are the same. However, our time together has been much more than the workshops and activities … What's made this week special is you. We"—he pauses to look at Dominique—"are grateful you have trusted us to assist with your journey." Again, he bows. Dominque does as well.

"Before you leave tomorrow, we wish to offer each of you a token of our appreciation."

"This is the best part," Juliette says with a giggle. It's so strange how she can transition from one state of being to another. It's as though there are two different Juliettes in one body.

Dominique moves toward the table, takes an item, then hands it to Francisco. He calls someone named Terrence O'Brien, motioning for the young man to join him in the circle. "Terrence, I know coming to Elevar was not your idea. You attended because your wife asked you to do so."

I hear a few sweet sighs, no doubt from women wishing their husband or boyfriend had joined them on this retreat.

"But if I am correct," Francisco says with a slight smirk, "you have uncovered answers you did not expect to find." He hands Terrence a small pair of binoculars. Annie snorts in response. Quickly, she covers her mouth with her hand.

"These are awesome—thanks!" Terrence replies, then gives Francisco a hug.

While I don't know the significance of the binoculars, apparently Terrence does. And that's all that matters. This process repeats itself, as Francisco bestows a meaningful gift to each guest. He then calls Marlee's name. I watch as she eagerly stands and walks toward him.

"My dear Marlee," he begins. "I believe you have found some direction this week, correct?" Marlee slowly nods her head yes as her face glows, not from the fire, but from her beautiful essence. "I offer this to you," he says, handing her a leather-bound book. "This journal is empty, waiting for you to fill the pages." Marlee graciously accepts the gift, then hugs Francisco before offering a warm embrace to Dominique, who gives her a bouquet of flowers. As Marlee returns to her seat, Francisco says, "I cannot wait to read your first novel. Be sure to send me a copy." She laughs, giving him the thumbs-up sign.

"You're going to write a book?" Annie leans over me to ask Marlee. Marlee shrugs her shoulders as if to say *who knows*, but there's a determination in her eyes. I know the true answer is *most definitely*.

Next, Francisco beckons Sophia to join him. In a majestic manner, she glides toward the center of the circle. I watch Dominique's expression as she offers Sophia flowers. Standing next to one another, they almost look like sisters. It's strange I hadn't noticed this before.

"The lovely Sophia. For you, I have an amethyst pendulum. If you ever find yourself unsure of anything ... such as whether someone is suffering from a physical or energetic ailment ... this pendulum will help guide you. Her name is Faith." He smiles, then winks before whispering something in her ear. Sophia embraces both Francisco and Dominique, giving each a kiss on the cheek.

"Annie Thompson ... come on down," he says with a laugh, doing his best impression of the host from the TV show *The Price is Right*.

Annie scurries toward Francisco, only to pause and turn back, as if looking for encouragement. I watch as Marlee motions for her to proceed.

First, Dominique hands her a bouquet of flowers, and then Francisco shows her what appears to be a fabric bracelet. I'm too far away to clearly see what it is, but it doesn't look like a typical bracelet.

"Annie, my mother-to-be." She blushes, placing her hands on her belly. "You have come far this week, confronting many fears while becoming open to new ways. But most importantly, I believe you are accepting your special gift. However, should you have concerns, I want you to wear this bracelet." He holds something up to the group before placing it on Annie's wrist.

Squinting, I realize it's a worry doll bracelet. I remember seeing those in a boutique in Shadyside while doing some

Christmas shopping last year. What a perfect present for Annie. I watch as she lifts her hand closer to her face, carefully examining the individual fabric dolls sewn together to form the bracelet. Annie goes onto her tiptoes to give Francisco a huge squeeze, something I wouldn't have expected.

Only Juliette and I are left. Butterflies flit about my stomach. Not a fan of attention, I feel myself shrinking into my chair.

"Maggie Carr, please join me," Francisco says as Dominique reaches for a bouquet and a small box.

I walk across the circle and around the fire to stand between Francisco and Dominique, who graciously offers me the second to last bouquet. Francisco holds up a small beige box, motioning me to open it. Instead of dread, there's a surge of excitement. I wonder what he has for me.

Cradling the bouquet in the crook of my left elbow, I take the box with my left hand, and carefully remove the lid with my right. Inside is a stone pyramid, though I have no idea what it means. Dominque offers to take the lid so I can remove the pyramid from the box. It's gorgeous. This bright orange stone, with grains of white running through it, must be three inches wide and equal in height. There's a heaviness to it, though I doubt its purpose is to secure piles of papers.

"Maggie, the sweet architect. The top of this carnelian pyramid signifies that you are limitless … You can do … be … achieve … whatever it is you desire. And the strong foundation is to remind you that no matter where you go or what you do, you have a solid base holding you up. Yes, you have friends"—he pauses to look at Marlee, Annie, Sophia, and Juliette—"but more importantly, you have yourself. Everything you will ever require is within *you*. Now go and build your future." He leans down to hug me. At that moment, if I could choose my father, I'd want him to be exactly like Francisco.

As I return to my seat, I watch Juliette sit up straighter as she pushes her hair behind her ears. She is the only one whose name has not been called.

"And last but not least, my dear Juliette."

Juliette practically springs off her folding chair and saunters toward the couple as if she's about to receive an Oscar.

When she joins Francisco, Juliette's wide-eyed, looking like a little girl anxious to see what Santa's brought her. Dominique hands her the final bouquet, then gives a folded piece of fabric to her husband. In a wave of his hand, Francisco opens the bundle, revealing the most gorgeous turquoise and rose tapestry. But it's what's woven into the tapestry that catches my eye—the profile of two women with a large heart in the background. Juliette looks at the tapestry, then back at Francisco. He merely nods his head. I watch as she bites her lower lip, then nods back at him. Unsure of what's going on, I turn to Marlee, hoping she may be able to interpret Juliette's bizarre reaction. However, Marlee's cheeks are wet with tears. What does she know that I don't?

Juliette slowly returns to her seat, eyes cast down on the sand, as though she's purposely avoiding us. I've never seen her behave this way. As soon as she sits down, her hands fly to her face, and I can hear her crying. Annie, who is seated next to Juliette, gently rubs her back.

Everyone seems to notice Juliette's behavior. Francisco, who must be aware of what's occurring, calls for our attention and asks us to stand. He then offers a few words of thanks, honoring our ancestors, spirit guides, animal totems, and others.

By now, the sun has almost set, perhaps symbolic of the end of our retreat.

"And now we celebrate each other!" It's Dominque who breaks the silence after her husband's final blessing.

Music begins to play. To my surprise, Juan is playing the guitar, and Ricardo is at the drums. I hadn't noticed a five-piece band set up during our ceremony.

"Shall we join the festivities?" Marlee asks, motioning to the people already dancing.

I turn and grab Juliette's hand, hoping to lift her mood. "Come on—let's have some fun. Soon you'll be an old married lady," I tease as I pull her toward the band.

***

My phone alarm sounds. It's six o'clock. I'm exhausted—mentally, emotionally, and physically. After the party, Annie and Sophia went back to Marlee and Juliette's room. As much as I wanted to join them, I couldn't keep my eyes open one more minute, so I called it a night.

Right before I left, Juliette said she wanted advice regarding her session with Francisco. I'm not sure why she didn't mention it earlier. But I guess that's the way Juliette is. She seems to compartmentalize her feelings, only allowing them to surface when it's convenient. Nevertheless, I'll have time to catch up on what Francisco told her. I'm on the same flight to Houston as they are. Plus, we can talk on the way to the airport.

Luckily, I packed after the paddleboard trip, so there are only a few items to tuck into my suitcase. While breakfast is normally not served until eight, the kitchen is opening at six thirty to accommodate those with early flights.

The sun's rising as I make my way toward the main hotel. It's quiet; the only sounds come from birds chirping in the trees.

Annie and Sophia are already having breakfast when I arrive. Before joining them, I grab a plate, filling it with fresh fruit, eggs, and delicious pastries. Tomorrow, I'll be back to cereal and black coffee.

"Good morning," Annie says, sounding chipper. "Are you taking the seven-thirty shuttle to the airport?"

"Yes, I believe we're all on the same flight to Houston. What time is your connection to Philadelphia? My flight to Pittsburgh doesn't leave till six thirty."

"I believe our plane departs at 5:45. We do not have much time in between flights," Sophia says.

"Are Marlee and Juliette still sleeping?" I wonder if I should have knocked on their door before coming.

"I suspect they were up late talking after we left their room." Sophia pauses, as if wondering whether she should say more. "I assume you are not aware of what happened yesterday during Juliette's session with Francisco," she says, though it's more of a question than a statement.

I shake my head no.

"Juliette asked Francisco if she could become a shaman. It's been a dream of hers," Annie blurts out.

"Juliette told me about the energy work she was doing, but she never mentioned anything about wanting to be a shaman. Isn't that a huge commitment?"

"It is. Francisco emphasized that to Juliette during their session," Sophia says before taking in a big breath. "Additionally, he shared that before she could embark on this journey, she must face her biggest fear."

"What's that?" I ask, my eyebrows scrunching together.

"Abandonment. She must find her mother and reconcile," Annie says, wide-eyed.

I'm frozen. Juliette is faced with the exact dilemma I am. Of course, the details are different, but the concept is the same. For each of us to proceed, we must find a parent and see if we can have some sort of relationship with them. Knowing how much I dread contacting a man who has no idea I exist, let alone that I'm his daughter, at least I have a good shot he *might* be receptive. But Juliette's mother *left her*. She already has a tainted relationship with her mom. What are the odds that this woman will want to reunite? Now I realize the significance of Francisco's gift. That was a mother and a daughter on the tapestry. And the heart, behind them, signified the missing love.

"But can Juliette do it?" I ask. "Her mom sounds pretty troubled."

"Exactly," Sophia says before blotting her lips with a napkin. "Juliette's mother left her child and husband. I know she suffers from addiction, but she refused to seek help." Sophia's voice trails off. I believe this is the first time I've ever heard Sophia be critical of another.

"Juliette knows what she must do. She's just dreading it." Annie's surprisingly firm in her statement.

"Does she still want to be a shaman, knowing it's contingent on her reaching out to her mom?" I inquire.

"That is what weighs so deeply on Juliette. She is beginning to question her journey and doubt her dharma," Sophia says. She places the napkin in her lap, then takes a sip of coffee.

As if on cue, Marlee and Juliette enter the dining area. While Marlee looks a bit tired, Juliette looks absolutely drained. When Juliette removes her dark sunglasses, her normally radiant face looks sallow, and there are large circles under her eyes.

Juliette heads directly to the coffee station, bypassing the food. Marlee, however, takes her time going through the buffet line. I watch as she seemingly sighs, no doubt aware this is our last meal at Nueva Vida.

Juliette sits at our table, coffee in hand, head cast downward. She's wearing a baseball hat, backward, and her hair is pulled into a ponytail.

"Tough night?" I ask, unsure what to say.

"Yeah," Juliette mutters, then brings the brim of the cup to her lips.

"Do you know what you want to do?" Annie asks, perhaps a bit too impatiently. Something tells me Juliette's not quite ready to talk about it.

She merely shakes her head no.

Marlee joins us with a plate full of fresh fruit, poached eggs, a variety of seasonal vegetables, and the most delicious-looking corn scone. She sets her breakfast and mug of coffee on the table, pulls out an empty chair, then sits.

"How's everyone this morning?" she asks. Her voice seems a bit forced, unnaturally cheery.

We all murmur contrived phrases, those used when no one knows exactly what to say. Small talk ensues. However, Juliette remains silent, staring into her mug of coffee.

"They said they'd get our bags, correct? All we need to do is meet by the van?" I already know the answer but am running out of things to say. It's more than Juliette's mood, which feels enormously heavy. Soon I must leave four of the most incredible women I've ever met. I know I'll see them again, but it won't be for a while. Unexpectedly, tears fill my eyes.

It's Marlee who reaches across the table to give my hand a squeeze. "What's wrong?" she asks, then says, "I know ... you also have a lot to deal with when you return."

In between sniffs, I whisper, "Yes." But it's more. I don't want to leave my new friends.

"Isn't it strange," Annie begins, "how two of us now have a huge burden, a difficult task that needs to be completed in order to move forward on our ... what is that word called?"

"Dharma." Juliette speaks, but her eyes remain glued to the floor.

"Yes, *our dharma*, thank you." Annie pauses, then a confused look comes across her face. "Sophia, Marlee, and I have been given different challenges. It's as if we must go within to trust ourselves to move forward ... Marlee to write, Sophia to shift to a more naturopathic practice, and me to embrace my clairvoyance. And we're the oldest." It's then a grin emerges. "Perhaps that's the difference ... You two are still in your twenties. You have so much time and so many decision points ahead of you. Maybe that's why your work is harder."

Juliette lifts her head, eyes squinted, as she turns to Annie.

"What I mean is ... the three of us are all happily married, and soon, we'll all be moms. So much of our path is already decided. Sure, we can make tweaks here and there, but mostly in our professional arenas ... and how we wish to spend our time. Both you and Maggie have so many options ahead of you. The sky's the limit. That's why Francisco wants you to clean up your past so you can forge ahead, free of any baggage."

"Baggage?" I ask, now totally confused.

"Yes. So much of *our* past cannot be changed. It is what it is. But if you or Juliette have stuff holding you back, you'll never truly find what it is you're here to discover ... that dharma thing ... until you release the pain inside."

Annie's last statement causes Juliette to shift. Her eyes light up a bit, and her scowl softens.

"I believe what Annie says is true," Sophia adds. "Much of our trajectory has been decided. Of course, we always have the option to make *significant changes*, but I do not think any of us want to do that." She pauses, looking at Annie and Marlee, who both shake their heads no.

"I like my life," Annie says. "Sure, there are things I must deal with, but I love being married to Jonathon, and I can't think of having a better job, even if I need to learn how to set boundaries." She offers a brief laugh. "And now that I know I'm having a daughter with special gifts like mine, well … that only prompts me to want to better understand my clairvoyance so I can help her navigate her path." It's as though Annie's transforming before my eyes.

"I agree with Annie," Sophia says before she takes a sip of coffee. "My family is everything to me … The only thing I would change is having my children closer." For a brief second, her glow dims, but then it resurfaces. Now I understand her comment regarding Juliette's mom. "I am elated to study with Jack. It is exactly what I require to move forward and create the practice I know is possible. While this is significant, it is not a life-altering change for me."

I turn to Marlee, who has been unusually quiet. Maybe she's just exhausted.

When she sees me searching in her eyes, she speaks: "I think I have found exactly what I've been missing." The muscles in her face relax with these words. "I am giving myself permission to quit working at the *Inquirer*, so I have time to figure out a few things." Now she's grinning.

"Like what?" I ask, eyes wide with curiosity.

"Like what my book is going to be about." Her face illuminates when she announces this, all signs of tiredness suddenly disappearing.

"You're seriously going to write a book?" I ask, amazed with how effortlessly she committed to this task.

"I am," she says with a new air of confidence. "I'm still toying with the topic, but already, I'm creating characters in my mind." As she says this, her eyes sparkle, and there's a hint of mischief in her voice.

"So the three of you are all leaving with a clear path?" I ask before glancing toward Juliette, who's hunched over the table with her head propped in her cupped hands, looking somewhat desperate.

"I believe we have found direction," Sophia says, tilting her head toward Annie and Marlee, perhaps for support.

"I'd call it a blueprint ... with lots of missing details," Marlee adds.

"But that's what's so wonderful ... the mystery ... not knowing what is next. It's exciting!" Annie says.

Annie's words shock me. I cannot believe she's no longer afraid of the unknown. I mean, she *is* kind of old to be having a baby. Plus, this isn't an ordinary baby ... She's supposed to be clairvoyant. And, from how Marlee described Annie's hesitation to come here, the Annie that is leaving seems to be at totally different person than the one who arrived Saturday.

"But what about us?" Juliette asks. "I'm really glad the three of you have a game plan." She swallows hard. "But now mine's shattered. I believed I was meant to be a shaman," Juliette says before swallowing again several times. "But after my session with Francisco, I'm not so sure."

"What if you chose a different path?" Sophia asks.

"What do you mean?"

"From the little I know, becoming a shaman requires extreme sacrifices; perhaps sacrifices you are not prepared to make. Yet there are many other avenues for you to be a healer, Juliette. Already you are doing this exact thing at your yoga studio and through energy work."

Juliette remains quiet.

It's then Annie who chimes in: "And do you really want to leave Michael to go live in the jungle and study with a shaman?" She looks at her in a perplexed fashion, as if that is the last thing on Earth she'd ever do.

Juliette's head drops. "No. I love him. Being apart like that ... I think I would miss him too much."

I watch as Juliette's eyes dart to Marlee. For a brief second, I sense a change in her expression.

"Exactly. You love him. Admitting this is a good thing, Juliette. It's what marriage is all about," Marlee says. Something's definitely going on between them. "Maybe the biggest message from this week is to accept how much Michael means to you, then decide how you can *honestly* follow your dharma *and* maintain a fulfilling relationship. When it's only you, it's easier to see things in black or white. However, when another—someone who means the world to you—enters your life, that's when you begin to see the importance of gray."

Listening to Marlee, I sadly realize I have no need for gray. Those in my world have gone. My mother's dead, my grandfather has no memory of me, and I'm about to break up with my boyfriend.

"But what's my message?" I finally ask, feeling my throat tighten. "I know I've got some big decisions to make." I pause, reminding myself I've already chosen. "Actually, I've decided what I want to do."

My new friends look at me with tender eyes.

"But if I follow through and do what I believe is best—contact my dad, break up with Pete, and take the job in Oregon—it's still only me. There is really no one in my life anymore."

"You've got us." Juliette extends her hand to touch mine. Magically, her negativity seems to dissipate, along with her tough exterior. As she reaches out to let me know I am not alone, I sense an innocence in Juliette that I've never before witnessed.

MARLEE
Saturday, April 24 – Sunday, May 1

My phone pings. Tom's in the cell phone parking lot, asking that I text him as soon as we have our luggage. I reply with a heart emoji.

Twenty minutes later, once all our bags are accounted for, I let him know we're ready. I suspect he drove our old Suburban, the one I used to carpool Patrick and his friends to soccer practices. Now Tom relies on it to haul firewood and other messy items for various home projects.

Seeing Annie struggle with her bags, I once again grab the smaller roller before heading toward the exit sign. A frigid wind practically accosts us when we walk through the revolving doors. This cold rush of late April air makes me long for Costa Rica's tropical breeze.

Still, it's good to be home. I don't mean the Philadelphia airport. I find that to be depressing. Rather, back in Pennsylvania, where I live with my husband and son.

The large gray SUV pulls up. Tom hops out of the driver's seat and envelops me in a sweet embrace. My lips reach for his. I've missed my husband.

After loading everyone's bags into the back, we climb into the Suburban and share bits and pieces of our trip with Tom. Our first stop is Annie's apartment building, a high-rise near Rittenhouse Square. Jonathon's standing by the revolving glass doorway, clearly happy to see his wife. Next, we drive to Fishtown to Juliette's. Michael's car is parked outside of the four-story building. A part of me cringes, knowing what's ahead for these two ... that is, if she chooses to confess. But by the look on Juliette's face, I believe that's exactly what will happen this evening. I get out of the car to give her a long hug, knowing how difficult tonight's conversation will be.

"I'm scared, Marlee," she whispers into my ear. "What if he won't forgive me?" A tear falls down her cheek.

"Then it was never meant to be," I say with a wince.

Last night, Juliette seemed so sure of her decision to come clean to Michael. She claimed she needed resolution. Juliette also told me that she and Francisco talked about how her marrying Michael would impact her ability to become a shaman. No doubt this is also an issue for Juliette. It's not solely about reconciling with her mother.

"Juliette," I say, taking hold of her hands, "people make mistakes. But if we own them ... and do our best to make amends ... sometimes things have a way of working out." I give her another hug.

Juliette nods as she wipes her cheeks.

"I'm here if you need me," I say before getting back into the car.

Juliette mouths, "Thank you," then puts on a happy face and waves goodbye to Tom and Sophia.

Not wanting either to pick up on the seriousness of the situation, I also force a smile as I fasten my seatbelt before asking Tom about the forecast for the upcoming week. Fifteen minutes later, we're outside of Sophia's house, saying goodbye.

"So how was it?" Tom asks as he interlaces his fingers with mine. It's nice to be alone after a week apart.

"Perfect," I say, then add, "I cannot imagine a better retreat. Being there helped me find some answers to questions I didn't realize I had."

"No boyfriends?" Tom teases, not inquiring what these questions might be.

"Ha, none at all, but I almost had an interesting encounter with a crocodile." I tell him about the paddleboarding excursion and my tumble into the river.

"You know you were safe, don't you?"

"I do now, but in the moment, I wasn't so sure."

"It's good to have you home. I missed you. We missed you." He leans over to give me a real kiss.

"And I missed you ... both of you. How's Patrick?" I ask, noting Tom hasn't mentioned him at all.

"Well ... now that you're back ... I can tell you." The lightness in his voice fades.

"Is Patrick OK?" Immediately panic floods my mind, as I revert to my mama bear persona.

"Physically, he's fine."

"What happened?"

"Last Saturday night, he told me he was sleeping at Matt's. Of course, this seemed typical, so I didn't question anything."

"But ..."

"Apparently, there was a party—a friend of a friend was watching someone's house. Let's just say one text inviting a few people quickly became a hundred-kid event."

"Patrick went to a party at someone's house when they were away?" Shock and disappointment fill my heart. Patrick's never done anything like this before. "Were they drinking?"

"Yep ... he and all of his buddies." Tom shakes his head before letting out a long sigh. "But if I remember correctly, we did the same thing when we were his age." With that, he turns toward me and raises his eyebrows.

"Yes, but the rules were different then. When we were kids, you didn't get into big trouble if you were caught drinking. Now schools will suspend you, especially if you're on sports teams. And that affects college applications." I feel a dread within rise. I've been back for only an hour and already the peace I achieved in Costa Rica is beginning to fade. "Tell me the whole thing."

"I got the phone call around ten thirty," Tom says, then pauses. "The police received a complaint about noise and a bunch of cars parked on a side road. So they responded, finding a ton of kids partying in someone's house who was away on vacation."

"Patrick was arrested?" Every ounce of air leaves my body as I ask this question. I clench my eyes shut, knowing this will have lasting consequences.

"Not arrested, but he's in trouble. And so are his friends."

"Is the school involved?"

"The other parents and I have been trying to work with the principal to come up with an alternative punishment, one that doesn't go on their record. We read the school board's policy, and since this event had nothing to do with school or an interscholastic activity, the district has no authority to punish the kids. Still, all the parents are upset, so we're looking at a community service project the kids could do—clean up a park or something like that."

I'm extremely disappointed in Patrick, but at the same time, I'm aware he did what many teenagers do—including Tom and me when we were his age. Still, we've never had to deal with this stuff before. Our son was the kid who never got into trouble.

"Thank you," I say, touching my husband's cheek. "I know you handled this better than I ever could have." I let out a big exhale.

"Oh, and I grounded Patrick for the next month. Guess I'm not the only one who did that. Seems like all of us parents are working together to give the kids a similar message."

"That's good. Kids need to be held accountable for their actions. Because soon they'll be off to college. And then, we can't fix their problems." As the words come out of my mouth, I'm taken aback. Did I really say that? Could it be that I'm beginning to let go and accept that I can no longer keep Patrick safe ... and ultimately, he must deal with his own consequences? Tom squeezes my hand.

When we arrive home, Patrick's awake, waiting for us in the kitchen. As soon as we walk in, he looks up. Instead of my normally carefree kid who would be excited to see me, he remains seated, shoulders hunched.

"I'm sorry, Mom." Of course, he knew I'd be upset. We'd talked about how being caught at a party could impact applying to college.

I take a deep breath, walk over to my son, and wrap my arms around him. "I guess you're human," I say, then pull away to look him in the eyes. "I'm not happy about what happened, but I understand how it did. You're growing up, and sometimes you'll make decisions that don't turn out in your best interest. Luckily, you've made your first big mistake while your dad was here to help."

"And punish," Tom adds, his lips pressed firmly together. He must still be angry, as I'm sure this is the last thing he wanted to deal with solo, while I was with friends on a retreat in Costa Rica.

"I get it, Dad," Patrick says, his voice quivers a bit. "I messed up … and I lied to you. That was wrong." He hangs his head.

Tom walks over to us, then places his arm around his son. "You certainly aren't the first to do that," he says. "When I was your age, I got in trouble because some buddies and I caught a bunch of water snakes and put them in a neighbor's pool. The guy was a real jerk, and we were fed up with his bullying."

A slight grin comes across Patrick's face. "Really?" he asks. "You did that?" He laughs. "How did you get caught? And what did your parents do?"

"Apparently, another neighbor watched the whole thing from her kitchen window and couldn't wait to rat us out. I spent the next eight Saturdays working at my dad's veterinarian office, cleaning the bathrooms and mopping floors," Tom says, causing me to laugh as well. I have trouble imagining my meticulous and smell-sensitive husband scouring toilet bowls. It's the one household job he abhors.

Fifteen minutes later, we call it a night. I'm exhausted, but not that tired that we go straight to sleep. I've missed my husband, and he missed me.

***

After a quick run, I shower, then head downtown to meet Juliette. I woke up to a text—which she had written at 2:00 a.m.—asking if we could have coffee after her morning class.

I arrive at the café before Juliette, so I order an oat milk latté, then find a small table in the back corner, where it is a bit more private.

Five minutes later, Juliette, wearing black sunglasses and a long gray sweater tightly wrapped around her black yoga tights, enters the coffee shop.

Juliette gives me a brief wave before placing her order. Several minutes later, Juliette's approaching with a mug of tea in her hand.

"Hey," I say as I stand up to give her a hug.

"Thanks for coming downtown." After taking a seat across from me, she takes off her sunglasses. I can tell she's had another night of little sleep. Still, in true Juliette style, she does her best to offer me a smile.

"How are you doing? Did you tell Michael?" The words blurt from my mouth as soon as she sits.

"I did," she says, looking directly at me, but I cannot discern the expression on her face. She doesn't look sad, yet there's no sign of relief for having confessed what had happened.

"He said he needed some time alone ... to think about it." She lets out a breath, then bites her lip. Still, her face does not reveal what she's feeling.

"That's better than calling everything off," I say in what I hope is an encouraging voice. But knowing Michael and his ego, it could go either way.

"Actually, Marlee," Juliette begins before pausing. "I think I need some time too."

Shocked by her comment, I find myself leaning across the table, inches from Juliette's face, as I whisper, "You do? Are you second-guessing your relationship?"

"No. But I've realized how marriage would complicate everything. As I shared Friday night, it would be difficult for me to become a shaman *and* Michael's wife. If only I had completed the steps before I met him." She lets out a loud sigh. "The two times I'd cheated on past boyfriends was because *I wanted it to be over* ... Being unfaithful was my way to self-sabotage the relationship. Recalling this caused me to realize I wasn't ready to get married."

Juliette's pronouncement blows my mind. All along I thought she was head over heels in love with Michael. Perhaps becoming a shaman is more important to her than he is.

"Does Michael know you feel this way?" My eyes widen as I ask her this.

Juliette hangs her head. "No. I hurt him enough by telling him about René. If I'd said there was a subconscious reason I'd cheated ... or that I wasn't ready to get married..." She lets out a sigh. Juliette remains silent for a minute.

As much as I wish I could pause and wait to receive sage words of advice, I cannot refrain myself from reacting. "What are you going to do? Do you think you're afraid to commit, or is Michael not the one? Do you still love him?" After firing one question after another, I suddenly feel sorry for Michael. *If* he decides to forgive Juliette, will she even be there for him?

It's then Juliette looks up at me, tears streaming down her face.

"Oh, honey," I say as I move my seat closer to hers to wrap my arm around her shoulders. "It's all going to work out." Even as I say these words, I have absolutely no idea what's ahead for Juliette or what she must do to figure this out.

"But there is one thing I've decided," Juliette says with resolve before clearing her throat. "I'm going to find my mom, reach out to her, and see if she wants to talk."

I smile as I gently wipe a tear from Juliette's cheek.

"I figured, until I get my shit together ... you know ... figure out my whole mother abandonment thing ... well, how can I know if I am meant to *be a shaman* or if I am supposed to *be with Michael*?" She rubs the back of her forearm over her face, drying the remaining tears.

"Of course, that makes total sense." I then get an idea. "Do you want me to go with you ... to see your mom ... for moral support?"

In response, Juliette flips her flaxen hair over her shoulder, momentarily returning to the confident, headstrong woman I am so familiar with. Yet I watch as her shoulders drop and the sharpness in her brow softens. "You would do that for me?"

"Absolutely. And who knows—maybe it will turn out better than you expect."

Instead of saying anything, she merely lets out a long, loud sigh.

I then ask another difficult question, the one that Juliette struggled the most with on our last night in Costa Rica. "Do you *really* want to become a shaman? It's causing so much confusion regarding your relationship with Michael. Isn't there a way you could be together *and* follow your soul's purpose?"

Juliette gulps, then scrunches her shoulders. "I haven't let myself go there." Juliette looks up at me. "As much as I think I'm called, there's too much I need to deal with first. Sometimes I wonder if it's meant for me ... or if it's merely my ego wanting more ... *to know* ... to be able to *do things* I can't currently do."

"Be like Francisco?" I ask, cupping my chin in my hand.

"I guess so," she says as her shoulders round forward. "He's incredible ... how he helps people ... *I want to do that*."

"But you can," I say, reaching across the table to touch her arm. "And you already are ... with what you do at Bliss."

"But lots of people have yoga studios. *I want more.*"

"I know you do," I say, unable to suppress my grin. "But it must be what fits your path. Following in Francisco's footsteps is not *your* dharma," I say, giving her arm a squeeze before taking a drink of my latté.

"I know you're right." She brings the brim of her mug to her lips. But before taking a sip, she says, "I used to be so sure of what I wanted. But after last week, and everything I experienced ..." She pauses as a wave of uncertainty comes over her face. "Well ... it's as though my path now has a fork ... and I don't know which road to take."

*****

"You seem happy," Tom says as I take the bunch of yellow tulips I bought at Whole Foods, snip off the ends, then place them into a crystal vase we received as a wedding present. I set the vase on the dining room table. Carefully eyeing the six place settings, I pause, then adjust several pieces of silverware.

"But you're a bit quirky. You know that, don't you?" Tom takes me into his arms, gently kissing me on the lips.

"I guess I like things a certain way," I say before returning his kiss, this time with promises of something more.

"What time are they coming?" Tom asks, perhaps also wondering if we might have some alone time. But then his expression changes. "Oh yeah ... Patrick's here, I forgot."

A demure smile comes over my face. "The downside to grounding your teenage son." I let out a loud exhale, momentarily second-guessing the punishment. "And to answer your question, I told them to come around seven. I'd have suggested an earlier time, but I know how hard it is for Annie to get away from work." However, maybe things are different now that's she been away. Has Annie changed too? Juliette certainly has.

"Well, I don't need to go in to do rounds tomorrow, so maybe we can sleep in." Tom gently pats my bottom as I squirm to return to the kitchen to check on the large clay pot inside of the oven. I'd decided to make a cassoulet with a pork shoulder, ham, beans, prosciutto, and of course, fresh spring vegetables.

I return to preparing dinner, washing mixed greens for the salad before adding chopped asparagus, fresh peas, radishes, and shallots. I take a bowl from a lower cabinet and combine a heaping pour of olive oil, the juice from a lemon, a touch of honey, and generous amounts of salt and pepper. Whisking it until it froths, I cover the dressing, then place it to the side. All that's left to do is to heat the baguette. Earlier today, I made the raspberry ricotta cake that's now sitting on the counter.

Knowing I have an hour before I need to shower, I decide to take advantage of the beautiful sunshine and go for a walk. As I grab my jacket and head toward the door, Roxie, our border collie, nudges my calf.

"Of course, you can come," I say as I pat her head. She responds by vigorously wagging her tail.

Once I'm outside, it's clear spring is finally here. Trees are budding and tulips are in full bloom. The forsythia has dropped its yellow flowers, allowing the green leaves to sprout.

Roxie and I begin our walk. As much as I love the summer and fall seasons, there's something special about springtime. I guess it's because everything's new, alive, reborn … the way I now feel.

My mind returns to our final night in Costa Rica and the beautiful leather-bound journal Francisco gave to me. Of course, this gift was only a confirmation of what I'd already realized. Maybe that's why it was easy to tell the others about my plan to write a book. For the past few days, I've been having fun playing with possible characters and various settings. But it's the plot that has me confused. That and the fear of whether I can write authentically, the intention I'd written for the Full Moon Ceremony.

Roxie pulls me left, toward the park. She loves our community's green space because of all the dog walkers who pass through. When we arrive, people and their dogs are everywhere. But that's to be expected on a beautiful Friday. No doubt everyone has spring fever.

While doing a loop around the pond, Roxie confidently approaches each dog we encounter, conducting a sniff test as she wags her tail. When she spies children playing T-ball nearby, she lets out a playful bark and pulls toward them. I'm pleased with how gentle she is with kids. Not all dogs can handle their quick movements. But then I remember how Patrick used to roughhouse with her when she was a puppy. Sadly, he rarely does that anymore. I let out a sigh, acknowledging he's growing up.

That's it. Why don't I write a book about what I'm experiencing—how it feels to have your first child, or only child, get ready to leave the nest? I know I'm not the only one who struggles with this. Besides, after years of being a child's primary caretaker, it's tough to let go and allow them to grow up without you, especially after you realize the dumbass decisions they may soon be making. Surely, I could write as my true self on this topic.

Let go. Letting go. That sounds like a good title for a book. And what if it's not only about having a son go to college? I guess it could be about letting go of all sorts of things. Patrick's leaving could merely be one example I use to illustrate our struggle to release what we hold so close.

Roxie stops to relieve herself by a small bush. I wait until she's done, still sorting out possibilities for my first book. *First book*, ha! I guess I'm now committing to writing more than one. But best to focus on this one before I start dreaming of others. A surge of energy courses through my veins.

However, something still bothers me, I think as I reflexively tuck a strand of hair behind my ear. How is cooking connected to my story? I stare down at the gravel path as we make our way out of the park. Several moments later, I recall Daniel's words: "... *it is what you bring when you step into the kitchen. What makes your approach unique? It is the process, not the product.*"

I let Daniel's—or Zecheal's—wisdom reverberate in my mind as we head home, considering ways to incorporate this message into my book. Do I write about how I nurture others through cooking? Or is there more?

Glancing at my watch, I realize I'll have just enough time to shower and put out the appetizers before the Thompsons and Robbinses arrive.

The answer lies within. Be aware of your thoughts and actions when you are in your kitchen doing what you love.

My body freezes. Has it returned? I thought the few times my intuition spoke while we were in Costa Rica was a mere coincidence. But maybe it wasn't.

***

"So, Marlee," Jared asks, "tell me about the retreat. Sophia shared her experiences, but I'm curious what it was like from your perspective." He raises his graying eyebrows as he waits for my response.

I set my glass of pinot noir on the table before answering Jared. "To be honest, I had no idea what to expect. Juliette gave us a preview, but she left a few things out ... like the fact that she and I would be staying in a tree house." I roll my eyes, which causes everyone to laugh.

"But was it not lovely ... waking to the sound of the ocean?" Sophia asks before taking a bite of salad.

"It was amazing." I sigh, momentarily returning to that bedroom in the sky. "I think Maggie was happy we were next door," I say, smiling, then take a sip from my water glass. "But back to your question. The retreat was fabulous. And it was so much more than learning about different healing modalities. I believe everyone there received individual guidance ... to help them move forward on their path." Maybe this response is a bit obtuse, but I am still unpacking so much of what occurred last week.

I pause, looking around the table. While thrilled to have the Robbinses and Thompsons for dinner, I can't help but reflect that we are a group of six and not eight. Unable to keep the thought to myself, I say, "I invited both Juliette and Michael tonight, but they declined, being that their situation is ... well ... complicated."

"It does seem strange," Annie says in a soft voice. "I hope she and Michael figure things out."

"We all do, Annie," says Tom, surprising me. "Michael's not himself at work. His usually upbeat personality is gone. Instead, he's been quiet, reserved."

"You're right," Jared adds. "I think this is truly affecting him."

After a few moments, it's Jonathon who breaks the awkward silence. "What was your favorite session, Marlee?" he asks, leaning closer to me. I assume Annie's shared a bit about the workshops.

"That's a difficult question because each presenter offered something unique." I rest my elbow on the table, propping my chin in my hand as I take a moment to think. "My favorite workshop may have been with Daniel, who channels. I also did a private session with him, and it was amazing. However, my one-on-one meeting with Francisco gave me significant insights ... I guess you could say I now have a game plan."

"Ah, the shaman," Jared says, nodding his head as if he's well versed in shamanism and all it entails.

"What about you, Sophia?" Tom asks. "Marlee told me about all the workshops and her private sessions. From my perspective, some seemed a bit out there. But who knows?" Slowly I'm detecting a change in Tom. While initially skeptical, he's now acting more interested in what I learned.

"What a difficult question." Sophia takes a sip from her wine glass before continuing: "Meeting with Francisco was quite instrumental, as he provided guidance and connected me with Jack Keeler, the naturopathic doctor I will be interning with." She pauses as she straightens her spine. "Yet I *believe* the person who impacted me the most was Dominique."

"What did Dominique discuss during her session?" Tom asks, looking confused, as I don't believe I mentioned Dominique to him, except perhaps to say that she and Francisco own the resort.

"Dominique was not a presenter ... She is married to Francisco." Sophia's emerald eyes sparkle as she relays this couple's story.

Once she finishes, Jonathon says, "Now that's quite a 'how I met your mother' tale." Everyone laughs.

"It was a conversation Dominique and I had that helped me the most." Jared merely smiles as his wife speaks.

"You didn't tell us about this," I say, somewhat confused with where Sophia is going.

In pure Sophia fashion, she merely grins, tilts her head, then softly says, "I greatly benefited from each of the workshops and private sessions, but it was Dominique who provided exactly what I required." Her shoulders slide down her back, elongating her neck, as she begins to explain her statement. "After meeting with Jack, I took a long walk in the gardens." Sophia lets out a breath before continuing: "While wandering along the path, I came upon

Dominique sitting on a bench, writing in a journal. When she saw me, she asked that I join her. We sat and talked for quite some time." Sophia stops to look to Jared.

"I admitted my fear regarding practicing holistic methods. Was it too late in my career to make such a shift? Additionally, Jack lives in Costa Rica and I in Pennsylvania. Would the distance between us be too great, or could we manage with technology?" Once again, Sophia pauses. "But I believe something deeper was holding me back. I did not trust my ability to know when traditional medicine was required and when a more natural approach would be the preferred course." Jared, who is seated next to her, gently takes her hand in his.

"She helped you believe in yourself," Tom says with a knowing in his eyes.

"Yes," Sophia replies. "Dominique fully understood my predicament. She made a significant choice in her midfifties ... when she decided to leave her first husband and travel to the rain forests of Peru. Of course, had she not done so, she never would have reunited with Francisco, nor would they have founded Nueva Vida. And while magical in many ways, managing a spiritual resort required a great deal of work, drastically different from her life of luxury in Santiago."

"So Dominique empowered you to follow your path?" Tom confirms.

Sophia nods her head.

"She is quite inspiring," Annie adds before taking a forkful of food from her plate.

Allowing time for Annie to chew her food, Jared then asks Annie the same question Tom had asked his wife.

"As much as I loved all of the presenters"—Annie giggles as she says this—"I know, at first, they terrified me ... but they were all really normal people." She lets out a quirky laugh. "Anyway, I think

I most enjoyed meeting Camille." Annie pauses, then scrunches her nose, as if contemplating the reason behind her statement. "When she showed me the school and explained how she and her husband are making this progressive educational program available to the kids of Nosara, well, I was totally impressed. Still, something was missing. I thought, *How could this school be even better*? That's when I realized the answer."

Four of us look at one another in confusion. Where is Annie going with this?

"Our schools in the United States have guidance counselors available to the kids. But this tiny innovative school has no emotional support services. That's when I knew I could help."

I turn to Jonathon, whose eyes are locked on his wife as he slowly nods his head. Whatever she's about to say, it seems he fully supports her.

"While I cannot physically meet with the kids, I can Zoom in and have virtual guidance sessions." She shrugs her shoulders, then blushes. "And I'll be able to do it from home, after I have the baby."

"I thought you were cutting back," Sophia says, her eyes narrowing.

"I'm referring all new patients to other therapists in my practice," Annie says before gently wiping her lips with her napkin. "And I've hired one of those consultants who help people who aren't tech savvy to learn strategies to lighten their load." With that, she waves her hand through the air. "This guy tells me I can easily save ten hours a week if I begin using voice recording for my notes instead of hand typing them on my laptop. Did you know that there's a way for you to do that and then have a written report compiled? That alone will save me gobs of time. For years, I've stressed over writing follow-ups to my sessions. I don't want to forget anything ... or misconstrue what a client said."

Good for Annie. She's finally figuring out a system that will work for her, *and* she's sharing her talents with the children at Camille's school.

Once everyone's finished with dinner, Sophia and I clear the plates before I bring the raspberry ricotta cake—and six dessert plates—to the table.

Sophia announces she's spending three weeks in Costa Rica this September for an intensive in-person training with Jack.

After learning the details of her internship, Annie asks, "Have you heard from Maggie? Did she break up with Pete? With all that's been happening this past week, I haven't had time to check in with her."

I let out a sigh, then empty what remains of the red wine into my glass. "Maggie's fine. But she's had a few tough days. Pete didn't take the breakup well, which of course devastated Maggie ... Sometimes she's too nice for her own good." When I say this, Tom begins to laugh, then both he and Annie roll their eyes.

"What?" I ask, oblivious as to what is going on.

"I know someone else who is often too nice for her own good," he says, winking at Annie, who starts to giggle.

"Stop it. I'm not that way." I let out a sigh, then shake my head. Jonathon seems amused by the antics. "Anyway, she's accepted the job offer and is moving to Oregon. Her bosses were thrilled. I can only imagine how talented Maggie is. Even though she's in the beginning phases of her career, she's smart, and she certainly seems as though she'd be a team player."

"When does she move?" Annie asks before taking a bite of the raspberry ricotta cake.

"Maggie booked a U-Haul so she can drive to Bend at the end of May. But I believe she flies there on Thursday to look for an apartment." I pause, momentarily returning to our conversation yesterday morning. "But she sounded good, like she's at peace with her decisions."

"What about her father—did she contact him?" Sophia asks.

The three men stare at us, looking confused.

I explain Maggie's situation and how she recently sent a letter to a man whom she believes may be her father, adding that she's not heard back yet.

The rest of the conversation is lighthearted. As before, Tom invites Jonathon and Jared to the porch for cigars, allowing the three of us time to talk.

"Have you spoken with Juliette?" Sophia asks as soon as we are alone. "I left several messages, but she has not returned my calls." There is concern in her voice.

"She hasn't returned my texts either," Annie says as she furrows her eyebrows. "Why is she shutting us out?"

Two days ago, Juliette texted all of us, announcing she and Michael were taking a break to figure things out. Of course, this came as a huge shock to Annie and Sophia. I pretended to be equally surprised, realizing they have no idea I'm aware of what Juliette's going through. While determined not to betray any confidences with Juliette, I do offer a few words, hoping to help Annie and Sophia better comprehend the complexity of the situation.

"I met with Juliette the day after we got back. I believe she realized more during this retreat than she shared. Before she can fully commit to Michael, she must resolve some issues from her past."

While Annie gives me a perplexed look, Sophia slowly nods her head as her eyes fall to her lap.

"Yes, Juliette must find her missing pieces." Sophia's response is plain and simple. While I doubt Sophia has a full grasp on the situation, she definitely understands Juliette.

Annie's expression still shows confusion.

"Sometimes when we dig deep, we don't always expect what appears. I believe this is what happened to Juliette last week." I smile, then add, "But I have faith all will work out. She just needs some time."

***

Tom and Patrick are deeply entrenched in a Sixers versus Celtics game, giving me an excuse to retreat to my office and contemplate *the book*. While I like the concept of writing about letting go, I have no idea how to incorporate cooking into a story about surrendering. Maybe I'm on the wrong track.

I focus on my session with Daniel. I remember I didn't *think* about what to write. In fact, there was no effort at all. Instead, the words merely came through me.

Determined to re-create the experience, I go to the kitchen and retrieve Sophia's hostess gift from last night—several bundles of sage, a large clam shell, and a container of sand she brought back from the beach in Nosara. In the gift bag was also a box of matches; its cover is a beautiful picture of rain forest plants.

After assembling my new sage kit, I light the bundle and allow the smoke to flow. Then, ever so carefully, I sage my office, my laptop, and myself before setting the tied bundle of dried leaves inside of the shell filled with sand on top of my desk. The lingering smoke fills my nostrils. Then I light the candle Annie brought while saying a small prayer—asking God, my Guide, and my intuition to direct me.

While Daniel had me use a pen and notepad, I prefer to type. Placing my fingers on the keyboard, I shut my eyes and wait, wondering if anything will happen. If something occurs, will it be me writing as my authentic self? But instead of doubting whether words will come through me, I do my best to trust and believe, letting go of trying to control what transpires. I inhale slowly, hold my breath, then exhale.

Several moments later, my fingers begin moving, though I have no idea what I'm typing. Instead of questioning, I allow.

Finally, my hands stop. I open my eyes and read what's on the screen.

> The older I get, the more I realize life is not only about learning, but it also involves unlearning.
>
> Perhaps this concept seems strange, even outlandish. After all, aren't we supposed to be lifetime learners, constantly open to new ideas and concepts to broaden ourselves and our minds?
>
> In some ways this is true. Yet we have certain ideas— limiting beliefs—that we must examine if we hope to evolve. After all, life is not a competition to fill our heads with facts. Rather, our time on Earth is an opportunity to witness experiences in new ways, open our hearts, and see the oneness between ourselves and those around us.

I pause, totally unsure of what is happening. It's as though these words are magically forming on the screen in front of me. Still, I don't question. Instead, I trust. Once again, I clear my mind and allow whatever this is to continue.

> I had quite a bit of unlearning to do. This is not to insinuate that I've been wrong, bad, or ill-advised. Not at all. In fact, had I chosen to stay on the same path

and do the same things, all would be fine. I'd be happy … content.

But somewhere along the way, I realized I wanted more than happy and content. Searching for something greater in meaning, I began to look within to examine who I truly am, what I believe, and what I want during this lifetime. Never before had I given myself permission to do this. However, a voice inside told me it was time to pay attention and begin asking myself questions. So I took a deep breath, found an untapped courage within, and paused. Only when I became still was I able to consider where I needed to surrender in order to discover a new way—letting go of beliefs I'd clung to—so I could find my reason for being here.

I stop writing, taking a moment to read what I'd just typed. As the words reverberate in my mind, I know this is exactly what I'm meant to do. What transpired occurred without effort on my part. Instead, there was flow, grace, expansiveness—everything I've yearned for.

I repeat this process several times. Eventually, words stop coming, no doubt a signal this "session" is complete. But tomorrow's another day. I can only hope the words will flow again.

MAGGIE
Monday, May 2

For twenty-eight years, this house has been the only home I've known. But soon it will belong to someone else. I'm meeting with a realtor at seven o'clock this evening to list it.

I've lived in this brick duplex in Brookline my entire life, except for four of the six years I was at Pitt—two in the dorms and two in off-campus apartments. While completing my master's, I lived at home ... with Mom. Still, home was less than a fifteen-minute drive from campus, except during rush hour. I exhale, returning to my college days, when life seemed simple. Sure, I had a full course load and worked part-time as a waitress at Pamela's Diner, but it was all manageable. In fact, I graduated magna cum laude—both times.

The kitchen, though small and compact, was sufficient for Mom and me. Not known for her cooking skills, Mom never cared that our oven was tiny or that the burners were small. Mom preferred to use the microwave. She claimed it was easier.

The square wooden table, barely big enough for four, is pushed against the wall. The fourth chair is upstairs, at her desk. I take a moment to smile. Mom was a pro when it came to managing her affairs. She always preferred paperwork to cooking or anything house related. I still remember what her boss, the lead partner at the law firm where she worked, said to me at her funeral.

"Your mother was the finest administrative assistant I've ever seen. Her attention to detail ... and her work ethic ... was like no other."

I smile, knowing he described Mom to a T. While every birthday cake was made by the corner bakery, and my grandmother did all of our mending, Mom did her best working a demanding job while raising me.

The living room is long and narrow. A worn leather sofa faces the brick fireplace. On the left is a La-Z-Boy recliner, Mom's favorite chair. That's where she'd sit at night, watching Fox News before transitioning to *NCIS* or some other detective show. She loved those crime series, always prided herself in knowing who was guilty. I guess that was due to her ability to focus, listen, and home in on every detail.

Turning toward the right, I climb the stairs to the second floor. Her bedroom, the first room in the hallway, was small, but she said it met her needs. She loved the view of the dogwood tree in our backyard. I remember how she'd crack her window so she could hear the birds singing first thing each morning. The other room on this floor, besides her bathroom, was her office. I walk toward it and poke my head inside. There, in the corner, is the huge oak desk she found at a flea market. I smile, recalling it took Pete and two of his friends to haul this heavy piece upstairs.

That pit in my stomach reappears. I'd hurt him. But that was never my intention. I didn't think we were that serious. Sure, we spent a lot of time together. Yet I never told him I loved him. Still, he'd tell me … but I always changed the topic. Perhaps I hoped my feelings toward Pete would change. But they never did. My mind returns to last Saturday night.

"Pete, there's something we need to talk about."

"Sure, Maggie, what's on your mind?"

His expression was sweet, kind, naive … I still remember how he patted the sofa cushion next to him, as if asking me to sit beside him.

He'd picked me up at the airport. It was late. I know he wanted to sleep over. But I couldn't. Not now. I knew what had to be done.

"Pete ... Mark and Sandy have decided to move their office ... to Bend, Oregon."

"Oregon? That's straight across the country. Why are they doing that?"

"Well, they love the town, and it's an amazing place to raise their sons ... skiing, mountain biking."

"OK, I get that." But that's when it hit him. "But what about your job?" He shrugged. "But you're the best. I know you'll find another position right away." An encouraging smile, thoughtful words ...

"That's the thing." I tried to be brave. "They asked me to go with them ... move to Bend."

"Move? But this is your home, Maggie. I'm here. This is where you belong. I thought we—"

I stopped him before he could continue. "No, Pete. I've made up my mind. I'm going."

"But what about us? I mean ... I was going to propose ... next weekend ... I had it all planned out."

I watched as the nicest guy in the world began to crumble. I'd done this. It was my fault. I hurt the person who loved me more than he ever should have.

"I'm so sorry, Pete ... I ... I care so much about you," I said as I hung my head and stared at the floor. "But ...." I paused, looking up before gently touching his face.

"This is it? We're done?" He pulled away from my hand as tears welled in his eyes. However, I knew Pete. He was too proud to cry in front to me.

I couldn't say yes, so I nodded my head, diverting my eyes from his.

That's when he became angry. I should have known this wasn't going to be easy.

"What happened this week? Did you meet someone?" His eyes narrowed as his voice grew shockingly aggressive.

"No. There's no one else." I shook my head, then took a big in-hale and decided to speak my truth. "I need to do what is best for me. I need to leave Pittsburgh, start fresh … in all areas of my life."

"But I'm what's best for you." He paused, and his puppy dog eyes appeared. "Don't you love me?" His question echoed a mixture of hurt and realization.

"Not the same way you love me," I admitted. A lone tear fell down my cheek.

He nodded, stood up, and headed toward the door, never once looking back.

Since then, he hasn't called. But his mother has, asking what happened. So did two of his closest friends.

While I did my best to explain, I suspect they didn't want to hear what I had to say. Perhaps they merely wanted to change my mind, hoping I'd return to Pete and things would go back to the way they were.

There's no denying the guilt, but I trust it's better than regret. I had to be true to myself.

I climb the final set of stairs to my room on the third floor. Standing at the doorway, I remember all the different colors my bedroom had been painted. First it was light pink when I was a little girl. Then it became purple before I chose a lemon yellow. Now, it's a light gray, so indicative of my mood these past years—almost a replica of Pittsburgh's weather. I shut the door, perhaps to close this chapter of my life, the one I'm about to leave.

But as I descend the two flights of stairs to the bottom floor of the only house I've ever known, I realize it's time. While these memories are beautiful, they are my past. I'm ready to find my future.

***

"So what did you think?" Sandy's standing by my office door, waiting for me. She must have seen me pull into the parking lot. After
all, she has a full view from her office window.

"Bend's amazing. Honestly, I had no idea what to expect."

Sandy rushes over to give me a warm embrace before saying,
"I'm thrilled you like it. You're going to be so happy there!"

My brief trip to Central Oregon was a whirlwind. I left
Thursday after lunch, flying Delta through Phoenix to the Redmond
airport, which was a mere twenty-five-minute drive to where I
was staying.

I'd made a last-minute reservation at Loge, a small motel
about ten minutes southwest of town. It's on the way to Mt. Bachelor,
the local ski mountain. I'd read Loge had been recently refurbished.
Once settled in my room, I sensed what a special vibe this motel had.

Before leaving Pittsburgh, I scheduled to meet with a realtor
on Friday afternoon to look at rentals. However, first, I wanted the
morning to explore Bend on my own.

After going for a run along the Deschutes River, I drove to the
west side of town and had a delicious breakfast at an amazing diner.
I then spent the next two hours driving around Bend, checking out
the different neighborhoods. Before I knew it, it was time to meet
with Tabitha, the realtor from RE/MAX. Together, we toured seven
rental properties: two downtown, three on the east side, one south
of downtown, and the last—which was the winner—in Northwest
Crossing. By five o'clock, I'd signed all the paperwork. The space was
mine, at least for the next year, beginning June 1.

The apartment is perfect. It has two bedrooms, one and a half
bathrooms, an ample kitchen, and a nice-sized living space. Located on the second floor of the building, it's above a small home goods
store. The building was built in 2009, and there are hardwood floors,
up-to-date appliances, and central air. But it was the stone fireplace
that sold me … and the back patio that faces the mountains.

Comforted by having secured a space to live, I spent the rest of the weekend playing ... leisurely walking downtown to peruse the stores, then sampling different restaurants, food trucks, and breweries. Each morning, I ran on a new trail before having breakfast at one of the local coffee shops. Those few days were jam-packed. I left Sunday evening at eight for Seattle, then took a red-eye back to Pittsburgh.

Bend felt good ... No ... it felt amazing. Fresh and full of opportunities. In some ways it reminded me of Shadyside. Yet being that it's nestled in the middle of Oregon, there's a spontaneous freedom that comes when nature surrounds you ... and you're in an entirely new space where no one knows you.

But what called to my soul are the views ... and the sunsets. I suppose those who live there might take them for granted. But I cannot imagine ever doing so.

***

Today after work, before I head back to the house in Brookline to meet with the realtor, I make a detour out of the city, in the opposite direction. Knowing this may be even more difficult than listing the house or ending things with Pete, I must now say goodbye to my grandfather. Of course, it won't be goodbye forever. I've committed to making sure I visit him, at least every few months. But it will be different. I won't be able to be there at a moment's notice in case he needs me. Still, he has no idea of who I am—or where he is for that matter. Alzheimer's is a cruel disease.

The woman at the front desk waves as I pass. She's used to me stopping by.

When I open the door to his room, my grandfather—rather a shell of the man who was my grandad—is sitting in a leather chair, on top of a blue pad, just in case.

"Granddad, it's me, Maggie," I gingerly say, hoping that may-be, this time, he'll show some sort of recognition. But he doesn't. He never will.

Instead, he tilts his head toward my voice. But his eyes remain vacuous, unable to comprehend who is in front of him.

I go into my normal babble, updating him on my life, my work … but then I stop. I realize everything is changing. I'm changing.

"Granddad," I begin, having no idea if any part of him will understand, "I'm going to be leaving for a while. Moving to Oregon. But don't worry. I'll come back … to see you … to make sure you're OK." As the words flow from my lips, tears follow. My throat tight-ens, but I push on, wanting so dearly to say those things I've been keeping inside.

"You see … I must do this … for me. I love you. And I'll miss you." I stop, unsure how to continue. But I find the strength. "I'll always be here," I say as I gently place my hand on his chest. At that moment, there's a flicker in his eyes as he places both hands on top of mine, as if he's imprinting my handprint onto his heart.

Moments later, his arms fall to his side. The empty look re-turns. I've lost him.

I stay for a bit, rattling on about things that aren't important. But I feel the need to say something to fill the lonely space.

Granddad starts to doze off. I understand. He's lived a full life—lost his wife and his daughter, though the latter is something he does not know. And now I'm leaving. But I'll be back.

MARLEE

Wednesday, September 7 –
Tuesday, October 17

Lying in Shavasana, Juliette slowly guides the class back to the present moment. She instructs us to wiggle our fingers and toes, circle our wrists and ankles, then hug our knees to our chest before gently rolling onto our right side. After several moments of creating a rebirth of sorts, I follow her lead and sit cross-legged at the front of my mat, palms together at my sternum.

Instead of the typical salutation that Juliette usually ends her classes with—"May you be safe, may you be healthy, may you be happy, may you know peace"—she pauses for several moments too long. But, of course, this is her last class before she leaves for Peru for an eight-month training with a famous shaman, one Francisco introduced her to.

"Place your right hand on your heart with your left hand over the right. Inhale deeply. Feel the energy in your fourth chakra. This is the love and light I will hold for each of you while I'm away. Namaste." It's then Juliette's voice cracks. I'm surprised it's taken this long.

I hear several sniffles. But, of course, Juliette's yoga students have come to rely upon her, and no doubt her absence will impact them deeply.

At the beginning of class, Juliette shared that Sabrina, one of the instructors whom I've worked with for gemstone healings, will be the point person while she is away. However, as lovely as Sabrina is, her teaching style is quite different from Juliette's. My dear friend will be missed.

I look over at Annie, who, at eight months pregnant, struggles with our weekly restorative class. Juliette's helped her modify poses and taught her how to incorporate bolsters to better support her growing body. However, I noticed that tonight Annie spent most of the class on her back. But she looks content, and besides, yoga is so much more than the asanas, or poses.

After we roll up our mats and place the blocks and other props on the shelves at the back of the studio, I watch as each person pauses to say goodbye to Juliette. The three of us wait until Juliette's finished. We have a seven-thirty reservation at Vedge, her favorite restaurant. We wanted to make tonight's last class special. Juliette leaves Friday morning and won't return until the middle of May.

Thirty-five minutes later, changed and seated at a window table, the normally composed Juliette begins to cry.

"I'm going to miss you all so much," she says as she loudly sniffs.

"It won't be the same without you," I say, placing my hand on top of hers.

Nodding her head yes, she turns to Annie. "You better send me pictures when that baby's born. And I want weekly updates. Promise?"

"Absolutely," Annie responds, visibly holding back her own tears.

"Dominique shared that Francisco will be visiting you during your training," Sophia says, no doubt hoping to add some ease to the conversation.

Juliette loudly sniffs. "I think Francisco knows how nervous I am. Plus, when I told him how I'd reached out to my mother, and she said she would meet with me, but never showed… you remember how Marlee and I waited four hours for her at that diner outside of Albany … well, I think he felt sorry for me. I had done what he had asked … you know, what he said I must do before I could begin this journey to shamanism."

I momentarily return to that Sunday afternoon. Juliette's mom had promised to meet her at a diner off of Route 87 in New York, near a town called McKownville. When we arrived, Juliette texted her mom, letting her know she was there. Her mom confirmed she was on her way but was running a few minutes late. We watched every car as it pulled into the lot. But Juliette's mother never came. Finally, at four o'clock, we left and drove back to Philadelphia. Juliette was silent the entire way.

"It will be wonderful for you to see him," Sophia says, "and it appears he will be doing additional training with this shaman." Sophia pauses before explaining: "Dominique said Francisco desires to take his knowledge to another level." With this statement, Sophia sits back in her seat, tilting her head to the left. "I never thought shamans would have a need for additional training." She pauses before continuing. "Yet it is required for doctors and many others in health professions. I find it quite impressive that Francisco is seeking this on his own."

"Yes," Annie chimes in. "In fact, after I have the baby … while I take a few months away from my practice … I plan to enroll in courses to keep my license up to date. That, and begin my counseling sessions at Camille's school."

"How will that work?" I ask, cognizant that Annie's only done in-person, one-on-one therapy sessions with her clients.

"Well, Camille and I identified topics the students struggle with. While I may eventually work individually with some of the children, for now, I'm creating thirty-minute 'guidance classes' … you know, addressing issues like friendship, collaboration, conflict … things all kids encounter."

"And you'll Zoom in to teach these classes?" Juliette asks.

"Yes. We've decided to hold classes each Wednesday at noon our time, during my scheduled lunch break. Each child at the school has an iPad, so it will be easy. And I'll be able to see their faces, which will help me better gauge how each is processing the information from the lesson."

"Or if they're paying attention," Juliette says with a smirk. It's nice to see the "old Juliette," considering how much of her life has changed and will continue to over the next months.

"I think this is fabulous, Annie. And from what you have already shared, it appears you have transformed your practice, allowing for more deliberate interactions with your patients." Sophia seems genuinely impressed with how Annie's shifting her ways.

"I knew I had to, with the baby coming and everything. Plus, Jonathon's committed to taking off one afternoon a week to be with her. Oh … did I tell you we finally hired a nanny? Her name is Mary. She's fifty-two and from Ireland … and her résumé is impeccable." As Annie shares this, there's an ease in both her tone and expression, telling me she's at peace with this arrangement.

"But have you been using your gift?" Juliette asks. "I mean, has your clairvoyance been helping you meet your clients' needs?"

A devilish grin comes across Annie's face. "That's one of the reasons work is easier. I can *see* the problems more easily, so I don't have to take so much time figuring things out. And the solutions, or the steps I must take to work with my patients, are becoming crystal clear."

"Sophia, when do you go to Costa Rica?" Juliette asks right before a woman comes to take our drink order.

After the server leaves, Sophia says, "I leave in four days and return October 1." She pauses, then turns to Annie. "I will be back three weeks prior to your due date." Sophia then continues: "Jack and I agreed to three weeks of in-person training each fall for the next several years. However, we communicate daily. Each evening, I send him a recap of my appointments, summarizing which holistic approaches I've applied and why." She smiles, then takes a sip of her water. "Our system works beautifully. And when I have questions, Jack provides me with immediate feedback. Still, having a concentrated period to work together will allow me to proceed to the next level." Although she doesn't share what that means, it's clear Sophia has a plan.

"Have you been using the pendulum Francisco gave to you?" Annie asks Sophia, wide-eyed.

"Yes … and no. While his beautiful gift has been beneficial in several situations, I am hesitant to become reliant on it for answers I have within."

"That seems wise," I say, realizing how one could become dependent on using it for everyday decisions, a habit that would actually be disempowering, the exact opposite of a pendulum's purpose.

"How is the book coming, Marlee?" Annie asks, turning the attention to me.

"Well … I sent it to my editor yesterday." Merely saying these words aloud cause butterflies to stir in my stomach. I'd revised the manuscript so many times, worried readers might not understand my message. Yet I finally realized I have no control how others react to my work. All I can do is write as my authentic self, the intention I tossed into the flames during the Full Moon Ceremony.

"Did you decide on a title?" Juliette asks, knowing I'd been struggling with the wording.

"I believe I have. I'm calling the book *The Best Is Yet to Come*. The title's somewhat vague, but I think it's the picture that will capture potential readers' attention." I take out my phone and show everyone a mock-up of the cover. Endless wildflowers surround a tranquil pond. To the right is a beautiful two-story white cottage with a gorgeous stone fireplace and a wrap-around porch—complete with old-fashioned rocking chairs. Majestic mountains, graced by an old pine forest, complete the background. "I commissioned an artist to create this cover. In fact, I have the original watercolor hanging in my office."

"It's amazing. For me, it invokes feelings of peace, grace, and gratitude," Sophia says as she looks more closely at the picture. "There is something so very familiar about it, but I cannot say what it is." Her eyes squint, as if looking closer will provide her with the answer.

"You know," Annie begins, after Sophia passes my phone to her, "it kind of reminds me of a fairy-tale version of Eagle's Landing. While the cottage is surrounded by a meadow, there *is* a forest in the background. And even though the home's a different color, it *has* a big porch ... *and* a stone fireplace. Plus, there's a pond. Sure, it's not a lake, but it's still a body of water."

"Yes!" Juliette chimes in. "You've nailed it, Annie ..." She takes my phone, holding it closer to her face. "Of course! There they are ... two eagles ... perched on top of the tall tree, right behind the quaint house." Juliette passes the phone around, her finger next to the two eagles.

"So you understand," I say as a warmth fills my body. "The cover shows something more beautiful than what I know, perhaps something beyond my wildest dreams. While it incorporates elements of my current life, it elevates it to a new level. That's what the book is about ... letting go of what *we think should be* so we can be open to new and unforeseen possibilities."

"Oh, Marlee, your book cover perfectly illustrates this concept." Hearing Annie's acknowledgment only solidifies what I felt when I first came up with this idea. But I cannot take all of the credit. My session with Francisco was the impetus to this idea.

"There is one thing I have been meaning to ask?" Sophia says, her eyes slightly narrowed and lips somewhat pursed. "I remember Conor said you would incorporate cooking into your writing. Have you done so in this book?" Of course, Sophia would remember this detail.

I let out a laugh, then say, "Actually, it took me some time to figure out how to do so. But once I began writing the book, it became obvious. Basically, for 'the best' to come our way, we must trust, let go, and believe, correct?"

All three women nod their heads.

"As a way to illustrate this concept, I compare it to cooking without a recipe or using your intuition to create your own tasty dish. Of course, this requires trusting you have the correct ingredients, letting go of fears that the final product will be undercooked or unsavory, and believing in your abilities as a chef. In essence, if we're afraid to trust, let go, and believe and instead resort to following a proven recipe, while we may bake something nice, it will never be amazing." The volume of my voice rises as I try to make my point.

"However, if we release the need to listen to others and adhere to a prescribed way of doing something for their approval, then we are free to discover other ways, explore paths that are *best for us*. Maybe it's how we create our signature dishes, adding our own special sauce to make it unique to us. And if we possess the faith that something higher has our backs, then we can find the confidence to leap forward and leave our comfort zone. This is following our inner-knowing … helping us discover what lies beyond our wildest dreams. Hence, the title, *The Best Is Yet to Come*."

Sophia lifts her glass of water. "To Marlee … may this book be the first of many."

Water glasses clink. But after a few moments of celebrating my upcoming project—which is still far from being published—I shift gears, asking the question we all have on our minds.

"Are you seeing Michael before you leave?"

Juliette quietly says, "Tomorrow night." She pauses and looks at her left hand. She eventually told Sophia and Annie about what happened in Costa Rica. She also shared her aha moment—how she was not ready to commit and had unconsciously self-sabotaged her engagement to Michael. Juliette also claims she's now at peace with her mother, no longer hoping to have a relationship with her. While it hurts, she acknowledges this was her mother's choice. Juliette understands her mom did not leave because of her—instead, her mother deserted her daughter and husband due to her own problems. No doubt this has eased the abandonment issues that have been holding Juliette back and causing her to doubt her own ability to commit to Michael.

When she carefully explained all of this to Michael, he began to understand how fragile and complicated Juliette is. It took some time, but eventually he forgave her. And while they officially called off the wedding, Michael insisted that Juliette keep the ring—and asked that she continue wearing it. He told Tom how much he still loves her and how he hopes that when Juliette returns in May, she'll be ready. Tom admitted he's a bit worried what will happen to Michael if Juliette is not.

"Saying goodbye to Michael," Juliette begins, "is going to be torture. I don't know how I'll be apart from him until May." She heaves out a big sigh and rubs her temples with her thumbs.

Annie asks, "So are you guys together, or are you only friends? I'm so confused."

"Well, we started off with the intention to be *just friends.*" Juliette rolls her eyes. "But that didn't work." She chuckles. "So we took things down a notch and tried to remain in the present moment, knowing I'm going to be gone for eight months." The tone of her voice drops as she once again reminds herself of this extended absence.

"Do you think that … well, maybe … when you get back …" a wide-eyed Annie begins, but it's Sophia who interrupts her.

"I am sure Juliette and Michael will figure out what is best for them."

Juliette shoots Sophia an appreciative look. I can only imagine how taxing this is on both her and Michael.

The waiter sets down three glasses of wine and one club soda with lime. We give him our dinner order.

The rest of the night is spent rehashing our special weekend together with Maggie at Eagle's Landing. We laugh as we reflect, shedding a tear or two that Maggie's so far away. But having her with us in the Poconos, well, it was as though we hadn't missed a beat. She truly is the fifth musketeer of our group. And life in Bend seems to be agreeing with her. I couldn't be happier for Maggie.

***

"Marlee." Tom nudges me. "Wake up. That was Jonathon on the phone. Annie's in labor. Her doctor said she should have the baby within the hour."

I sit up, shake my head, then bolt out of bed. "How is she doing?"

"Jonathon said she and the baby are doing well. Of course, they're being closely monitored, but all signs point toward a normal delivery."

"Is Sophia there?" I ask, knowing how much Annie wanted Sophia with her during the delivery.

"Yes," he says. "Jared texted me. He's in the waiting room; they've been there since eleven last night.

"Well, we've got to go. Hurry—get dressed." I throw on a pair of jeans, a long sleeve shirt, and a comfy sweater before going to the bathroom to brush my teeth and comb my hair. "I'll write a note for Patrick," I say, realizing he might be worried if we're not home when he wakes up in the morning.

After arriving at Jefferson Hospital, Tom drops me off at the front entrance while he parks the car in the section reserved for doctors. Moments later, I'm sitting next to Jared in the maternity unit's waiting room.

"Don't worry, Marlee. Annie will be fine. Sophia's been monitoring her pregnancy since the beginning. She's shown absolutely no signs of any distress." Jared's soothing words help comfort me a bit.

Only then do I take a big breath, center myself, and ask the voice—my intuition—if Annie and her baby will be OK. Within moments, a lightness fills me, my shoulders drop, and I can feel my pulse slow. I *know* all will be well.

Right after Tom arrives, Jonathon walks into the waiting room.

"I'm a father!" he proudly announces. "And Annie and Ella are doing beautifully."

Ella ... how beautiful! As much as we tried to pry the baby's name out of Annie, she insisted that it be a surprise.

A tear falls down Jonathon's cheek. No doubt our friend's emotionally and physically exhausted, watching his wife in labor *and* his daughter's entrance into this world—two things he never imagined would happen.

I reach for Tom's hand, but he instead pulls me close into him, kissing the top of my head. Realizing how much life has changed these past ten months, I can only imagine what the future holds. However, no longer am I fearful. I wrap my arm around my husband, giving him a solid squeeze. This is what's important in life ... those you love ... standing side by side, hand in hand, as you each walk your path.

Trust, let go, believe ... The best is yet to come.

Instead of Margaret's harsh tone, I now hear a beautiful soft whisper. Encouraging and filled with hope, my intuition speaks.

MAGGIE

"You'll text me as soon as you book your flights?"

"I promise."

"Mark and Sandy know I'm taking off the first week of February. We can ski at Mt. Bachelor … or go snowshoeing … or cross-country skiing… whatever you want."

"It will be amazing. I can't wait to see you, Maggie."

After saying goodbye to Marlee, I realize how much I've missed her. I like having an older friend. She helps ground me, remind me of what's important in life.

"Is Marlee coming?" Bobby asks as he takes two salmon filets from the wrapper, places them in a Pyrex dish, and begins adding his special marinade.

"She is." I move into the kitchen, wrapping my arms around Bobby's waist. Things have been moving fast—perhaps a bit too fast—but it feels so right. I've never met anyone like him. Bobby's amazing *and* I've finally discovered my passionate side.

"Hey, babe," he says after returning the bottle of olive oil to the lazy Susan in the cabinet. "I forgot to tell you … A letter arrived today. It doesn't look like junk mail." He hands me an envelope.

Not recognizing the handwriting, I look at the return address. "Pensacola, Florida? I don't know anyone there." As I casually open the letter, unfolding the cream-colored stationary, I see the

271

monogram of *JTM* on top. "Oh my God, Bobby. I think this is a letter from my dad."

Dear Maggie,

I am so sorry that I am only writing you now. Your beautiful letter did not arrive until two days ago. We moved to Florida this past May, and I assume there was a problem with forwarding our mail.

First, let me begin by saying thank you. I know it took courage to contact me, and I am so grateful you did. You are correct. Your mother never told me about you or that she was pregnant. I had no idea. But had I known, things would have been different. I would have made sure to have been a part of your life.

No doubt you hated me, unsure why I wasn't there. Right now, I hate myself for not knowing I was your father. A part of me feels robbed of the experience of witnessing you grow up, watching you become the beautiful woman I know you are.

If you are willing, I would love to meet you. You tell me where and when. I will be there.

And if you decide you prefer never to hear from me again, I also understand. I cannot expect you to suddenly be open to a father who was absent your entire life.

My phone number is 850-214-5593, and my email address is jmcintyre1967@gmail.com.

I would love to tell you about your mother's and my relationship. It's a story you deserve to know.

With heartfelt gratitude,
John

I hand the letter to Bobby. As he reads the beautifully scripted penmanship, he places his arm around me, drawing me into his muscular chest. When he's done, he sets the letter on the table, then rests his chin on top of my head.

"What are you going to do?" he asks, yet something tells me he already knows my response.

"I want to meet him."

***

Ten days later, I'm standing inside the Redmond airport by the baggage claim, waiting to meet *my dad*. I texted him a picture of me, so there's no awkwardness and to ensure he'll be able to recognize me right away. He texted me a picture too. John's so handsome. His hair is starting to gray, but in a distinguished way, almost like Francisco's, though he's much younger.

I arrive early, checking my phone to see how far his flight is from landing. It says two minutes. That means he'll be here—next to me—in less than ten. My body feels flushed, and butterflies swarm inside my core.

Having practiced several speeches of sorts, I'm not sure which one I'll use or if I'll totally ab-lib it. But that's OK. It's not every day that a twenty-eight-year-old meets her father for the first time.

Bobby wanted to come with me, to help with any possible awkwardness. But I said no. This is mine to do alone. It's important for me to show up as I am, without a bodyguard of sorts, in case I begin to crumble. Deep down inside, I know I'm strong enough to handle this. And besides, isn't this what I've wanted all my life ... to meet my dad?

I look at my watch. If my calculations are accurate, he should be walking through the revolving door at any moment. Passengers from his flight begin to trickle into the baggage area. I stare straight ahead, not wanting to risk missing him as he comes through the door. Carefully eyeing each person, I glance at the photo on my phone for clarification. But that's not necessary. His image is etched onto my brain. I've memorized every curve of his face and crease on his forehead, as well as the sparkles in his blue eyes. No, I will recognize my dad immediately.

It's then I see him. He's carrying flowers, a bouquet of pink Gerber daisies, tied together in a beautiful lavender-colored ribbon.

"Maggie?" he says.

But before I can respond, I find myself running toward this tall man, opening my arms, ready to embrace my father for the first time.

"Dad!" However, there is no question mark after his name. I know who he is. And he knows me.

***

After spending four amazing days together, my dad returns to Florida. But he made me promise that Bobby and I would come and visit him and meet his wife, Alyssa, and their children, Hannah, Lizzy, and Sam. I told him I couldn't wait. Then I asked if March was too early. This made him smile.

Bobby and I are going to his parents' home in Bozeman, Montana, for Christmas. A part of me is nervous to meet them. But if they're anything like Bobby, then his mom and dad will be amazing.

I signed up for an astrology course which begins in January. I feel called, especially after reading the book Francisco gave to me.

Unsure what I'll do with the certification, all I know is it's what I'm meant to do.

The only thing that's "wrong" with my life is that I miss Marlee, Annie, Juliette, and Sophia. I haven't yet made friends in Bend who come close to the connection I feel with these four. But perhaps that's because of how we met and what we experienced together. No doubt when you discover who you are with people you trust, you create bonds that are like no others.

When we all got together last August at Marlee's house in the Poconos—before Juliette went to Peru to study with some famous shaman—I dubbed these four women "The Healers." After all, each one seems to possess a special gift. Annie's clairvoyant, Sophia's becoming an intuitive doctor, Juliette's on her road to shaman-hood— if that's even a term—and Marlee, well, I believe she's a channeler in her own right.

Maybe The Healers can visit me this summer. While I'd love for them to come with Marlee in February, Juliette doesn't return until May. Besides, I doubt Annie would enjoy the winter months in Bend. A trip here this summer will be better for everyone. There's so much to do—hiking, paddleboarding, concerts. Plus, Ella will be older. Of course, I'll offer for Annie to bring the baby with her, but she may want a bit of time away from being a mommy. I chuckle; the concept of motherhood seems so distant to me. But then, I think of my mom and how much I miss her.

My grandfather passed in August. Luckily, when I returned for settlement on the house mid-July, I was able to see him one final time. I was shocked by his appearance—he was propped up in his bed with an oxygen tube in his nose. Still, Granddad showed no signs of recognition. He only stared straight ahead. The doctor, whom I spoke with weekly, had prepared me for his decline, but there's nothing like being there and witnessing it for yourself.

There were only six of us at the funeral—four old friends who had survived him and were still able to get themselves to the church, Marlee, and me. I couldn't believe it when she told me she was coming. Marlee drove to Pittsburgh—two days before the funeral—and picked me up at the airport. She stayed downtown with me, helping with all of the arrangements.

More importantly, she was there, by my side, every step of the way. While I would have been able to do it alone, Marlee made everything easier. She helped me laugh when I wanted to cry, and she sat with me as I went through old photos I found in the bottom drawer of the dresser in Granddad's skilled care room. I suppose my mother brought them, hoping they'd help him to relive his memories. Afterward, Marlee took me to lunch, making sure I ate.

I walk toward my bedroom, pausing at the wooden nightstand to pick up the carnelian pyramid Francisco gave to me during our closing ceremony. Holding it tightly in my left hand, I finally understand the significance of his gift. I am like the pyramid—strong, solid, capable of nurturing myself and weathering unforeseen storms. And while I prefer not to travel my journey alone, I know I am able ... *I've got this.*

ACKNOWLEDGMENTS

This book is dedicated to Janice Miller, my mother, who in 2016 took me to Miraval Arizona Spa and Resort for my first "retreat-like" experience. Never before had I heard of Ayurveda, Reiki, or the concept of energy healing. However, once I was introduced to these practices, my life began to shift.

I believe I've unconsciously woven a piece of my mother into each of the main characters. Sophia reflects her wisdom. Her concern for others can be seen through Annie, and Maggie possesses her independent streak. Yet it's Marlee who embodies her love.

ALSO BY MICHELLE DAVIS

Learning to Bend

The Dog Walkers

The Invitation

Made in United States
Troutdale, OR
03/14/2025

29748243R00163